The Iceberg Presi
By Caroline Corfield

Cover Art by Shaun Giblin 2021
All image rights reserved.

Special Thanks to my friends, husband and daughters.

9 781739 929824

The Iceberg Presidency
By Caroline Corfield

(c) Caroline Corfield

Special Thanks to my friends, my son and daughters ...

Chapter One - Trawling

Senator Valentina Torres was standing on the bridge of her new ship on its maiden voyage. The MS Mercer had been in the yard at Saylon for six months. Freshly modified by the Antarctic Free State it was the flagship of its new inshore navy.

The creation of the navy and its air support of two helicopters had been the culmination of a campaign that Valla Torres had instigated nearly four years previously. She'd been pragmatic about where the ships might come from: speed of conversion and suitability for modification had been the main concern. Since the UN's failed incursion into AFS territory at McMurdo town, the need she'd already identified had also become apparent to a voting majority of the AFS Senate and they'd given her free rein to develop the specifications for this new force within a generous budget.

The Mercer, had been a survey ship, with a Polar Classification of seven. There'd been work to bring it up to three, but it already had a large helideck, and for Valla the added bonus of ocean going capabilities. The rest of her fleet consisted of three small modified trawlers, more used to continental shelf activities.

The weather was auspicious, a high pressure ridge had pushed out of the Antarctic interior and settled as a long wide finger towards the south of the Indian Ocean and the ship rolled to the deep ocean swells that had travelled southeast from the Cape of Good Hope. She was staring through the windows watching the swell.

"When's the helicopter due to reach us?" she enquired of the captain, without turning round from the hypnotic view.

She heard Captain Dmitry Beardmore answer with a hint of anxiety, "two thirty, in forty five minutes time. We'll be making a turn to shore shortly."

She turned to see what was making him sound worried, and realised it was her. She'd interviewed all the crew, for all the vessels, aided by a revolving group of experts on navies, ships and the psychologies of crew. Captain Beardmore was an experienced captain, he'd worked cruise ships in Antarctic waters for the last ten years and had sailed on a number of different vessel types before that. He'd naturalised as a citizen as soon as it had been feasible and had come across in the interview as fully aware of the changes needed to captain a defence vessel compared to a civilian vessel. She was quite certain it wasn't the ship that was putting him off.

"Dimitry, would you like me to leave? I should probably go deal with the press anyway."

"Senator, I didn't mean… I'm just not used to civilians on the bridge."

She smiled at him, she supposed cruise ships were a very different set-up to this, wealthy passengers could be awkward but they weren't often your boss.

"Captain Beardmore, this is your command, I defer to your orders. You don't want the politicians or the press on your bridge you just say so. We're running a navy now."

She headed towards the stairs that would take her to the decks below, passing by the large chair he was sitting in, surrounded by instrumentation. She saw him smile back and she thought he looked a lot happier.

She entered the large mess room, where the press had been allowed to gather. Most were local to Antarctica. She spotted Matt Green the New Zealand Times correspondent and Lee Tsang from the South China Herald who both lived in Saylon, but they'd been joined by some more properly foreign correspondents she didn't recognise at all. The ocean swell below decks was a less pleasant affair and some looked distinctly queasy in its long roll. They turned as she entered the area, most sitting on the fixed tables or on the chairs chatting in groups.

"Ladies and Gentlemen of the Press. Thank you for coming out with us today to welcome the MS Mercer into the new Antarctic Free State Navy. I'm open for questions now, and we'll be able to get you sorted for photo opportunities when the helicopter turns up in about three quarters of an hour."

"Matt Green, New Zealand Times. Senator Torres, can you explain why the AFS has suddenly decided it needs a navy?"

Good old Matt, you could rely on him. She fielded that question with the carefully worded answer that had been put out several times so far to the local press and the press of their immediate neighbouring states. Matt had clearly asked it again because he knew there were journalists from more far flung parts of the globe. As if to emphasise that, the next question had been from a Canadian journalist, asking primarily about the modifications to bring it up to the Polar class 3. The English journalist, who had been at pains to point out he was from Greater Kent for some reason, wanted to know about the armaments that had been added. She then realised that was because they'd bought the guns from a weapons broker in Greater Kent. Well, she thought, it's not exactly a secret, the things are sticking up out of the deck for everyone to see.

She checked her watch, as she felt the ship turn in the swell. Not long now.

"Could Senator Torres please return to the bridge." The voice of the executive officer, Martin Kostov, came over the intercom.

She looked up from her watch at the expectant faces of the press.

"Excuse me, I'll be back and we'll get the photo setup sorted out."

She headed off.

When she arrived back on the bridge, both the captain and the executive officer were at the windows with binoculars.

Captain Beardmore turned to her, holding out his binoculars, "We appear to have some unexpected company."

She focussed and looked out towards where the executive officer had pointed. She saw a deep sea trawler, a decent size, not quite a factory ship but certainly able to stay out for more than a couple of weeks at a time. It looked like she had a lot of storage space.

"They're not answering our hail."

"Oh," said Valla turning away from the window, her memory trying to drag up the name of the vessel that was smuggling for Freddie Tran before Freddie ended up in prison. "Are we in territorial waters still?"

She saw Dmitry watching her, she could tell he knew exactly what she was thinking. She searched for hesitation on his face, and was pleased to see nothing like that. He looked more than happy to fully christen his ship. The name came to her, she remembered thinking it was an odd name for a ship.

"Can you make out the name?" she asked, "is it the Iron Prestige?"

"I'll check the AIS code," said Captain Beardmore, tapping his console, "we're close enough now and they've not switched off their transmission. Yes. It's the Prestige."

She saw him turn to see her.

"Senator Torres, do I have your permission to engage?"

"Captain Bearmore, we must start as we mean to go on, smuggling will not be tolerated even if the press are onboard. I'll go and inform them of this new dimension to their story."

"Senator," said Captain Beardmore returning to his console.

Valla could hear the orders beginning behind her as she took the stairs and hurried to the mess room, entering as the all stations alert began to sound.

The press were looking interested, not a single peaky face amongst them now.

"This isn't for the helicopter is it, Senator?" asked Matt.

"No, Matt. You're lucky, we've spotted a suspected smuggler, not answering our hails and posting ID as a vessel already implicated in Frederika Tran's trial as part of their smuggling ring. We'll hopefully be witnessing our first bust."

She felt the ship heave to, some chairs slid away from the tables, but the press pack seemed to be taking that in their stride. The Greater Kent guy was now asking if the guns would get a try-out. She was hoping not.

Dmitry Beardmore was happy. He finally felt several of his passions had come together in this new command. Being at sea, a disciplined crew and a good reason to be at sea. The politicians and the press were a small price to pay, and they wouldn't be a part of the everyday running of the ship either. But now they were an added complication to the work that had suddenly popped over the horizon while they'd been out on these manoeuvres. He'd radioed the helicopter to stand by, and made a course correction to intercept the Prestige.

His XO was continuing to try and hail them using their name now too. He noticed after a minute of that the AIS code had disappeared from his screen. It would appear to be bad luck for the Prestige that they were out and about today. He had every confidence in his crew. He'd sat in on their interviews with Senator Torres.

The message that Martin, his XO, was now relaying over the radio included the information that the Prestige was being targeted. His small guns, two 30mm rapid fire Millenniums were mounted on the deck below the bridge to port and starboard and his big gun was astern, a 127mm Otobreda. He liked Senator Torres' idea of defence. He'd been concerned there'd be no teeth when he'd first heard about the idea of an inshore naval defence force, but the more he'd read about what was being discussed in the Senate, the more he'd wanted to be a part of it.

He ordered a dummy shot across the Prestige's bows with his big gun. They had a mix of dummy and live ammunitions: there'd been the chance they might show off for the press if the helicopter hadn't been able to land. The gun's firing reverberated through the ship. He knew it would sound louder in the mess room than it did on the bridge.

"This is the Iron Prestige, repeat this is the Iron Prestige, we surrender."

Dimtry wondered how anyone could be at sea off Antarctica and not know the Mercer was coming out of Saylon, or even just a little bit about her capabilities. But it had clearly surprised the Prestige that she could, or would fire on them. Well, he'd see them for himself when they got alongside. He could see the Prestige slowing and he ordered Martin to take the Prestige into their lee so they could board her.

Patrice Reilly felt he had rotten luck. Some people had told him he made bad choices, which he was self-aware enough to recognise, but he knew that on top of those bad choices he also had bad luck. If it was going to go wrong it would, and more than usually when he was up to no good.

He was making the run south from Singapore, he had some booze, some bio-tech and six shitting turtles that were stinking up his hold and wouldn't even be making the illegal animal market in Saylon. He could ditch the booze, maybe even the bio-tech but the person who'd bought the shitty turtles was not someone you messed with. Despite being the one thing he'd like to get rid of, and also the one thing that would really appreciate being dumped overboard, the turtles were staying. If he got them into the AFS, even impounded, then they stood a chance of getting into the right hands, and he stood a chance of staying alive.

He'd been surprised to see the Mercer appear on his radar, he was sure it had been delayed, Senate projects were never on time. He was more than surprised to be shot at. He didn't like this new approach to smuggling that had been part of the fall-out from Freddie's trial. He'd always had his suspicions about Freddie, she talked the talk and you couldn't deny the evidence that came out at the trial, but he never felt she truly believed in anything she said. It was like she was getting off on being someone else that nobody had yet figured out. He always felt he was being laughed at for his naivety.

His current occupation as a smuggler, he hesitated to call it a job, led to a deep suspicion of most people anyway, especially ones who could have you killed for smiling at the wrong time. People such as the shitting turtle guy. He mentally tried to untag Santiago Kooper, boss of the Clover gang as shitting turtle guy, because if he allowed that to continue he was going to get himself into bigger trouble than he was already.

Dmitry had sent Martin with some men onboard the Prestige to round up the crew. There were four; an engineer, two heavies and the captain, Patrice Reilly. He'd let the press onto the main deck to take their photographs of the crew being brought onboard. He felt that life was going to get more interesting as soon as those photographs made the front pages.

Smuggling was big in Saylon. It was a string to many bows elsewhere in the AFS and had been disregarded on the whole as a small town perk. But Saylon was different, it was a bigger port than Weddell City, almost as large a city, and had ties back to Vostok in the interior. Those ties were mostly organised crime ties, and the smuggling had become a key part of their infrastructure. The Senate had seemed powerless until recently to do something about it. The Larsen senator they charged, Leon Palma, he recalled, had seemed to have been the log jam and once he and Freddie had got put away everything had changed.

He ordered Patrice brought to the bridge and invited Senator Torres back. She was already there when Patrice arrived, more or less dragged up the stairs. Dmitry noticed he also had the beginnings of a black eye.

"Who hit you?" he asked.

Patrice looked sheepish, "Kawan. He didn't think we should have surrendered. This is how he explained it."

Dmitry rolled his eyes, the lanky mess in front of him must count for the world's worst smuggler. He reckoned Patrice was in his early twenties, a generation scarred by their early experiences of a world gone mad. The Carrington-level solar flares had taken the world backwards into a dark place for a while, and ripples continued to undulate through the world today. Organised crime and an unstable United Nations as world government propped up by Global Corp were just two things that directly affected the Antarctic Free State as a result.

"Mr. Reilly," said Valla, "I'm genuinely curious, why are you still at it? Surely you know the Iron Prestige was mentioned during Frederika Tran's trial?"

Dmitry heard the incredulity in Senator Torres' voice and he felt the same. But unlike Valentina Torres, he understood why sometimes people did un-strategic and downright stupid things. Sometimes, he thought, you just ended up in a place and only had stupid or suicidal to choose from.

Patrice spoke, "Yeah, you'd think, but Mr. Kooper can be a very persuasive man. I was trying to go legitimate. This was going to be my last run. It was the shitting turtles, he wouldn't trust anyone else with them."

Dmitry saw Valentina give him a questioning look.

"There were six Loggerhead turtles in a secret compartment. Although they couldn't hide the smell."

"Ah. Just as well, Mr. Reilly, that we're not going to hand you over to the UN. They don't take kindly to that sort of thing. What else can you tell us about Mr. Kooper other than his deep interest in endangered marine reptiles?"

Dmitry saw Patrice re-appraise his recent statement, and his realisation he had probably said more than he should have already.

"I'd like my lawyer now, thanks," Patrice said with complete resignation.

To be honest, Dmitry thought, we got more than we should have out of him. I don't fancy his chances of staying alive beyond any trial.

"Take him to the brig with the others," he ordered, "Keep Kawan handcuffed though."

He waited till Patrice was gone.

"Poor sod. He doesn't stand a chance," he said, looking at Senator Torres.

"Dmitry. I'd like to say I'm surprised but I saw your psychology scores. I agree, he's not who we should be locking up, but we've got to start somewhere. I could maybe call in a favour. Someone I know who could get him to talk, maybe enough to save his life."

"I think he's worth giving a second chance. And he certainly knows more."

"Okay," she said. "Let's get that helicopter down and give it some real work to do. I'll head back with Patrice. You can arrange the reception for the rest when you dock. That'll give them something to write about."

"Senator."

He turned to Martin to call for the helicopter and get in touch with the police. That was another change he'd approved of; the police had taken on more tasks from the Intelligence Agency, and had got a commensurate increase in funding. It felt to him like Antarctica was maturing as a country from a frontier to a fully structured state. He watched the senator disappear down the stairs, and ordered some men to escort Patrice to the forward deck area near to where the helicopter would land.

Valentina Torres liked flying. She preferred small jets, especially if they had weaponry, but a nippy little civilian would suit her fine. She didn't mind helicopters, so she watched with increasing amusement the look on Patrice's face as he realised he was going to be getting on the helicopter and flying over the sea to land in Saylon. He didn't look happy, and was becoming increasingly agitated.

"Never flown before?" she asked conversationally.

"This some kind of torture technique? I hate flying. Did it once, that was enough. This isn't even flying. It's barely controlled falling."

"Patrice. You need some basic physics lessons," she smiled at him, it wasn't much fun winding him up, it was too easy. She also realised she'd prefer a more relaxed travelling companion. "We'll be fine. We're going to land on the roof of the Intelligence Agency building. I want you to meet someone tomorrow."

She saw that get his attention. Good.

The downdraft from the approaching helicopter blew spray and loose dust up at them. It landed in a slow controlled movement, its wheels cradled inside the thick rope net tied across the helideck. The ship's helicopter officer waved at them to approach. She bent her head, but saw that Patrice was practically crawling towards it. She cast a glance towards the windows that the press would be up against to take their shots. She suppressed the desire to wave.

The more serious her role as the senior Torres senator got the more she wanted to kick back against it. Being head of the Family Torres, one of five Families that made up the political landscape of the AFS had changed since she'd assumed it on the death of her father. Membership was no longer hereditary, but it hadn't affected them too much, most members liked being in Torres anyway. However they hadn't recruited many from the other four Families either. It seemed not many people felt like Glenn Murcheson about their original Family. She was secretly pleased about that. She'd never admit it to him

13

though, and she did agree that the hereditary aspect was wrong. She'd been in the Resistance like Glenn, even while it had been a proscribed organisation, and the revocation of hereditary membership had been a key policy point.

She pushed Patrice inside and gestured to a seat he should strap into and that he should put on the headphones. She took the one opposite him. The helicopter officer shut the door and backed off to start arm signals for the helicopter take off. She felt it lift, and watched Patrice close his eyes tight shut.

Her headphones had a microphone. She talked to the pilot, asking him to put a message through to Alison Strang, the State Negotiator to meet them tomorrow at the Intelligence Agency building in Saylon. She knew Alison was in Weddell City and it was a long journey to take but she'd come if it was Senate business. And Valentina considered netting Santiago Kooper, head of the Clover Gang as Senate business even more than it was the job of the Intelligence Agency or the police.

Chapter Two - Sparks

Alison Strang received the call at four in the afternoon just before leaving the Environment Department building. The meeting between Global Mining and the AFS miners had recently finished and Glenn had yet to arrive. She was standing in the foyer, the sun streaming through the glass from a medium height. The meeting had gone well, despite the shake up in Family politics that the removal of hereditary allegiance had instigated. None of the mining representatives had changed Family, Torres and Glencor still had the biggest populations, and they still had two representatives to the other three Familes' single representatives. She sensed Global had been surprised and noted that briefly they'd tried to stir the pot amongst the representatives, but now she was a State Negotiator she'd nipped that idea in the bud immediately.

The call from Valla was a completely different set of intrigues however. At the time of Frederika Tran's trial she'd barely noticed what was being said but she did remember Glenn had suggested his grandfather, the current president, Gordon Murcheson had been working with Freddie and that she was undercover. But Freddie Tran went to prison and indeed was still in prison. If what Glenn suspected was true, the pair of them were playing a very long game.

She agreed to come directly to Saylon. The timing was good for a break in the negotiations, she could tell the miners were getting argumentative with each other despite her best efforts and Global were emboldened by that. A rest would give the miners time to think. Global, time to worry. She checked on the scheduled flights, there seemed to be a lot of coming and going between Saylon and Weddell City despite the distance making it the longest scheduled non-stop route. She wondered if Glenn wanted to come along. It sounded like the Intelligence Agency was already involved, since they were keeping Patrice Reilly. She waited to book seats until she could speak with him.

Gary, her son was back in McMurdo, boarding at the local school there. He'd liked it better than Weddell City, it was difficult to go outside in the city. Weddell City hadn't been designed for pedestrians or eleven year old boys newly arrived from Northumberland. He was nearly sixteen now and she felt he'd settled into life in Antarctica much better than she had. She continued to dread the winter, the months of twilight either side of the darkness were the worst. She could handle the dark, but not the murky half light. Gary seemed to revel in the changes, but then it was a young country, geared up for the needs of the young. For the first three years she'd travelled during the winter, getting some much needed light. Sometimes even doing small jobs for the AFS. Last year she had been in Kwazulu-natal helping to broker a trade deal. Nikau Burns, Valla's chief advisor, with his maori looks and friendly smile had been part of the delegation and it had been good to catch up with old friends.

She saw Glenn through the glass wall and waved him inside.

"How do you fancy a trip to Saylon? Valla has asked me to go. It sounds more like an interrogation than anything else, but the meetings here need some space to cook."

She watched him as he answered. He'd been preoccupied ever since his grandfather had decided to run for a second term, and she felt it was clouding his judgement.

"Sure. I heard Valla had captured a smuggler on her first trip out. The ship that dropped out of tailing the UN minesweeper because they were working for Freddie. I'd be interested in meeting the captain myself."

She'd got used to the judgmental side of him, but occasionally it hit her again that despite his excellent analytical skills he still operated on these more absolute terms first. He'd severed all connection with Wahid, a man she was sure he'd considered a mentor since he was ten just because he'd found out Wahid worked for his grandfather. And then there was that relationship, or rather the lack of one, between him and Gordon Murcheson, his paternal grandfather. She was however eternally grateful to Daniel Ektov, his maternal grandfather for welcoming him back into his life, and for welcoming her too.

"Good, I'll book seats on this evening's flight, we'll get there just after breakfast."

"We best get home and pack."

It had taken her a few days on her first arrival in Antarctica to get used to the stability of the technology. Elsewhere in the world everything was at the mercy of intermittent electrical supply and hackers. It had improved in the last five years. There had been an increase in the flow of technological innovations between the AFS and the UN states. What had taken her longer to adjust to was the AFS's seeming disregard for the planet's ecology. Flights in the rest of the world were strictly rationed, a lot of travel was now by ship, although there were some enterprising solar powered airship designs coming through. Here in the AFS, with a continent whose interior was ice sheet, air travel was essential. But it wasn't just that. It was almost as if the two entities occupied the same planet in parallel universes. She'd finally got used to the leather and the wood, but it had taken a long time to override her inbuilt misgivings.

The plane took off through the gathering snow clouds. It was early summer, most of the storms had passed but occasionally there were flurries; moisture had been dragged in over Weddell City because of the high pressure over Saylon. She was beginning to understand the importance of basic meteorological knowledge in a place like this. Everything depended on what the weather was doing and would do. They ate, read and dozed, comfortable with the length of journey, knowing that Antarctica had a single time zone. It was ten hours later that she saw the coastline.

Saylon was similar to McMurdo in that it was sandwiched between the land and the sea, but on a much larger scale. They flew over the city spread out in a squashed horseshoe shape with the harbour at its centre. The plane banked right and seemed to almost be turning around on itself, and she saw the city to the right and the ice sheet, a great cliff of white, ahead as the plane descended rapidly to the runway which jutted out into the sea, again like McMurdo.

The land here was still mostly covered by retreating ice sheet, two glaciers flowed either side of Saylon. Alison had done some reading on the flight to catch up on the city. There was a constant vigilance at the edge of the city for rogue ice flow and they had to monitor the katabatic winds while also trying to harness them for power generation. It sounded far more dangerous an environment than that surrounding Weddell City, and she wondered at the explosive development that had seen it begin to rival the nominal capital. Would it really have happened without organised crime and its money?

There was a car waiting for them when they got out the terminal building. Glenn seemed to recognise the driver.

"Colin," he exclaimed, "how're you doing? Does this mean you're not co-opted anymore?"

She saw the stocky figure, shoulders straight, waiting in a stand-at-ease pose next to the car and recollected that this was the ex-UN marine, Colin Nguyen who had defected during the attack on McMurdo. They'd asked him to help locate remaining UN agents shortly after and he'd been co-opted to the Intelligence Agency for that job, but obviously he'd decided to stay on when they'd asked him. Glenn had told her his sister lived in Saylon. She saw him bear hug Glenn. She declined an embrace and offered a hand instead.

"Hi Colin, I'm Alison Strang. Valla asked me to come over. I only know a bit from the press and a bit from Glenn, perhaps you could fill me in some more on the drive?"

She saw his grin widen.

"Sure. Anything for our State Negotiator. Anything for a fellow immigrant. And anything for Glenn's lady."

She decided to smile back despite his final reason. She'd accepted the job and the citizenship that was true. But she'd always thought of her and Glenn as a partnership not an ownership. She knew it was simply Colin's old

19

country talking. It took everyone who arrived as an adult a while to adjust, to leave old ways of thinking behind, and sometimes people didn't even realise what cultural assumptions they still carried with them.

She got in the front to make it easier to listen to Colin. They turned out of the airport and onto a road which, as its name suggested, Boundary Road, acted as a boundary to the city. Away to her left was the ice sheet in the distance, a cliff of white: she could barely make out the wind farms through its reflective glare. Colin explained what had happened when Valla had taken the MS Mercer out for its first trip as the flagship of the AFS navy and then Alison had asked him if he'd met Patrice. Colin reminded her a little of Enya Zhao, very no nonsense, but she was keen to get as many impressions of Patrice, before meeting him, as possible. It gave her sharp mind more to work on.

Her sharp mind was a bio-implant in her brain. Something that had nearly killed her, and something she had subsequently managed to incorporate into her own psyche. It could no longer shut her body down via external triggers, and it was entirely at her disposal. She had Glenn to thank for that.

They turned down onto Lucky Avenue. She'd noticed they'd already passed Fifteenth and Fourteenth Avenue, and now she smiled at the way they'd got round naming the Thirteenth. Back in Weddell City there was a real suppression of superstition, but here they worked with it. She realised some parts of the AFS were as removed from each other as it itself was removed from the UN. She didn't envy Gordon Murcheson trying to preside over these disparate parts.

The car turned almost immediately into an underground car park beneath a tall building. It was no skyscraper, the katabatic winds made sure of that, but it was tall for Saylon. She'd read that the winds rushed down off the ice sheet at nearly 200 kilometres an hour. The city intercepted the dense cold air powered by gravity with various designs of windbreak and then at the wind farms. The great blades of the wind turbines turned every day.

They entered the foyer and went through the security with minimum fuss. Colin was ushering them towards the lifts and she saw he'd pressed for the even floor car.

"Floor six. Valla'll meet you. Sorry, I've got other things to do. Here's my number if you fancy a drink later, though."

She saw Glenn take the proffered bit of paper and pocket it.

"We will. Definitely," said Glenn as the lift doors opened.

She saw Colin wave and stride off as they went inside. Valla was waiting for them on the sixth floor but when the doors opened she looked more worried than Alison expected.

"What's wrong?" she asked.

"It's not been officially released but last night somebody killed Freddie in the high security wing of Denam Prison," said Valla, "we don't know who, or how. It's a mess. And Patrice might be next."

"It's best we get as much out of him as quickly as possible then," said Alison, "I can amend some of my questions to assist in that. Colin filled me in on some of

21

the details missing in official press releases, but I want your take on this too, Valla. Before I meet him."

"Come in here," Valla was opening a door, and Alison could see it was a small room to the side of the one with Patrice, a large one way window showing him pacing up and down.

Alison chose to sit with her back to the window. She wanted to concentrate on what Valla had to say. But Glenn it seemed couldn't stay away from the window. She sensed his analytical mind would be churning over the body language. When Valla had finished she felt she was ready to meet Patrice. But Glenn spoke.

"He's hiding something," he said, "something big, he's not just scared for *his* life. There's something, maybe some*one* else. But he's getting desperate."

"Valla?" Alison looked over to the Senator, seeing for the first time how tired she looked.

"I'll get someone to dig into his background some more," Valla was looking at Glenn, "You okay to observe?"

"Yes. I'll be fine," he said.

She saw Valla look at him harder.

"I'll be good. I promise."

She watched Valla leave and remembered when she would see Valla swoop out of rooms with such purpose, you'd expect the dust to self-actualise in response. Something had ground down 'The General', as those who'd fought the UN marines at McMurdo had taken to calling her. Alison made a mental note to find out what. She liked Valla a great deal and didn't want to see her like this. It seemed to Alison, that the news about Freddie had been a final straw for Valla and she needed to know what the whole load was.

Alison spen an hour in the room with Patrice. At the end of it, she felt she had a very good idea what or rather who Patrice was hiding. He'd not really tried to obfuscate, in fact he sounded resigned. She could understand why Valla, or maybe it was someone who'd persuaded Valla, wanted to try and help him. When someone believes so strongly in their Fate, and its inescapability, it's hard to resist trying to snap them out of their fatalism. Patrice was resigned to being killed on the orders of Santiago Kooper, she thought. But hidden from Santiago was someone who depended on Patrice to stay alive and that spark was enough to keep Patrice pushing against what he considered his fate. Alison knew that whoever it was, Patrice wanted them not just safe from Santiago but hidden in general. Patrice was as hopeless a case as she'd ever come across, and yet he still kept going.

But the real information she'd garnered was about Santiago. The man at the top of the Clover gang. A man with overriding ambition, that could blind him to his own mistakes. A man who, of course, did not believe he made mistakes, but Patrice was one and she knew there'd be others. She knew Santiago would expect Patrice to talk, that he was weak. Santiago was blind to the sparks that kept people going in the darkest winters.

Alison also knew that none of them were safe in the Intelligence Agency building. The Agency had been cleaned out in the wake of the UN's attack, but that clearance could never be as thorough as it needed to be. Bribery was always effective in a country that lacked for some of the luxuries available elsewhere in the world simply because they were not feasible in Antarctica. Hyperplane seats and cruise ship cabins were relatively expensive items to reach such luxuries too. When she had re-entered the small side room, she'd immediately asked Glenn where would be safe to go to. He'd looked worried, then pensive and eventually he'd said he had no idea.

How were they going to protect Patrice? And ensnare Santiago? What was she going to do about Valla? And who had killed Freddie?

Chapter Three - Deep Game

Daniel Ektov was watching from the side of the stage as Gordon Murcheson talked to the press. He'd always been wary of Gordon, ever since his daughter Ruth had brought Bruce Murcheson home. But they had been so in love and Bruce had been nothing like his father Gordon, he'd never thought they'd be in danger from Gordon's ambitions. Bruce seemed determined to make his own life; studying engineering, setting up the geothermal station. Together he and Ruth had built a life in McMurdo and then Glenn had been born and Daniel had almost relaxed.

He was surprised when Gordon had approached him to be the campaign manager. In the first Antarctic presidential elections four years ago there hadn't been any real competition. Gordon had been elected on the back of the new pacts with their neighbours, and the new relationship with the UN. Whoever had been campaign manager last time, it was clear Gordon knew they weren't up to the job this time. Senator Christine Frome, a senior Moss senator standing on an anti-corruption ticket was an entirely different kind of competition.

Daniel'd had some respect for Christine, until she'd ran for the Presidency. Since he'd negotiated directly with the UN from the beginning of the discussions, he knew it still required someone like Gordon Murcheson to be president. Someone who could multi-layer beyond the depths of their adversary. Someone who quite possibly was corrupt but who was also clever enough to never leave any evidence to prove it. Daniel felt the UN would eat Christine for breakfast. So he'd said yes when Gordon had asked him to be the campaign manager. He'd not yet been able to talk with Glenn about that, and having only just re-connected with him, he wasn't looking forward to the conversation. His misgivings were only assuaged by having met Alison Strang, Glenn's partner. If anyone could turn a Murcheson's mind from what it had been set to, it was Alison Strang.

The press questions were mostly about the impounding of the deep sea trawler, Iron Prestige, and centred around what would happen to the crew, the AFS's new attitude to smuggling in general and organised crime specifically. They were hard questions, but Gordon was fielding them with an expert ambiguity. The trouble was, Daniel knew, the press could see that too. They'd go back and write entirely speculative articles instead. Then he realised this was part of Gordon's plan. Gordon was stirring the hornets' nest that was the organised criminal gangs of the AFS based in Vostok and Saylon. Daniel felt that was dangerous. He would have eliminated the gang heads slowly but surely through assassinations and then influenced power-plays until they technically still existed but were actually under state control. Again he felt that Christine's presidential ambition was driving Gordon at a pace that was not his own. It was unlike Gordon to allow himself to be driven. Daniel dived deeper into the machinations that he felt were most likely, but it was still too obscured. However, he felt Gordon was now playing the deepest game of his life and so much was below the water line, Daniel was worried it could sink the AFS.

The press conference was over. Gordon invited Daniel back to his office in the Senate building. He'd retained his old office even after becoming president, not least because the senate hadn't been built for a presidential structure, but also to make a point. He saw Daniel busy watching him, while he poured them both some whisky from the decanters he kept on the bookcases to the side of the room. His eye caught as it always did, the charred copy of the Frobius Turbine manual, up on the top shelf. He breathed in deeply and let the breath out slowly, knowing it would add to the concern he could already see was a permanent fixture on Daniel Ektov's face these days. He considered Daniel as close to a friend as he felt able to allow, given what his plans were.

"Freddie Tran is dead," he said, handing Daniel a cut crystal glass with the amber liquid rolling greasily inside.

"Inevitable. Why was she still in prison?"

"I felt it was the safest place for her. I'm troubled that it still wasn't safe enough."

"Do we know who? How?"

"Valla's on the case. But no. Not yet."

"You can't keep piling things onto Valla. She'll only keep taking them on. Domingo wouldn't have thanked you for that. Anyway, she works better in single-minded mode."

"I'm hoping Glenn will pick it up."

"Ask him Gordon. Just ask him. What's so hard about that?"

"You know."

Gordon rolled the whisky round some more in the glass, as if further agitation would transform it into something new, in a way he hoped would also happen with his thoughts.

"I do," said Daniel, "but I can't help thinking it's time to stop avoiding each other."

"This is a conversation for another time," he said dismissively. "We're going to have to release the news about Freddie by tonight. Denam prison might be remote, but it's not on the moon, people talk. Do you think Christine'll be able to make much out of it?"

"Yes. Freddie should have been shot as a traitor. It's always going to be a point for discussion, plea bargain or not. How did you get mixed up with her?"

"Ah, Daniel, trust me, it was the other way around."

He saw Daniel put his head into his hands and run them backwards through his grey hair.

"You're already stirring it with the gangs, Gordon, just name the one you think most likely. If the game is to poke them with a stick, this is a nice big stick. Although you know I already disagree with that direction," Daniel said. "Christine can't make too much noise about that. She'll be forced to condemn them too, making her a target, so she'll be careful how she does that. It could even help us. We'll look tougher. The tide is turning against the criminal gangs, they're taking too big a cut these days, and the population is becoming more settled and civilised."

"What's Valla said so far?" Gordon asked.

"I haven't been in touch with the Intelligence Agency in Saylon today, but I know Alison and Glenn are there now. Valla asked her to come and interview Patrice Reilly."

"That's good news. I've not met her yet, maybe I won't ever... but I'm pleased he found someone."

He knocked back the rest of the whisky, and put the glass down on the bookcase. The Senate Chamber lights were being switched off and the large picture window behind him turned from brightly lit to black and now reflected the interior of his office. He turned to look at the reflected view, seeing Daniel sitting in the leather wingback armchair nearest the door, his desk obscuring the bottom half of Daniel. He saw the full bookmarked cut stone wall opposite the bookcase wall. The red garnets were the size of cherries studding the grey and white contortions of the schist. Gordon had handpicked the slabs, and for him the stone had always summed up the Antarctic Free State. Born out of pressure, dotted with blood, twisted by time, but still beautiful.

Daniel decided to call Valla once he was back in his office. When they'd been given an allowance for decorating the senior senators' offices, he'd donated his money to a fund set up in the aftermath of the pirate raids on the McMurdo coast. His concrete walls showed the marks left by the form-boards used when the concrete had been poured. He enjoyed looking at the marks. He remembered the summer they had built the Senate. It had been warm, the first year when the temperature was warm enough for the new cold weather concrete mix. It had still been a gamble. He thought the whole project of the AFS had been a gamble back then, and now... Now he was still waiting for the bet to fail.

Criminal gangs were the most likely candidates for the murder of Frederika Tran, but the UN designated states which retained strong nationalist ties amongst themselves, making up the supra-states of Australia, England and India, were just as likely. As was an east coast grouping of former US states, whose membership fluctuated too much for anyone to agree a supra-state name on. He knew Valla would have thought of all the options too. But he wanted to give her as much help as possible. He was worried about her.

"Valla, how are you?"

"Good Daniel. Alison and Glenn are here. We have some good leads to follow up on too. Nothing so far on who killed Freddie. But I have agents going over all the footage we've collected. They must have arrived by sea, there's nothing unusual by air and it all checks out."

"Who identified the body? And what's happening with it?"

"Well, the guard did initially. We've been in touch with Tanya, her former partner, she's agreed to travel to the prison for confirmation. Do I detect suspicions, Daniel?"

"Ha. Hanging around Gordon is getting to me. I'm just making sure. We're going to announce the death shortly. And Gordon is going to suggest the Clover Gang is involved. He reckons they're most likely at the moment. I don't know Valla. I think this will backfire on us. But I'm just running the campaign not the presidency."

"Daniel, let him get on with it, it's his funeral."

"Ah, your father used to say that all the time Valla. My advice, get Glenn involved in finding out who's killed Freddie, and you concentrate on Patrice. We'll concentrate on the Clover gang and the rest of them."

"I'll send you some stuff encrypted Daniel. Stay safe."

"You too Valla."

He put the phone down and knew he was more worried than when he'd picked it up. They'd managed to dig one thing up on Christine since she'd won the nomination out of the other candidates. She'd attended dinners and jollies organised by Global, more than the usual, much more and not all had been registered with the Senate. He and Gordon had agreed there was a time for making the most of that, but it hadn't yet arrived. He wondered if the right moment would ever come if they shifted the focus onto the criminal gangs? He made a call.

"Boss?"

Santiago Kooper was disturbed from his thoughts, by his second in command, Trigger. A long time ago he'd know Trigger's real name, but Santiago didn't live in the past. He made a point of it, there was nothing there for him.

"What?"

"They're saying we killed Freddie. Did we?"

"Trigger, how long have we known each other?"

"I don't know, Boss, you don't like it when I tell you."

"Exactly. And now you want *me* to tell you something *you* don't need to know. Do you think that's a good idea, Trigger?"

He saw the computational overload on Trigger's face, and relented. Trigger was dependable, loyal and the best contract-man he'd ever had, if he was a bit slow he still got there.

"You never mind, Trigger, go have a drink," he said.

He watched Trigger head off across the room to lean on the bar and chat to Davit the barman. The bar would open soon, and fill with young executives from the newly opened branches of South Asian finance houses. And he would continue to help them develop a sophisticated palate for expensive and exotic drugs.

He *had* been paid to kill Freddie Tran but it'd been entirely secondary to his primary goal of locating Doctor Canning within Denam Prison. There was a future project involving the doctor which would make him a lot of money. It was unfortunate that someone had guessed correctly when suggesting the Clover gang had been involved in the death of his previously close associate. He still felt uneasy when he thought about how exposed he'd been when Frederika Tran had been arrested.

She'd been his Vostok contact, everything had gone through her, he'd supplied the Resistance too. He'd spend some months during her trial waiting for a knock at the door, even while he'd doubled his own personal security. Eventually he realised he was safe. Freddie, for whatever reason had not squealed on him. It was therefore with a twinge of regret that he'd ordered the hit on her.

He'd used an external outfit that made it harder to trace back to him and anyway it'd required a finesse that Trigger didn't have. It also needed considerable logistical expertise to reach and get inside Denam Prison which he'd preferred to pay for. He still didn't know how they'd managed the hit and he didn't want to know. He'd not even used one of the Bud gang members since everyone knew they were his distributors in Vostok. No, he'd put the contract out on the Underside, the AFS version of the old idea of a Dark Web: of course the real World Wide Web had gone dark, metaphorically as well as physically some time ago.

He'd interviewed the guy from a shortlist of two. His credentials were impeccable, his references checked out, but Santiago remembered when he met him, he'd felt a niggle between his shoulder blades. By the end of the interview however he'd been satisfied that Jim Leavey was who he said he was, and was, more importantly, the right man for the job. And the job had gone off without a hitch. It was on the news now. Why was that niggle between his shoulder blades back?

Chapter Four - Encryption

Valla returned to the small room where Alison and Glenn had been waiting. She'd made sure there were refreshments, for them and for Patrice, and she'd hand picked the guard for the room with Patrice. Her mind was in over-drive trying to second guess everything that could go wrong. She needed to speak to Alison and get some clarity before any press descended on the Intelligence Agency. Ideally she wanted to be long gone from here at that point but she was planning for all eventualities.

"Well?" she asked.

"He's got someone he's protecting, They're back in Singapore. Santiago's conceit is his weakness, there will be other people we can pull in and lever against him. But we need to get Patrice somewhere genuinely defensible, I'd like to say safe but Glenn assures me that doesn't exist."

Valla nodded at Alison, "I agree with Glenn. I think the best place we could head for is probably Kunlun, organised crime hasn't managed to take root there. I'll think about where would be defensible. However, I have some news. Tanya has gone missing en route to identifying Freddie's body. Somewhere between Vostok and Denam, they lost contact with the jet. There was no mayday, and there's no ping on the black box either. Anatoli Dale was flying."

She saw Alison's face change and looked in askance at Glenn, who nodded back at her.

"Sharp mind," he said.

"Should I whisper?" asked Valla.

"No, it's fine. But hang on to any more information till she comes back. In my experience she does this in chunks with sections of information, and it's like an iteration process."

Valla fell back on the social niceties of polite conversation.
"How are you? How's Gary?"

"I'm good. We're good. Gary's doing well, passing exams, enjoying McMurdo. I hear he's quite the climber these days too. Still plays poker, but the school aren't keen."

She could tell Glenn played the social game just as well.

"Freddie isn't dead," said Alison, "and Tanya isn't missing. Gordon is moving his pieces around for an end game."

The room stayed silent for a few minutes. Valla caught up, and she felt Glenn work on his temper. She decided to preempt anything he might say.

"Are you sure? This is pretty fucked up even for Gordon."

She saw from the corner of her eye Glenn looking at her, she could see he was convinced it was true.
"It's seventy five percent chance over all it's true. It's ninety five percent that Tanya and Anatoli are safe. It's eighty percent that Gordon is involved in both incidents. There's less certainty about Freddie, but that's mostly down to Freddie being who she is," said Alison.

Her face, Valla was pleased to see, looking lived in again.

"I have one more piece of information, are you ready," she asked Alison.

"Yes."

"Daniel Ektov told me Christine Frome might be influenced by Global. He had nothing concrete, only suspicions, but they were strong enough he wouldn't say it in an open phone call. I received an encrypted text after we had talked by sat phone."

She watched fascinated as Alison's face changed to a vacant stare. It must make her very vulnerable she thought. And as she looked across to Glenn's face, she could see that Alison being in that state worried him. It had wiped all trace of his earlier anger at his grandfather's manipulations from him.

She saw Alison snap out of the state much quicker than before.

"It's sixty five percent chance that's true but I don't have enough data. I'm relying on what I know about Christine from the news reports. Daniel must have more information even if it's just rumours. I know Daniel so that's why the score is relatively high. I'd trust his suspicions."

"Thanks, Alison," she said. "So, what are we going to do?"

She saw Glenn start to speak then hesitate, like he was getting some part of himself under control.

"We take Patrice to Kulun, to someone we can trust, and then... No," he said, "no. This is what he'll expect. The old bastard thinks he's the master puppeteer, he thinks he can move us around and we'll behave the way he predicts. Alison, what's the most unlikely thing we could do?"

Valla saw Alison look at Glenn and saw the realisation on her face that he meant to take that least likely path. It looked to Valla that Alison nearly said no, but then she saw the vacant stare again.

Patrice Reilly thought he was holding it together quite well. He'd been left alone in the room since the woman who'd called herself Alison had asked him those weird questions. He was unnerved now whenever he replayed those questions and his answers in his head. He felt vaguely violated in a way he couldn't put into words. It was all just feelings. But he was beginning to get worried. The helicoptering off the boat, bringing him to the Intelligence Agency were actions he'd expected but this long empty pause was a thing he recognised from his own life. The hiatus of indecision surrounded the people he'd so far had contact with. They were clearly in control of what happened to him, and legitimately so, but their lack of action suggested any plan was undergoing change, and he was unsure there'd been much to begin alterations on.

As long as Kim was safe he felt he was winning. She was the one good thing in his life, the one thing not tainted by Santiago Kooper. He'd met her on a rare break from 'business' in Singapore. She'd no idea about his life, and to be fair he'd little idea about hers. They had simply avoided anything that normally complicated a relationship and together they'd made a fantastical story up. Patrice knew it was doomed. His life always turned out that way, but so far it hadn't and he wanted to live in that world for as long as possible.

The door opened and the woman from the navy ship, Valentina he thought it was, and the other woman, Alison, came in accompanied by a man. Patrice didn't like the look of him. He was angry, it stood off him like an electrical charge and he was looking at Patrice the way you looked at unexploded ordinance lying washed up on the beach.

"Patrice, we're going to keep you safe, but you have to help us," said Valentina.

He focussed on her, people had said things like that to him before, and they'd rarely been able to keep their promises, But, this was a Senator, he remembered the news articles now, this was Senator Valentina Torres, and she'd got a navy out of the Senate so maybe it was a promise she could keep. He looked at the angry man, he didn't look like muscle, which wasn't to say he didn't look like he couldn't handle himself. So who was he?

"Who's this? I know slippery question lady, but who's angry dude?"

He saw the question lady, Alison, nudge the angry man in the ribs. Clearly there was something going on there, because that was tiger tail territory. He saw the man calm down a little.

39

"I'm Glenn Murcheson. I'm an Intelligence Agent. You need to tell us everything you know about Santiago's operation. Places and people. It's a deal. You make deals all the time."

This Glenn guy didn't like him, Patrice knew that for sure, but he wasn't lying either. It was a deal, and he thought they would keep their end. For a change Patrice felt like this was one of his good decisions.

"Okay," he said.

Daniel Ektov was in his office, he'd given Valla as much as he dared, but he also had suspicions which at that moment were too outlandish to share. He wondered if Gordon Murcheson's paranoia was actually just a form of psychological projection? That Gordon expected everyone was out to subvert him because he was doing just that to everyone else. Daniel's recent call had only deepened his mistrust, and now he truly regretted becoming campaign manager for Gordon. He still felt Gordon was the best option, but it scared him. Where were the new politicians who had the critical thinking skills to take on the rest of the world? Valentina Torres was one, but where were the others? Had they, as senior senators thwarted the up and coming talent?

He thought through the junior senators, thirty in a straight spilt between the five Families. He knew all six of the Lomonosov junior senators, and only Mariko Neish showed promise. He decided he ought to get her up to speed. He felt that spreading his suspicions far and wide with trusted confidants was the best defence against Gordon's obsessive secrecy. He called to arrange a meeting, and invited the other two senior Lomonosov senators Dante Castillero and River Sampson to join them. Lomonosov was a small Family, and often overlooked, which was an advantage when playing the kind of games Gordon Murcheson played, even if it seemed he never overlooked anything.

He received answers from all three over the next hour while he worked on Gordon's next press conference. They were all available for the following morning which he felt was soon enough. There was another press conference tonight. There would be a lot of questions about Frederika Tran's murder, and he especially wanted to hear Gordon's answers in light of his own suspicions. The first recorded candidate debate was tomorrow evening, and he'd need to meet Gordon tomorrow to discuss that too. Suddenly he felt very tired. He'd been living on the edge for so long, the effort had become second nature, but now he realised he was too old for this kind of shit. He'd hoped by now the world and the AFS in particular, would have become a safer place, maybe like it was at the end of the last century. But at seventy five years old he had finally realised the past had never been a safer place. It was only that the past's dangers had faded in the memories of those who were there.

Glenn was watching Alison closely. She was wobbling imperceptibly as they stood in the room with Patrice. Every time she used her sharp mind lately he'd felt more and more worried. He dug into a pocket on the outside of his survival suit's leg, and pulled out a high energy snack bar. He handed it to Alison. She took it and it was eaten in seconds. He saw Valla quickly cover up her surprise. It was late afternoon, the sun wouldn't be setting, but just now, there was still a feeling you could call evening. The plan they'd agreed on was to be on the Mercer before then.

There was a knock at the door, and Colin entered, with two others. As a group they headed out of the building, Patrice flanked on all sides by agents, with Glenn bringing up his rear. Valla and Alison in the lead. When they got to the car, Glenn watched Colin wave off the other two back inside.

"To the docks," said Valla to Colin as she got into the front passenger seat.

Patrice was sitting in-between Alison and Glenn in the rear. Glenn couldn't fault the plan. The Mercer was certainly defensible. It was't under the control of anyone other than the state in the shape of Senator Valentina Torres. And its destination could change at any point it became necessary. Alison had agreed their most likely destination had been Kunlun, and that heading for the ship, simply because its newness wouldn't have been factored fully into account, would be the least likely thing they could do, bar the truly mad or bad options.

As the car approached the dock gates, he could see the size of the ship. To him it was a decent size, as big as the cruise ships that used to come to McMurdo. Nowadays the cruise ships were massive and they had to anchor offshore and come to the harbour in their small boats, but when he was a boy, this size could tie up alongside the breakwater. The Mercer brought him back memories he was now at peace with.

The guard wore a dock security uniform. Glenn wondered about the guard's loyalties, but was pleased the man gave Valla's pass a perfunctory glance and didn't seem interested in the other car occupants. Colin drove on and they came alongside where the gangway reached down to the dock. They didn't get out straight away. Valla went onboard first. None of their plan had been communicated to the Mercer yet. While the radio had always been an open network, the AFS phone network was becoming increasing liable to the same kind of eavesdropping. An unexpected import from the UN that had been less useful.

Glenn saw Valla come back down with the captain. He had all the bearing of military men like Colin but there was also something fatherly about him. Glenn could tell he'd been in command for a long time. He also reminded Glenn of Valla but he decided to reserve further judgment on the captain. As Valla and the captain got to the bottom of the gangway, he tapped Colin on the shoulder and they all got out the car. He and Colin in positions which covered Patrice from the shore side.

The ship had a conference room and Captain Beardmore had invited everyone to meet there, except Patrice who'd been re-acquainted with the brig. Glenn and Alison were following the deck map when they caught up with Valla.

"Are you still thinking of heading for Singapore?" Glenn asked Valla.

"It's an unlikely destination, don't you think? But I found out Patrice was born there. He stowed away on a cruise ship when he was eight. Ended up in the Naturalisation Amnesty after hiding out in Saylon for four years. Guess who was hiding him?"

"Santiago?" ventured Alison.

"Yes," said Valla. "It's a risk taking Patrice anywhere near there. Singapore is still in negotiations over extradition. It's a safe bet Patrice has his papers on him everywhere he goes though." She continued, "We've now got a reason to go there, which I've left in Captain Beardmore's hands. He's getting the Loggerhead turtles ready to be brought onboard. We're going to repatriate them to Singapore."

Glenn didn't like this plan. He'd argued for simply sailing round to Weddell City but Singapore did mean they might be able to get Patrice's lover or friend or whoever safe too.

"What's the latest on Tanya and Anatoli?" he asked as they entered the conference room.

The room had two square windows to port and starboard and nearly every other inch of wall was either whiteboard or map. He could hear the ship's engines change as the ship prepared to set off, the turtles presumably now onboard. A slight vibration settled through the bulkheads and floor of the room. He saw Valla take a seat at the head of the table and he moved with Alison to take seats opposite the door they'd just entered through.

"I checked my mail and I've got a fresh encrypted file from Daniel, let me put it up, I've not read it yet," said Valla.

She docked her phone and the projector whirred into action displaying the mail on a whiteboard. He saw her tap the icon and there was a slight pause while it was decrypted. They stared at the few lines.

Chapter Five - Impermanence

Detective Inspector Enya Zhao was working at her desk in Weddell City Police Central Station. Or at least she was trying. It had been 12 hours since she'd been told the jet piloted by Anatoli Dale had gone missing. She wasn't down as next of kin, but Senator Dale, Anatoli's father, had made sure she'd known, calling her at home, before she learnt it from her boss, Chief Inspector Houten. She and Anatoli had met four and half years ago during the UN's failed attempt to retrieve Alison, Alison's son Gary, and a scientist called Doctor Michael Canning. Before then she'd been content to police Weddell City for tourist crime and the basic petty crimes that the police had been allowed to pursue. Since then, the remit of the police in the Antarctic Free State had changed considerably. They'd changed to resemble the other police forces around the world, while the Intelligence Agency had turned from serous crime to concentrate on state versus state threats. Sometimes she wished it hadn't altered, but now she was keen to take advantage of that change.

She wanted to investigate the disappearance of the jet. She needed to assure herself that they were still alive; Tanya, the ex-partner of the recently deceased Frederika Tran and her beloved Anatoli. She'd also met Freddie and Tanya four and a half years ago and she didn't believe Freddie was dead. It made her even more keen to find the jet, because it was part of the same puzzle. How she wrangled herself onto such a case was not yet clear, but she was determined. She might even have to call in a few favours, but that was what favours were for.

She saw James Wylie come into the office and catch her eye. He looked furtive which was unusual for James.

He'd been with her when they'd killed two UN Special Forces guys in a shoot out at Wilkes Enterprise Zone and she'd been trying to protect him from the fall out of that and other things for the four and half years since. He still worked traffic, despite being a world class sharp shooter. He'd been scouted by the AFS Olympic Committee. Now that the AFS was recognised by the UN, they'd been invited to the games in two years time. James had been made up when he'd been invited to join the team. He didn't look made up today.

She got up from the desk and headed over towards him. He hadn't moved from standing just inside the door.

"What's up James, you look like you've seen a ghost."

"Maybe I have."

"What do you mean?"

"Not here. In the car park."

This was not at all like James Wylie. He had specifically turned down the offer to join the Intelligence Agency because he found the subterfuge so stressful. He'd told her he'd seen what it had done to Glenn Murcheson and hadn't wanted that lifestyle. She followed him down the stairs and out into the car park. The sun was shining, the ground was dry, the forecast air temperature had been 14 degrees but she reckoned that was an underestimate. Summer was here.

She caught up with James next to her car.
"I have something to tell you. You might not like it."

"Okay," she said, "I might not, but if you have good reasons, I will understand, James."

"You know I shot that bus driver, the Resistance smuggler in Vostok? You and I know it was hushed up. But Gordon Murcheson knew too. He sent the rifle, remember?"

She nodded, James had been seriously shook up when he found out he'd not shot the U.N. Special Forces leader, but someone else. It had taken him over a year to come to terms with it. The fact he'd been played by Freddie and Gordon, hadn't really helped as much as she'd hoped it would.

"I got a call a month ago from Gordon. I wanted to tell you, but I also wanted to deal with it on my own. You're in the shit...sorry... with Houten enough. Anyway, he told me he had a job and if I took it he would destroy all the evidence there was about me in Vostok and nothing would reach the Olympic committee. I asked him what the job was. He told me he wanted me to assassinate Freddie."

"God, Wylie, you didn't say yes? Did you?"

She could tell just by looking at him that he'd said yes. She felt bad for asking him to say it out loud. She knew now she had to get, not just on the case, but get in full control of the search for the missing jet. Anything involving Gordon Murcheson was liable to cost someone their life, she didn't want that someone to be Anatoli.

"I don't want to hear more here," she said. "I'm going back into the office to make some phone calls. Here's my keys stay in the car, keep it locked. We'll sort this. And we'll sort Senator Murcheson, for good this time."

She saw him relax a bit as he took her keys. Why did people like Gordon Murcheson have to mess up people like James Wylie, she thought.

When she returned to the car, she was waiting on one email from Senator Arne Dale to be in control of the case. She'd also sent Valla an update, but she'd no idea if Valla'd be able to help. They could travel by scheduled flight to Vostok, but they'd need to charter something to get to Denam. They'd have to get to Denam Prison as quickly as possible and avoid alerting Gordon Murcheson to that. Gordon wouldn't move against the suggestion she'd investigate the missing jet, and heading to Vostok was perfectly reasonable since Anatoli had left from there. It was the second part where she'd need help.

James had unlocked the car, and she was sitting in the driver's seat trying to get things clearer, before she started driving. She preferred to be focussed on one thing at time.

"You okay?" he asked, "I didn't want to get you involved, but I don't think it was Freddie I shot in Denam Prison, and I can't face that again. I want Gordon Murcheson to get what he deserves."

"Why do you think it wasn't Freddie?"

She herself hadn't believed the news when she'd heard it. Frederika Tran just wasn't that stupid, she had contacts inside and outside the prison, ex-Resistance contacts and criminal contacts too. She'd know a hit had been commissioned. She'd probably even know who it was, which would give her the knowledge that it was Gordon behind it. Enya knew Freddie wouldn't go quietly. And she also knew Freddie cared for Tanya, she'd make sure Tanya stayed safe. Which meant that Anatoli, if still alive might not be so safe.

"I don't know. I was pretty sure at the time. I had the free time schedule. It looked like her. I couldn't imagine someone would choose to take Freddie's place. But the more I thought about it, the more I worried it hadn't been her. First I put it down to what happened in Vostok, maybe I was paranoid. But then I got this posted through my door."

He passed her an envelope, which was addressed to Jim Leavey, inside was a four leafed clover cut from green paper.

"I don't understand?"

"Gordon arranged a persona for me, Jim Leavey, full back story as a hitman. It was fucking awful, I kept thinking they'd rumble me."

She saw him check her face, he'd sworn twice now, she didn't like swearing and he knew it. He continued.

"Somehow he'd got Santiago Kooper to commission the hit, I got the job from the Clover gang. Who would know that? Only Gordon, and only Freddie if she was still alive."

"Well that's conclusive. Gordon's manipulative but he's not sadistic, he didn't send this. He must believe Freddie is dead, and we need to keep it that way. My concern is what Freddie will do next."

"If I was Freddie I'd be tempted to try and take Gordon out in revenge, and maybe for my own safety too."

She thought about that, it was always dangerous assigning your own motives to a suspect, but it sounded a reasonable assumption. Even if Freddie might have more going on, those two things would cross her mind like anyone's.

"I agree. But I'm sure his security must already be tight, Gordon's annoyed a lot of people over the years. I can let Valla know, maybe she can tip the Intelligence Agency anonymously. But we need to get to Vostok, there's a flight tomorrow morning, your favourite time."

She heard him groan, and felt he was finally lightening up. However she was quite determined to see Gordon brought to justice for the attempt on Freddie's life. Who would enter into a plea bargain ever again if they knew the President might take it into their head to have you bumped off once you'd avoided the firing squad? No. His actions were criminal, just like all the things Freddie had done and went to prison for.

It was early afternoon the following day when they landed at Vostok. The last time Enya had been here there'd been a big spring storm tearing through the place, and she'd not seen much more than pastel shaded snow flakes. Today the sun was shining. They got through the airport without much trouble and into a taxi to take them to the local police station. Her orders had come from Houten with barely concealed bad grace. She reckoned her time in Weddell City Police was nearly through, and it would be wise after this to seek a new position somewhere else before Houten could really screw her career up. Maybe Vostok, she thought. Anatoli was spending more time out here. The richer tourists wanted to charter jets and they were coming to Vostok more than Weddell City these days.

It still looked tacky to her, the bright neon colours were everywhere on The Strip. Everything vied for your attention, till there was just overload. In a street running parallel with The Strip, the administrative buildings looked dowdy compared to the casinos and hotels. The taxi pulled into the vehicle airlock and she paid the driver. There were no private vehicles in Vostok, everyone took a taxi or used the buses that ran routes past every hotel and casino. Most of the drivers, like Toni who'd been shot by Wylie in error, had some connection to the criminal gangs that operated in Vostok. There was the Bud gang, a part of Santiago's empire, the Tchai gang worked the casinos with some protection on the side and the Bird gang ran the brothels. While Freddie was technically removed from all of this, and had been for four years, Enya knew people still owed Freddie.

How she was going to infiltrate this network was another matter though. She needed an in. It was possible there was someone in the police department she could use. There was going to be a few of them on the take, a place like Vostok had too many temptations. If she wanted to make a new career out here though, she'd have to move carefully. They stepped through the door airlock and into the wide foyer of the police station. It looked like it had seen some action. The floor was scuffed, there was only a few chairs screwed down tight against a wall. Ahead, the reception desk was high and had a grill. She had to stand on tiptoe to lean on the thin edge of the counter.

"Hi," she said "I'm Detective Inspector Zhao, from Weddell City. You're expecting me."

The desk sergeant looked up from the paperwork she was quite sure he'd not been reading.

"Yeah. Come through." He nodded to the right side of the counter and she could see a detector gate.

She and Wylie passed through, depositing their handguns into the tray and receiving them back.

"Chief wants to see you first."

They followed, as the desk sergeant who's name she still didn't know, wove in and out of desks that littered the large area behind the reception counter. Most desks were empty she noticed, but all looked like they were worked at, with piles of papers and discarded coffee cups sitting to the sides of old style monitors. He showed them into an office on the far wall and left.

Enya could see a woman with her back to the door, talking low on the telephone. They waited, Enya knew the move, and she was determined not to break first. Instead she studied the rest of the office, the disordered papers on the tops of filing cabinets. Paperwork that would be digital elsewhere. It looked like the gangs were more than capable of hacking the network here. That was one place to start looking for Anatoli and Tanya. Maybe they had never left Vostok at all. The logs for the airport were all digital, it would be an easy bribe to falsify a departure. But she also noted it was more difficult to disable a black box. She should look for who could do that.

Finally the woman swung around, and Enya snapped her attention back. The woman was older, old enough to probably not be native. She spoke, her accent a mixture of Vostok and presumably where she'd originated from, but it wasn't anywhere that Enya could place. Lots of people from India or southern Africa had ended up in Vostok but it wasn't them, it was different.

"Detective Inspector, I see I have little choice in letting you investigate the missing jet. We walk a tightrope here, I hope you've not brought anything sharp with you that could jeopardise that."

Enya saw her look at Wylie, and wondered what she might have gleaned from any criminal or Resistance contacts she might have had.

"This is Constable Wylie, Ma'am. He works for me. We're not here to make trouble, just to find the missing jet and the missing pilot and passenger. There are vested interests, as I'm sure you'll understand, in securing their safety."

Enya wondered if she should air her suspicions about Freddie, but she held back. Let her see that, maybe she'd work it out for herself, there must be rumours starting by now. It would be hard for Freddie to keep a cover and make contact at the same time.

"Okay. I've allocated you an office next door to work from. I'm Chief Inspector Chapman, everyone calls me Chief. The Ma'ams run the brothels round here."

"I'll remember that Chief. Thanks."

55

There'd been a tone of dismissal in the Chief's final statement and Enya waved Wylie out the door ahead of her, and into the room next door. Next door was too close for her to feel comfortable though, and that was also on purpose. She swept the room a brief glance, seeing the hasty marks left from emptying what must have been a considerable pile of boxes from the room. She wondered where they were now being stashed, and felt it would be best to show willing to using the room even if they did nothing vital here.

"Lets get to the hotel and refresh. We can start here once we've checked out the airport."

She saw Wylie nod in understanding, and she picked up the key left on the desk, locking the door on the way out. Let everyone know this was simply how she operated and not a comment of trustworthiness. Even if it was.

They had rooms in the Grand Hotel. Its foyer was a cold, noisy place, with the constant whine of the broken air seals on the airlock, but it had a public sat phone, and it had relatively cheap rates for a place on The Strip. The rooms were warm, the beds were comfy and the showers had decent pressure, all in all it would do. She met James in the foyer, zipped up in his survival suit. Vostok was in the interior, it was built on the ice sheet, constantly having to be readjusted as the ice moved beneath the buildings, which was why there were no private cars. You needed plenty of experience to drive in Vostok. The lake, was to the west of The Strip, ignored entirely by the city's development. You could buy a postcard of it, but that seemed to be the most interaction people wanted with it. They were here to have a good time, not look at the geography.

The only other habitation in the interior was Kunlun deep in the Progress Massif, a mining town and, as far as Enya could remember from her school lessons, partially underground. Vostok was the most exposed and least permanent settlement in the Antarctic Free State, and she felt its impermanence had seeped into the very life of the city. They took a taxi to the airport. Once inside they headed for the customer service desk. Enya flashed her ID at the man behind the desk and noted that she didn't get the same level of attention as Glenn had, when they'd been here previously, and he'd mentioned his last name.

"I want to speak to whoever arranges the charter jets. I'm investigating the disappearance of Victor Oscar nine seventy. I also want to speak to the traffic controllers who were on shift when it took off. I'll wait."

He looked at her and then at James. She thought she saw a flicker of recognition. She hoped the most that might get back to Gordon was that she was naturally looking for Anatoli.

"I'll get the Charter Hire Manager over right away. I can get you the shift list but you can't visit the tower. You'll need to catch them off shift."

She was worried that felt too easy. But she knew finding who could disable a black box was going to be much harder than simply asking customer services.

Chapter Six - Waves

Colin Nyugen and Captain Beardmore entered the conference room to silence. They immediately turned to the screen to see what had everyone so quiet. Colin understood straight away. This information was really bad for the security of the AFS. He saw the Captain looking slightly puzzled. Colin didn't think it was his place to explain, but he saw Senator Torres was about to say something anyway.

"This is dangerous. We all know what Gordon Murcheson is like but who'd have thought Christine Frome was working for Global? And having the cheek to stand on an anti-corruption ticket too. She must be relying on a lot of people not wanting a second term of Gordon Murcheson."

Glenn spoke next, "Do we know this is true? I mean it's come from Daniel, but where's he got it from? Alison?"

Colin saw Glenn turn to look at Alison Strang, the state negotiator. He saw Alison's face look really strange, like she was going to have a fit. It unnerved Colin, especially since everyone else, except for the captain seemed to be okay with it. Colin looked back to the captain who was sitting down into a chair as quietly as possible. He decided to do the same.

The information on the screen was brief; details of several large financial transactions from accounts linked to Global into Christine Frome's account, one last year, two ahead of the run-off campaign and one very recently. There was a follow up paragraph detailing not a single payment had been registered with the Senate as campaign funding or otherwise, and that Christine's association with Global went back more than a decade to when she was a junior senator, a long time by AFS standards. Colin was under no illusion that if this could be proved then Christine would be disqualified from holding any office. Even without proof, if it was released to the press, she'd be entirely discredited in the eyes of the electorate. They still considered the UN and Global to be hostile entities, despite or perhaps because many had been recent UN states' residents and plenty were ex-employees of Global.

He saw Alison's face change again, awareness come back to her eyes and saw Glenn surreptitiously slide her a snack bar.

Alison began, "I can only base this on knowing Daniel and knowing Global. Information can be hacked, there would need to be more evidence to disqualify Christine from standing, but I think this is real. Christine works for Global to all intents and purposes, and this is bad for the independence of the AFS on the world stage if she gets elected. I calculate that Global doesn't think its influence has been detected by anyone. They have no concerns about Christine's ability to be discreet. This was an error, as clearly she's not been careful to hide their transactions. I expect we will find smaller payments made to Gordon, but I imagine they will be much harder to come by, and be less damaging to Gordon. Those payments would be disclosed by Global in the event of action against Christine so nothing should be done till there is independent evidence she is working to their agenda. I recommend photographic proof of her meeting senior Global personnel and also a body of speeches and voting decisions in support of Global's agenda in Senate business recordings."

Colin saw Valla nod and write something down on her phone.

Captain Beardmore, coughed, then asked, "Are we still heading for Singapore?"

Valla answered "Yes, Captain. We have some turtles to return. I'll pass this on to someone I trust. But we shouldn't forget there's more to this presidential election than the manoeuvring of Gordon Murcheson. I've received confirmation that Frederika Tran isn't dead and Gordon ordered the hit. While we may be caught in the middle of this, we make our own decisions."

Santiago Kooper had heard the rumours. A person like Frederika Tran was always going to have rumours, dead or alive. However he had to decide whether the rumours about her being alive were true or just the beginnings of the myth that would spring up around her death. Was it someone in her organisation using the uncertainty to solidify their control? The remains of the Resistance in Vostok had coalesced around Tanya, maybe it was her and that was why Tanya had gone 'missing'? He didn't put much faith in the rumour being true, but he seldom gambled where his own life was concerned. He was moving to a more secure base, Trigger was driving, and he had a car in front.

It was late evening, the sun was skimming the horizon, the temperature falling rapidly. They were driving down Fifth Avenue towards the container port, where he had a small warehouse. It had security round it, and best of all a secret escape route into the harbour.

"Shit," exclaimed Trigger as the car skidded sideways, throwing Santiago across the back seat.

"What's up?"

"Someone's just taken out Pauli, came out of a service alley and his car's been smashed into a building."

He felt the car lunge as Trigger tried to pull it around from where it had skidded to. Then he was thrown forward as the car started reversing at as high a speed as it could be forced, down a service alley. He could see Trigger busy watching the rear cameras and the radar. The orange glow making his already craggy face positively grotesque. Santiago stayed down. He knew hits and this one wasn't over. His car was bullet proof but not indestructible. The car slewed round out of the service alley and onto Fourth Avenue. Horns blared at them.

He let Trigger concentrate on driving and worked on who this might be, and therefore how determined they'd be, and also what resources they'd have to hand. To ram Pauli's car took fanaticism, maybe even of the suicidal variety. Which pointed to the Resistance rather than a rival. So this looked like someone knew he'd taken the commission on Freddie and it was revenge. That was bad, he'd have to make the dock warehouse and get going immediately.

"Call the warehouse, get them ready for us and for an attack."

"Yes, Boss."

He racked his memory for what supply ships he had in port. The Iron Prestige was impounded so not that one. He had people on the Golden Key, a freighter due in tomorrow. But he needed something now. He felt the car shudder as it ran over something.

"Track buster, gonna be bumpy ride but we're nearly there."

The car bucked as the broken central track unwound from its castor wheels and the car slumped down as the road tyres took the whole weight of the car. It would be less manoeuvrable now. He felt the car slew sideways again, as Trigger fought the steering. He heard the screeching of metal on metal as the fencing scraped along the side of the car. Then he heard gunshot and the pinging of bullets against the car.

He heard the answering staccato of sub-machine guns as his men fired back and then it went very dark as the car spun into the unlit warehouse. He fumbled with the door and rolled out, drawing his hand gun and looking for cover in the gloom.

"Boss"

He looked up and Trigger was gesturing to the back of the warehouse. He ran towards him.

"Is the launch ready? Its going to have to be the Iron Prestige, we'll need men to take her."

"Jack, Vann, fall back with us," shouted Trigger.

Two men started to run semi-backwards, guns trained on the warehouse door. They were all running to the small dot of bright light Santiago could see at the rear of the warehouse. As he got there, he looked down into the hole, brightly lit by LED strips around its edge. He could see the launch bouncing on the sparkling water. Trigger was already on the rungs of the ladder and he saw him drop the short distance into the launch and head for the stern which faced the shoreside.

"Clear," said Trigger.

Santiago went next, joining Trigger in the stern, wary of further ambush. The freezing water of the harbour would finish a person even in a survival suit in about fifteen minutes and whoever was attacking him had already shown their disregard for personal safety, he couldn't imagine the Code would stop them. The Code, the idea that you saved a person from the environment no matter what, was becoming a thing of the past anyway. He doubted many people outside of Kunlun and the smaller towns bothered with it.

Jack and Vann dropped together, rocking the boat violently and, glancing round, Santiago saw Jack take the controls. The Iron Prestige was on the other side of the harbour, a journey across the open water. He hoped the launch was fast enough and they'd be a difficult target despite the light, but then they had to board the Prestige and gain control. There wouldn't be more than two police onboard he estimated, just to keep her safe. They might have heard the gunfire, or see the launch coming if the radar was on. He'd have to board her from the rear where the trawl nets were dragged aboard, so it might look from their bridge that he was simply passing astern of her.

"Go for the stern, get onboard take out anyone you find. I'm in a hurry."

The spray laden wind whipped across their faces. His cheeks were stinging, his eyes watering as he kept a look out for another boat getting close. He had always eschewed a visor, he felt they were a dangerous crutch that made you over confident. His men followed his lead. They'd left the protection of the container port side and were heading across the wide opening of Saylon harbour. A long deep swell started to roll the launch and he felt Jack shift the boat to crab across the swell, trying to keep a straight line to the City Quay. It felt like hours to Santiago, the cold had begun to penetrate through his survival suit just as they made the stern of the Prestige.

Trigger moved forward to take the controls as Jack and Vann jumped on a rising wave at the tied up trawl nets. Santiago watched them scramble away out of sight. He wrinkled his nose at the stench of fish coming from the nets. He didn't think Patrice had done that much fishing, but then he realised it made an excellent cover smell.

"Who d'you think they were, Boss?"

"Your guess is as good as mine," said Santiago, knowing his guess was probably better, "I think we've upset the Resistance."

"Is that because of Freddie?"

"Trigger, what have I said?"

"Yes, Boss."

He heard two shots come from above, then Jack reappeared at the top of the pile of nets.

"All secured."

He nodded, and Trigger brought the boat right into the stern so he could easily catch the netting. He clambered up, joined by Trigger who'd jumped as the now unpowered launch started to drift away.

"Get the engines started, and a course for Singapore set."

"Yes, Boss," said Jack.

Detective Inspector Enya Zhao was waiting for the Charter Hire Manager in the small room that the Customer Service guy had shown her to. She'd sent Wylie back to the police station, with the list of traffic controllers who were on shift when Anatoli's jet was supposed to have taken off, and told him to work out a route to go check on them all. The door opened and a rotund man bundled into the room, looking flustered.

"I'm told you want to see me?" he said, with the unmistakable accent of a Vostok native.

His job must take it out of him because she didn't think he looked young enough to be a Vostok native, most being under thirty. She saw him dab at his forehead with a hankie, which was so unusual as to make her wonder why he was sweating. There were very few occasions when you'd publicly sweat in Antarctica, and it was usually a stress tell rather than down to the temperature. He smelled of it, like he'd slept in his clothes.

"I'm Detective Inspector Zhao. Can I have your name?"

"I'm Manuel Delaval. People call me Manny."

"Manny. I'm investigating the disappearance of Victor Oscar nine seven zero. I understand someone chartered the flight at eighteen hundred hours. Was that by voice or text?"

"Err... Well. Now, let me try to remember. It's been very busy lately. The Dubai hyperplane got in yesterday and I can barely remember anything past that. Eighteen hundred.... Wait, yes, I remember now, it was text. It was an odd one. That's why it's sticking in my head, they asked specifically for Victor Oscar nine seventy, people don't often do that, and there were no passenger names. But they paid up front. This is Vostok you understand. It's not my business to go prying too deeply into what people want transported."

"Indeed," said Zhao, "And?"

"And I contacted Anatoli. He seemed fine with the charter. I spoke to him on the phone. He said he was free and... You know, now that I think about it, he usually asked questions about the charters and he didn't that time. It was like he already knew what it was all about. I never thought anymore about it, till I heard he'd gone missing. And then the hyperplane arrived and I haven't had a minute to myself. I haven't even gone home."

Enya Zhao was not convinced. The guy was scared. He might well have been busy, but she thought he had other reasons for not going home. And he was clearly trying to implicate Anatoli.

"Would you mind leaving your phone number and address in case I need to contact you again?"

She pushed a piece of paper and a pen at him, and gave him a look that dared him to create a fuss so she could arrest him. She noticed as he wrote how shaky his hand was. There was more to this guy than she'd so far uncovered, she thought. And he had more to tell her, she was sure. She watched Manny leave the room, and almost wished she had some of the skills of Alison Strang, but even without them she could see him untense his shoulders.

She called the station and got put through to James.

"James, work in one hundred and two, Monroe Street to your route. It's the address for Manuel Delaval, the Charter Manager, he's hiding something. I'll be along shortly."

"No problem, I have the three traffic controllers who were on shift that evening, one of them's also on Monroe Street."

"Interesting. Any luck on disabling black boxes?"

"Found a few methods with some overlap in mining tech. Looks promising. I'll keep digging till you arrive."

"Thanks."

Chapter Seven - Shots

Gordon Murcheson was waiting for a phone call. He didn't like waiting. He paced across the picture window in his office that showed the interior of the Senate Chamber. He'd heard that someone had tried to take out Santiago Kooper, and now he was concerned. He hadn't expected that reaction. It meant that some part of his plan was out of kilter. A plan should work like clockwork, and this one was in danger of coming un-sprung.

His sources were suggesting a remnant of Vostok Resistance had travelled to Saylon. The Resistance had melted away when the change to the hereditary membership of Families and the revocation of its proscription had taken place. As a political force they no longer existed, but there'd always been hardliners who'd wanted a fight, and they appeared to be happy to take on the gangs. Without Freddie he had no real inside to the Resistance anymore, just the chatter of the fringes. It was the one downside to removing her from play. If he had indeed removed her, he thought. He was beginning to suspect he'd not. Tanya's jet going missing had been his first clue but the attack on Santiago was further confirmation. He was now waiting to speak to the guard who'd identified the body first in Denam Prison.

He'd been waiting for an hour. It didn't bode well for the guard. In half an hour he'd be meeting with Daniel and discussing the strategy for the evening's debate with Christine. He tried to focus on that instead. They had the dirt on Christine but he had to choose when to reveal it. Usually he could feel the moment, sense the tension build, till his nugget of information would set off an avalanche of opinions and actions in his favour. He was not feeling it.

He needed to act. He called Wahid and told him to get to Denam and find out what was going on. Then he thought about who to contact in Vostok that could give him the information he required. He didn't need to trust them, they didn't have to like him, just a connection was enough. He paced some more as the Senate chamber filled behind him for the start of the day's business.

Daniel Ektov welcomed Mariko, River and Dante into his office, offering them seats around the small oval desk he used. Everything had been cleared from it and was now piled up on a nearby credenza.

"Thank you for coming. I'm sharing what I know with you all because I feel events are becoming dangerously complicated."

He saw them look puzzled.

"Let me explain."

When he'd finished he was please to see that Mariko was deep in thought, but more worried that River seemed to be out of his depth. Dante as usual was inscrutable, it was Daniel's favourite thing about him.

"You mean to say Christine is Global's candidate? And the man you're campaigning for you don't trust? That's kinda fucked up Daniel, if you don't mind me saying," said River.

"Of course Christine is working for Global, why else stand on an anti-corruption ticket if it wasn't to say 'Don't look at me, look at them'," said Dante. "and nothing Gordon Murcheson does would surprise me. The man's probably made a pact with the devil."

"But why?" asked Mariko. "What's their plan?"

"That's why I've invited you to join me this morning, I can't figure this out on my own. The attack on Santiago Kooper and the missing jet with the partner of Freddie and a senator's son in it, the assassination or not of Freddie, these are all either part of Gordon's plan or wrapped up inside his plan, and there's no way I'm letting it fail in a way that gets Christine elected. Do I make myself understood?"

"We agree, I'm sure," said River, looking at his fellow senators, "But what can we do?"

"We must expose Christine, not to the press immediately, that takes finesse, and I'm happy to let Gordon choose that moment. No. We must make sure the information is seeded around the senate, that it leaks out to the Resistance remnants, that in fine Antarctic style everyone knows but they don't recall how they found out," he said. "Lomonosov is a Family eminently suited to such things, it's how we've always had to work to get what we wanted."

He saw them nod in agreement. Lomonosov had never bemoaned their status as a small Family. Daniel had helped them all see it as a strength and most members felt a deep pride in what they'd achieved as a Family within the Senate and in Kunlun their political base. Daniel had simply tapped into that pride this morning and

71

they'd responded as he'd expected. He smiled. It didn't matter what else happened now, between Mariko, Dante and even Valla he was confident Christine would be thwarted. Though he was less sure about what would happen to Gordon. He mused on what Valla had said recently; it truly could be 'his own funeral'.

Daniel entered Gordon's secretary's office. It always smelt of its wood panelling, even after all this time. He wondered what the wood was, or how Gordon managed to keep the smell going? He knew there would be a psychological reason for it. Gordon never did anything purely for the aesthetic. Gordon's secretary buzzed through. Daniel noticed an unusual delay in the response. Something had rattled Gordon, another piece of the puzzle he had to put together. He entered into the stone clad office, seeing Gordon standing in front of the picture window, almost in silhouette against the bright lights from the Senate chamber.

"What's up?" he asked, walking toward the picture window.

"They can't find the guard who found Freddie's body. I've sent Wahid to try and find out what's happened. We must act as if Freddie is alive and loose. This could seriously affect the campaign. Do you think Global might have sprung her?"

"Global are capable of anything, let's not forget they were backing Dr. Canning and his experiments on people. But our efforts to remove UN agents must be making it a bit harder for them to operate. Maybe they're working with the remnants of the Resistance?"

"Yes. That makes sense. How do you think Christine is going to play this?"

"The corruption angle. Which we could turn round on her, but it wouldn't be wise to speculate too much in the debate. Highlight how inexperienced Christine will be as President, show up her naivety in her questions and statements. You have a reputation Gordon, use it."

Daniel stared into the Senate chamber watching the cleaners tidying up after the morning session. As if time had slowed, he realised one of the cleaners had lifted a hand gun up from somewhere and was aiming it at them. He pushed at Gordon. The glass shattered. He felt the heat in his chest. He breathed in heavily and wanted to cough. A burning sensation seared his left lung. He stopped the inward breath and coughed anyway. Blood spattered out of his mouth. He felt he was falling. He felt Gordon catch him and lower him to the floor. He could tell Gordon was saying something, but he couldn't make it out. His eyes felt heavy. He closed them. It would only be a minute. Just till this pain went away.

Chapter Eight - Empty

Frederika Tran was sitting in a swivel chair in the upstairs office of the warehouse. She was swinging idly from side to side, thinking. The only other person in the room was Tanya, her partner. They'd been together for twelve years, first in Kunlun and then in Vostok. When Freddie went to Denam Prison it was the first time they'd really been apart, and despite how she'd wanted it to go, it had hurt like hell. She'd tried to keep Tanya safe from the court case, but the way she'd done it had turned Tanya against her and Tanya had stood in the witness stand. She'd testified that Freddie had set up the hit on Toni the tourist bus driver, and so implicated Freddie as working with the U.N. Special Forces. When that had come out Freddie knew Gordon Murcheson had double crossed her, and she'd sworn revenge. She'd also sworn to win Tanya back, to make her see what had really happened.

Unfortunately it wasn't working, and Freddie was running out of time to come up with new ideas. She'd never had to figure someone out like this. She could figure out what someone wanted; what their weaknesses were, and how to manipulate that, but she'd never had to convince someone she was telling the truth, and she knew now it was because she'd never really told the truth before. Not the cold, hard truth, not the truth that tears at your heart while you tell it. Freddie had always protected herself from that till now.

"You've got to believe me. I'm telling the truth."

She watched Tanya's back for any sign she was listening. She saw her shake her long blonde hair, she knew her well enough to know Tanya's mind wasn't even in the room. Where was she? Was she thinking back to what happened? Maybe, Freddie thought, she was getting somewhere, maybe Tanya would see it was true. Freddie got as close to hope as her cynical mind dared, then pulled back to more mundane matters as Tanya continued to ignore her.

What was she going to do with the Dale boy? She didn't mind pissing Gordon off but she'd no mind to take on the Glencor Family in general. So far he hadn't seen her, they had him tied up and blindfolded downstairs in the warehouse. All he knew was Tanya wasn't with him, but that didn't really give him any clues. There could be a few different reasons he'd been hijacked without even taking to the air, especially in Vostok. The less he knew about what was going on the safer it was for him, and she'd impressed on the mixture of criminal and resistance lackeys she'd collected that he wasn't to be harmed.

Her mobile rang on the steel tabletop, vibrating away from her. She picked it up. It was Cheung, Pierre's man in Weddell City, the one Pierre had thought was dead, who'd turned up after all the fighting at McMurdo, as if nothing had happened. She didn't trust him one bit, but he was her only contact in Weddell City. She'd asked him to infiltrate the Senate building and to keep an eye on Gordon's movements there.

"It's done," he said.

"What's done?" she asked. Her mind whirred with the possibilities. She felt a rising panic. "What the fuck've you done? I didn't ask you to *do* anything."

"He needed taken out. He was a danger to the Antarctic Free State."

"Who? Who've you taken out? Not Gordon? Fuck. I'm having *you* taken out at the first opportunity. Tell me it wasn't Gordon."

"You ungrateful bitch. I risk my life getting inside the senate and I do you a favour and now you threaten me. We'll see. I've new friends who're more appreciative of my efforts. Fuck you Freddie. I hope they catch you and this time they do shoot you as a traitor."

The connection cut. The only word going through her head was fuck, on a constant loop, while behind it she was trying to draw in threads that would fix this.

"Another plan falling apart?"

Oh, not now Tanya, don't start this now, she thought.

"I'm trying to keep you safe, that's all I've ever wanted. I don't want Gordon dead, I want him discredited, his ego smashed. This is bad, bad for us."

"Bad for you, don't you mean?"

"Please Tanya, please believe me, if there was a way to undo Toni's death I would do it. Gordon double crossed me, he told me he was taking out the Special Forces guy. I couldn't admit that in court. Gordon always has back up plans, and it could be you he'd put in the dock next. I should have been straight with you. I'm sorry. I thought the less you knew the safer you'd be."

77

"Be straight with me now then. What's this all about Freddie? Why aren't you still in Denam Prison?"

"I got word there was a hit out on me, I couldn't stay there. I knew it was Gordon behind it too. He'd only relax if he thought it had been successful."

"Why set up Anatoli, why me?"

"You were going to identify the body. You'd find out it wasn't me and I didn't know how things were between us. You never visited. I was worried once Gordon found out, he might use you for leverage next. Anatoli's just a bit of extra insurance."

"Freddie you haven't changed. You've used someone associated with Pierre Cottrell to scout for you. Don't you remember how dysfunctional that bunch were? Hell, they were infiltrated by Glenn Murcheson. And now they've killed the president, and you're going to be fingered as the culprit. And this is keeping me safe?"

Freddie had never lost her temper with Tanya, ever. They'd had blazing rows, thrown things at each other, but Freddie hadn't really meant it, it'd been kind of fun, especially the making up afterwards. But now she did. Nothing got thrown. She didn't even raise her voice. Like the truth she'd been trying to tell, her voice was ice cold and sharp.

"I see."

She stood up, picked up the arms of her survival suit from where they'd been magnetically stuck on the legs, shouldered them on and zipped up to the chin. She picked up the mobile from the table and placed it in a chest pocket, then picked up her visor. She headed for the door.

"Where you going? Freddie?" Tanya's voice was anxious now, "It's going to get darker soon. You can't just walk out." Then it switched back to her earlier anger, "What the fuck am I going to do with Anatoli and your goons?"

Freddie opened the door and started down the metal stairs that ran against the wall at this end of the warehouse. Underneath the office were toilets, a kitchen and cupboards, the rest of the warehouse was full height and apart from Anatoli Dale strapped to a chair and some other empty chairs and cot beds, it was also entirely empty.

"Freddie," Tanya screamed.

Her name echoed off the walls. Fuck thought Freddie, bang goes Anatoli's passport out of here. She walked passed Anatoli and stopped, bending down close to the side of his head.

She whispered in his ear, "Tanya won't let anything happen to you."

Then she straighten up and continued to the air lock door. Behind her she could hear the door of the kitchen open and Casey and Phil piling out, the rustle of their suits as they shouldered them on and the clicks as hand guns were pulled.

"Boss?" Phil shouted.

"We're leaving," she shouted back.

"What about him?"

"Leave him. He's Tanya's problem. Come on we've got to get to Weddell City, there's a fresh bag of shit that needs to be fertilising flowers."

She'd every confidence they'd follow her and wouldn't ask too many questions while they did it. She still knew how to get some people to do as they were told. Outside was Tanya's car, she opened it up and they all got in. How Tanya left the warehouse, was now Tanya's problem. She'd tried, she told herself, she'd really tried.

Tanya watched the three of them leave through the airlock, and realised that Freddie would take her car. She'd no phone either, Freddie had destroyed her's and Anatoli's before they'd even been brought into the warehouse. What was worse was she knew this warehouse. It was one Freddie had used for smuggling, because it was on the edge of the airport warehouse district and not covered by any airport security. Freddie's reputation had been sufficient. She had to get Anatoli free and together they had to think of a way of getting far from the warehouse before Freddie's next goons showed up. Without direct instructions they'd want to kill Anatoli and maybe even her.

She went down the stairs. The loud clanging of her survival suit boots echoing around the empty space and increased her panic. She ran to the chair and took off the blindfold and gag on Anatoli. He blinked a few times.

"Untie me," he croaked.

He was looking at her with suspicion.

"It's cable ties, I'll have to check the kitchen for a knife."

"Was that Freddie?"

She couldn't answer him yet, she needed to think her story straight. She ran into the kitchen. It was brightly lit compared to the main space; there was a microwave on a small table, a sink and a kettle on a small counter with a cupboard below it. There were two cups next to the kettle waiting for the hot water that hadn't got poured. She crouched down and opened the cupboard. Inside was a giant mug with a motley selection of cutlery, some plastic, some from airline in-flight meal trays. None of it looked like it would cut a heavy duty wire tie. She picked the small metal airline knife. At least it had a serrated edge.

"You've got to be kidding," said Anatoli, as she started to saw at the wire tie with the knife in the space between his wrists.

"It's all there was and we have to be gone before more of Freddie's guys turn up. We didn't leave on the best of terms…"

"I heard," interrupted Anatoli. "Where's she gone?"

"You heard that too, Weddell City, Pierre's old mate killed Gordon."

"Fuck," said Anatoli, "we have to leave right now."

"There's a bit of problem with leaving. She took my car. She's smashed our phones. It's forecast to be minus fifteen and we're at least a forty minutes walk to anywhere with other people."

"Shit."

Detective Inspector Zhao asked for a driver from the pool. They had four properties to visit in the residential sector. She'd asked James to map a route, but now she was going to override him. She'd done some digging on Manny the Charter Manager and she'd been right, he was too old to be a Vostok native, but clearly he was an excellent mimic. So where else could he have been in the AFS? There was some delay in getting a driver, but they ended up with the same guy who'd taken them out to the airport earlier. She knew now they were being watched. The driver pool had five names in it when she'd put in the request. It was nothing she hadn't anticipated, it was just annoying.

"One hundred and two, Munroe Street, thanks," she said to the driver.

She saw James look sideways at her but he never said a word.

It was late, the sun was as low as it got, but still early in the twilight: the municipal buildings they passed on Lazarev Road had subtle LED signs, nothing like the brash neon colours on The Strip. As they were driven north she could see the apartment blocks ahead on their stubby stilts, part of the apparatus that allowed them to shift slowly, keeping in the same place even as the ice sheet moved. Larger buildings were more like ships moored in position and capable of being slid but the expansion of Vostok had needed new ways of keeping the city located at the side of Lake Vostok. They turned right onto Munroe Street, behind them was the main residential sector all named after nineteen fifties film stars, Vostok channeling its Las Vegas vibe again. The police car entered a vehicle airlock under one of the new apartment blocks.

"Stay here, please. We'll be in radio contact."

"Roger that, Boss."

She almost did a double take so used to being ma'am-ed by the uniformed officers back in Weddell City until she recalled what the Chief had said about 'ma'am' back at the station.

She and Wylie headed for the apartment airlock and entered. It seemed that in order to get inside you needed either a code or to buzz a resident, she sent Wylie back to get the code. Funny the uniform didn't mention that. Wylie came back faster than she'd expected.

"Buggered off," he said. "I suppose he'll claim it was an emergency if questioned. But I'm not happy, this feels like a fit up."

"Nevermind, James. We have ways."

She buzzed a random set of residents till she got someone home.

"Delivery for Delaval. They've given me the wrong code, can you buzz me in? It's time dependent. Thanks."

The inner door swooshed open and they started to look for Manny's flat. The building was only two storeys high and his flat was on the top, close to the stairs. She took out a set of lock picks and had a go at the basic lock. It gave up easily. The door however remained shut when she went to push it, like there was something behind it. She and Wylie pushed against the door until it moved, opening a quarter of the way. There was a smell of burnt metal, melted plastics and stale damp clothing as they entered the darkened room.

She turned to see what had kept the door from opening. It was a heap, too big to be a body she realised with some relief. It looked like a mattress. Yes, it was a burnt, soggy mattress, or rather two. She motioned James to switch on the lights. He flicked the switch but nothing happened. Then she noticed the floor was damp too, everything had been soaked, she looked upwards to the sprinkler system and saw the tell tale activation LED blinking in the dark.

"Shorted. They set something on fire, between these mattresses. Help me shift them."

The mattresses were heavy with the water and smelt of soot, flaking and breaking as they pulled them away. Massive scorch marks climbed the door, and she realised, because it would be a fire door, it had been the best place to set on fire whatever had triggered the sprinkler system. Why had it not alerted the fire department? A report at least, and one that should have also been logged on the police system. Their disappearing driver made more sense. She saw Wylie shine his torch over the space they'd cleared, his hands shaking the light beam slightly from his effort in shifting the mattress.

"What *is* that?" she said, kneeling down to get a closer look with her own torch. She saw the lettering, V, O and three numbers nine, seven and zero etched into it.

"It's something out of Anatoli's jet," she said, puzzled.

"It's the cockpit recorder, the black box. Someone has disabled it, with..." and Wylie now joined her, kneeling down, fingering the debris. "Yes, with a concentrated mining charge. It was one of the things I found out could disable them."

"So Manny was more than he seemed. Not surprised. Maybe there's something here can tell us where Tanya and Anatoli are."

She took some photographs of the mattresses, scorch marks and black box. Wylie headed into the bedroom. She set about the kitchen area, Manny was disgustingly unhygienic. Empty take away boxes in various stages of decay littered the counter top, something was smelling rank in the sink. She decided she didn't want to know what and instead she scanned the wall cupboards. In these kinds of apartment the wall material couldn't be punctured, and usually didn't respond well to adhesives either, this meant residents often used the wall cupboards for notes, art work and reminders the way she'd seen on T.V. shows people elsewhere used their fridges.

There was a tourist map taped up on a door. Why would Manny need a map? She looked closer and saw a small pen marked 'x' in an empty space to the south east of the airport. She got her mobile out to see what was out there. It had tracks marked on it but no further information. How useful if you didn't want anyone snooping about to have empty bits of map to hide things in. But how were they going to get there now?

"Come see this?" James called through from the bedroom. When she got to the door he was shining his torch on a faded photograph showing Freddie, Tanya and a much slimmer and younger Manny posing under a sign.

"Where was it taken?" she asked.

"Sign behind them says Innonnox Mine, Kunlun. No date."

"Interesting. Keep the photo," she said. Then waving the creased tourist map at him, continued, "We need to figure out how we're going to get here, though."

"Where?"

"Somewhere Manny needed a map to get to, out by the airport. My guess is smuggler warehouses. So safe they're not even on the phone maps. That's a lot of clout. Something Freddie's more than capable of."

"Do you think that's where they're keeping Tanya and Anatoli?"

"I hope so."

"I'll call a taxi," he said, "it's a risk but it's worth it if we're so close."

They waited in silence at the apartment airlock for the taxi to enter the vehicle airlock. She didn't want to speculate what was at the warehouse. James seemed unnaturally quiet too, she wondered why. The taxi arrived and it all seemed legit, she sat up front with the driver, her hand resting on her handgun in her pocket just in case.

"Take us to here."
She showed the driver the map, pointing at the small mark.
"And don't give me any bullshit about no roads out there or you'll find yourself arrested for impeding an investigation."

She saw him start the taxi, nodding his head vigorously. She'd no intention of letting him drive off when they got there either. No way was she going to get stranded in a part of the map marked 'here be monsters'. It was a light turquoise twilight, but cold. She stole a glance at the taxi dashboard and saw the air temperature was already at minus twelve. There was an illusion there was less here than there was, the way the warehouses had been arranged. The taxi driver seemed perfectly comfortable driving the route, she noted. Another reason not to let him go.

The taxi eventually stopped. She peered out, the shape of a building loomed to the side of the track. She drew her hand gun and pointed it at the driver.

"Out. You're coming with us. I need transport back out of this dump."

"Ma...' started the taxi driver, then clearly thought better of his choice of honorific, "Lady, I don't want any trouble. I'm just making a living."

"Me too, Bud," she said, "me too."

She noted Wylie was at the driver's door to escort the driver away from his vehicle. Together they moved towards the building. She adjusted her zipper up over her chin, the air was biting. Nobody would want to spend time out here tonight. They got to the airlock.

"Stay here and don't let him do a runner."

"Yes boss."

She entered the warehouse. What she saw made her heart leap. Two figures, one was definitely her Tolli, his short dark curls were unmistakable. The other she was less sure, long blonde hair obscured most of whoever it was, but at least they were trying to free him, they couldn't be all bad. As the airlock hissed shut the figure turned around, and Enya could see it was a woman holding what could be a small knife. Enya ran towards them.

"Tolli."

She could see him try to turn on the chair.

"I couldn't find a proper knife, just this," said the woman waving what Enya now saw was an airline knife, the kind you get with in flight meals. The woman looked familiar but Zhao couldn't place her. The woman continued, "We've got to leave. Freddie's men will be coming soon."

"Enya," said Anatoli.

"Hold still, Tolli." She whipped out her knife and sliced along the groove that the airline knife had been making slow progress at. Then she flicked it up across the ties holding his feet to the chair. He turned as he stood grabbing her in a tight embrace.

"We've got to go," he said, "this is Tanya. You remember her?"

She nodded as he let go. She stayed beside him. He seemed in pain, walking stiffly and slowly. He only seemed to loosen up as they reached the airlock.

"We've got a taxi but also its driver," said Enya, "Freddie has the town totally sewn up or at least that's how it seems. Our police driver buggered off earlier. It won't be safe to stay much longer in Vostok."

"Story of my life," muttered Anatoli as they exited the airlock.

There was no sign of Wylie, then she heard a hiss from the deeper shadows. She looked into them and could make out two figures. She pushed the others towards them.

"We've got company. Two guys got dropped off by a taxi down by the corner. I think they saw the taxi, and I don't know where they've gone now."

"Bugger," she said, receiving looks from both James and Anatoli, "Tolli, do you think you could keep a hold of Squirmy here?"

She pushed the taxi driver at Anatoli.

"Yes. Any friend of Freddie's is a friend of mine," he said with a hint of malice.

She saw the taxi driver flinch as Anatoli grabbed his arm and rammed it up his back.

She motioned to Tanya, "Stay as far back as you can. James and I will see if we can flush them out."

Together she and James moved along the edge of the shadows. The taxi they came in still sat out on the track. She asked James to point to where he'd last seen the men and pulled her visor down. She'd succumbed to buying her own after McMurdo, principles were all well and good but equipment could save your life and it was worth buying the best. The visor she now had was equipped with a basic digital zoom. She also moved to thermal imaging. There was the faintest trace of something, fading fast in the dropping temperature, a hand print on a door. She discounted making a run for the taxi. If it got shot up they were stranded in a hostile environment and she didn't mean being outside.

Chapter Nine - Echoes

The MS Mercer was twenty six hours out of Saylon and had shifted its time four hours ahead of Antarctic time, when the satellite phone rang. The mate on duty had taken the call and buzzed it through to Captain Beardmore immediately. Dmitry had snapped awake as soon as the President had introduced himself. Given all that was going on and the other half he didn't know, but felt certain was just as bad, it was not just with deference that he answered. He hung up after the call, got dressed and headed for the bridge. He called Valla from there. He didn't want to make this particular decision on his own. He wasn't afraid of hard decisions but this required a delicacy he didn't have enough insight for.

"Senator Ektov is dead."

"Oh no."

He could see Valla's face crumple even in the mix of pre-dawn light and instrumentation glow.

"How? Who?" she said.

He could see her trying to rally.

"Someone tried to shoot the President in the Senate and the senator got in the way. I don't know if they caught them. It was the President who called. He wanted to speak to Glenn, I said I would get Glenn to call back. He didn't even argue."

"He must have had to do a bit of digging to find out we were at sea. I bet he wasn't happy."

"You know Valla, I've never heard him sound like this. Granted I don't know the man personally, but he sounded old. He's never sounded old to me."

"Shit. What are we going to tell Glenn? And Alison had a soft spot for Daniel too. They're going to be heartbroken. And Glenn is going to be dangerously pissed off."

He could see Valla begin to strategise. He decided to keep his own counsel for the time being. A few minutes later Valla asked him what the top speed of the Mercer was.

"Seventeen knots. Are we turning around?"

"Absolutely not. Under no circumstances do we head back to Antarctica at this moment. That's an order. But I want that speed. Get us as far as you can on our original course. Give me an hour."

"Senator," he acknowledged, glad that he hadn't just acquiesced to the President after all. This job was getting more complicated than he was comfortable with.

"I'm going to make a call. Any chance of some coffee?"

"I'll get the AB to bring up fresh," he said, waving the sailor over from the window where they'd been watching ahead through binoculars.

He watched Valla disappear into the radio room to make her call on the sat-phone.

Valla was numb, the news about Daniel seemed to pass through her, emptying her of emotion as it went. She sat down in the radio room and realised she wanted to cry but it wouldn't happen. She sat up straight, took a big breath in and exhaled, letting that desire go through her as well. Then she picked up the sat-phone and dialled through to Nikau Burns. He answered after a few rings, as if he was expecting her call.

"Valla. Have you heard?"

"Yes. But second hand. Who's picking up Daniel's reins? I need to speak to the Lomonosov senators we can trust. Find out if they know about Christine, if not tell them. Do we know who it was?"

"You're not going to believe this, it was Arnaud Cheung, Pierre's friend, the guy he thought was dead. Turns out he wasn't but nobody knows where he's been. They don't have him. They identified him from CCTV but he escaped in the confusion. They initially thought it'd been Gordon that'd been hit."

"I bloody wish it was."

"Valla, you don't mean that. Not right now. We can't let Christine get in."

"I'd bump her off in a heartbeat, State Assassination."

"Valla, can I just remind you this isn't a particularly secure call. Calm down."

"I am calm. You want to see angry just wait till Glenn Murcheson finds out. If you see a mushroom cloud on the horizon you'll know it was us."

"He doesn't know? You *do* like danger. When are you going to tell him?"

She looked at her watch, "In fifteen minutes. Get me the Lomonosov numbers Nikau, we need to build a new Resistance."

"Will do."

She hung up and went back out onto the bridge. There was a small sofa and coffee table set to the rear. She could smell the freshly brewed coffee from the flask set with mugs on a tray. She sat down and poured herself a coffee. She could feel the quickening of the ship's motion, the extra hum in the engines. She knew Alison would pick up on that even if she was asleep. It wouldn't be long before Alison was on the bridge. Whether it would be with Glenn or not was something Valla couldn't foresee. She'd have to play this by ear. She noticed Martin the Executive Officer was now sitting in Dmitry's chair, and she heard footsteps in the stairwell.

It was Alison and she was alone. Secretly Valla was pleased, she wanted to postpone telling Glenn for as long as possible.

"Valla," said Alison, "What's up? You're on the bridge at three in the morning and we've increased speed. Something has happened, don't make me work it out myself."

"Ah, Alison." She couldn't keep the grief out of her voice. "I wanted to let you sleep for as long as possible. It's not good. Daniel Ektov was shot in the Senate. He's dead. Alison, I'm really sorry."

She watched the same emptiness take a hold of Alison, stripping the emotions from her face. Then she told her the how, the why and the who of it all. And then they held each other on the sofa for a while. There was a comfort in the closeness of another's heartbeat.

"Have a coffee," said Valla pouring into an empty heavy-base mug and topping her own up.

"And Gordon wants Glenn to call him?" Alison asked, "I don't think that's a good idea. Nothing good will come of that. Gordon can just grieve on his own. How did he find out Glenn was on the Mercer?"

Valla really appreciated Alison as a person but she was in awe of Alison's mind. The sheer computational power. She had to resist the urge to just fill her up with everything at once. She knew it took its toll on Alison.

"Gordon has spies everywhere, he'll have heard from someone in the Intelligence Agency in Saylon, then probably someone in the docks. Nobody onboard. I made sure of this crew. He probably read and filed the information, thinking we would sail round to Weddell City, like Glenn wanted to. And will probably now insist on. It's not happening."

"Good," said Alison patting Valla on the hand, "I'm going to tell him now. I expect he'll be up in about ten minutes."

"Tell me what?"

The both looked up to see Glenn standing at the top of the stairwell.

Valla was sure her face was telling him everything. She knew she looked guilty and that was because she felt guilty.

She watched Alison stand up and move towards him, taking his hand and pulling him towards the windows at the front of the bridge. She decided to leave.

Glenn stood at the window. The dawn was upon them, a spectacular sunrise, a flaming orange ball, pale pastels in all the colours of the rainbow radiating up into the still dark sky. He didn't see it. He didn't see anything that was there. He was right back at the smoking remains of his parents' geothermal power station. Standing in the busted-open doorway of the Rest House, seeing their bodies lying on the floor, his father's arm reaching out towards his mother's.

"Sweetheart."

Her voice. He dragged himself back. He saw the steel grey sea flecked with gold tips. He turned and saw Alison. She could always rescue him from that place.

""He didn't call to let me know," he said. "He called to try and change what we're doing. I'm not ten anymore. And I'm not going to let my anger sway me. But I am angry. What a fucked up mess this is. A choice between Gordon and Christine is no choice at all. I'm going to make sure neither can continue to stand. For Daniel."

He felt her lean in to him and he put his arm around her shoulder.

Enya Zhao motioned to James to head over to where she'd seen the thermal image handprint. He had a similar visor and would see what she meant. They moved in a way to keep each other covered from any shots that might come from there. She wondered what was inside that warehouse? Could they find a way to simply trap Freddie's guys inside and get moving themselves?

A shot rang past her ear and she flattened against the wall of the warehouse she'd been skirting. James had run to the other side of the track, out of sight of the shooter. She edged back along the wall, looking for cover. It was just like back in Wilkes Enterprise Zone. She seemed to be spending too much time having gun fights in warehouse estates. She watched James shuffle up to the corner of his building. She decided to draw the fire, maybe give him a best guess angle. She moved close to where she'd nearly got shot already and waved an experimental outstretched hand. A fresh bullet pockmarked the wall in answer, but she watched as James readied his shot. She saw him flip over the corner, fire and flip back in one fluid movement. It was hard to remember this was a guy who couldn't string a sentence together before ten in the morning when you watched him take a shot like that. She waved her hand again. This time there was no answer. One down hopefully, one to go.

She gave James a thumbs up, and watched him crouch down and turn the corner fully. Then she saw him stand up and return her gesture. She ran across the track.

"I think the other one's inside. Do you think we can jam the door?" she asked.

She watched James approach the door and examine it.

"It's an airlock door, if we can jam this outer door open, it'll be difficult to get the inner one to open while it's registering an open outer."

She looked around for something to jam into the door, everything was snow or ice.

"Wait here, I'll be back in a minute."

She jogged back towards Tanya.

"Do you still have the cutlery knife?"

Tanya looked at her then patted an outside pocket on the leg of her survival suit.
"Must have pocketed it automatically," she said fishing it out and handing it to Enya, "old habits and all that."

"Thanks."

She got back to James at the airlock door.

"This do?"

"Perfect," he said jamming it into the almost shut outer door at its opening edge.

"Right," she said, "let's get the proverbial out of here."

They jogged back towards the taxi, waving the others out of the shadows.

She was sitting up front with Tanya in the driving seat. Tolli and James were sitting either side of the reluctant taxi driver in the back.

"Tolli, what happened when you got captured? Was it at the airport?"

"Yes, in the hangar, Tanya arrived and then some guys turned up with guns. Manny was with them, so at first I thought maybe they were our security. Then they started pointing them at me and I was sure they weren't. I don't know what happened next I got knocked out."

"Let's check out the airport first, see if the jet is just sitting there. I'm prepared to work round it not being available, but it'd be foolish to assume they didn't simply strip out the black box and leave it in situ."

Tanya started the engine and they headed off down the track. It was a bumpy ride, the ice sheet sped up during the summer, and ridges could suddenly appear out of nowhere. So far there'd been no crevasses this far into the interior, but many commentators on the AFS wondered what would happen to Vostok if they did become regular occurrences.

The charter hangers were to the side of the main commercial hangars, set back from the shared apron area. Tanya waved the taxi driver's pass at the barrier and they drove to the hangar Anatoli used.

"Tolli and I'll check out the hangar and the jet. Stay in the taxi."

She popped open the taxi door and the icy blast hit her. Five bodies in the taxi made a big difference even with the survival suits' insulation. She pulled the zip up over her chin, seeing Anatoli do the same. She recalled rescuing Alison at the Enterprise Zone where she'd been held without her survival suit: it said a lot about Antarctic natives that nobody thought to strip Anatoli of his. She drew her hand gun and edged inside the airlock door with Anatoli behind her.

The inner door sucked open, she peeked round the door frame. It looked empty except for Anatoli's jet. She was relieved. They'd still have to check the fuel levels, and figure out what to do with the taxi driver, but if the jet was intact then it was one less problem. They jogged across to the jet and Anatoli opened the door latch then pulled the steps down. She continued to scan the hanger interior, as she saw Anatoli from the corner of her eye disappear inside the fuselage.

"Fucking animals. What've they done to you?"

She heard him swear and wondered how bad it was. As far as his jet was concerned it didn't take much to upset Tolli, they could have left something up that should have been down, or the entire electronics could be sitting in a spaghetti pile, she had no way of knowing.

She shouted to the inside, "Is it fixable?"

"Yes," he replied.

"Quickly?"

"An hour, maybe hour and a half."

Not ideal she thought, but better than trying to stay alive in Vostok till the commercial flight took off.

Chapter Ten - Dead Men

Christine Frome was sitting in her lounge catching up on the news. She twirled her fingers through her tight blonde curls absentmindedly: the news was a mere background to her thoughts. An hour ago she should have been with Gordon Murcheson, taking part in the first televised Presidential debate, but it had been cancelled. She hadn't been in the Senate building when the shooting and subsequent chaos ensued, but the whole building had only recently come out from the security lockdown. Not that it had helped them catch the killer, she thought. A small part of her wondered if the target had been Daniel all along. Everyone knew how deep a game Gordon could play and only the naive took something involving him at face value. Still, she mused, it would be pretty low even for him.

She felt mildly afraid, almost but not quite sure that she wasn't a target. Every senator had had their security tightened whether they were senior or junior. A few of the junior ones had made noises about that, suggesting it was an infringement of their liberty and one or two of the more conspiracy minded had suggested Gordon would use the guards as spies. As if Gordon needed to individually spy on senators.

She hadn't been looking forward to the debate, and the delay was only giving her time to be more uncomfortable about it. She was fine with debate, fine with live T.V. but she hated Gordon. She knew it would be a very hard thing to hide in such an intimate situation, just his face and hers, in close up after close up, as they answered the questions submitted by voters and chosen by the independent panel. It wouldn't look statesmanlike, it would look petty and he would take advantage of it, she knew.

She was younger than Gordon by fifteen years. Elected eight years ago to her senior senator position for Moss after the incumbent Clarissa Roth died. Despite the pretence of elections a senior senate position was strictly dead man's shoes. There'd been quite intense competition for Clarissa's position and she'd been glad of her decision as a junior senator to cultivate a relationship with Global. They'd helped ease her way into the position. She'd rationalised the feelings of guilt about what she'd done since to help Global get a toe hold in the Antarctic Free State on the basis that if it wasn't her it'd be somebody else anyway.

A few votes in the Senate where she'd leant on the Moss junior senators and allied with Senator Palma were hardly sedition. It had been a worry when they'd arrested Leon Palma, but he'd been stupid, he'd got mixed up in the Canning affair. She drew the line at helping scientists who experimented on people, even if she'd drawn that line after she found out that's what Global wanted him for.

Her phone rang, she checked the number, it was unlisted. Probably Global, which was unusual, but maybe not at this moment in time. They must be shitting themselves at what had happened too. She connected and an electronic voice spoke in monotone.

"Senator Frome. Greetings. We are sending you a package which we would like you to take care of for us. Come to the car park alone. Your friend."

She got a shiver down her spine. Those voices were always so creepy. But it made sense. She'd no idea what the package might be. Maybe it was something that would help her campaign. She picked up her car keys and headed to the door. Outside in the corridor the senate security guard was sitting on a chair the apartment block concierge had found for him.

"Just going down to the car, I left something. Do you want a coffee or a tea when I get back?"

"No Senator, thanks. I have my flask. Do you want me to accompany you?"

"No, it's fine. The car park has its own security so I'll be perfectly safe. Why don't you take a break?"

"I might use the rest room while you're gone, thanks."

She smiled at the guard and headed for the lift. The apartment block was favoured by a few senators precisely because of its already good security, she felt sorry for the guards they'd posted here. It must be so hard to stay awake with nothing to do. The lift door opened into the cool air of the underground car park. The building had its own geothermal plant providing power and background heating. The car park was part of the waste air heat reclamation. It never smelt particularly pleasant as a result. She looked around for a sign of this mysterious parcel.

A figure moved out of the shadows to her left. He looked like a janitor. With a dawning realisation she saw that he was the cleaner from the CCTV images shown on the news. He was the man who'd shot Daniel Ektov. Shit, what had Global got her into?

"Senator Frome, our mutual friends thought you were the best person to help me. I need to lie low for a day or two. Then I'll be out of your hair."

His voice was dripping with insincere camaraderie.

"Jesus, no," she exclaimed. "This is unacceptable. Do you know what this could do to my campaign? Aiding and abetting a murderer? No. I refuse."

Now his tone had changed to annoyance.

"I'm afraid it's too late to refuse. If you don't hide me they can implicate you in the assassination attempt anyway. Don't you want to be President?"

"Not like this. I want elected, not there by default because the other candidate was assassinated."

He moved towards her and she could see he still had the gun. Surely they had to get rid of that?

"You're not bringing that into my apartment," she said pointing to the gun.

He was very close to her now. She was scared. Her mind was starting to dart about. Worried about being discovered. What would the guard do if she was seen with him? She couldn't think straight. He was intimidating. It wasn't his size, it was the way he was holding himself. She felt he was dangerously unpredictable, almost on the edge of madness.

"Need the gun," he said in a flat tone.

She was losing control not just of the situation but also her nerve.

"Okay. But hide it. There's a guard outside my apartment, I'll have to distract him so you can get inside."

Fuck, she thought, I can't believe I'm going to do this.

"We take the stairs," she said. "You stay in the stairwell, at the door, till I signal it's clear to get in the apartment. Okay?"

"Sure," he drawled, his demeanour suddenly an exaggerated insouciance.

It was like he was playing a game, she thought, switching from role to role, and at any moment the game might change to 'kill Senator Frome'. A proper madman and now he was going to be in her home for maybe two days. She was determined to get in touch with Global. They'd gone too far if they thought.... And then it hit her. He'd tried to shoot Gordon and Global knew this. Did they know before or after? And worse, they'd sent him to her.

She came out of the stairwell and into the corridor. She didn't see the guard anywhere. She hurried to her door and opened it, all the time looking up and down for the returning guard. With the door propped open she frantically waved towards the stairwell door. He appeared, his janitor uniform ill fitting and making him look extra suspicious. He ambled toward the door, as she spiralled her hand in encouragement.

He was inside. She shut the door. Right, she thought, what next? She noticed him head over to her kitchen area and start opening doors and drawers.

"What are you looking for?" she said with exasperation.

"Food. I'm starving." A wall cupboard door was slammed shut. "You don't have any food."

"No. I eat out. Or take in. I might have some biscuits."

She was getting very worried now, she could feel the anxiety begin to seep into her body, making her arms shake inside. Her legs too.

He drew the gun and pointed it at her.

"Where's the biscuits?"

"In... in the tin," she stammered, pointing at the large cake tin on the counter top.

She relaxed slightly as he pocketed the gun to use two hands to open the biscuit tin. She watched him take the tin and slope over to sit on the sofa. He began to flick through the T.V. channels. Stunned, she looked over at him wondering if her day could get any shittier?

She locked the apartment door, if only to protect the security guard from accidentally finding him and getting shot. She'd no doubt this man was completely unhinged and would shoot anyone without hesitation. This was Global's idea of working together?

"The door's locked. Don't open it. I'm going to bed."

"Night," he replied, his tone suggesting it was a friendly sleep-over.

She lay on top of her bed, swearing over and over again. Nothing else was coming into her head. No plan. No idea to base a plan on. Nothing except her panicked swearing. She forced herself to think but now there were only questions. Could she kill him? She didn't know if she could kill someone. He'd have to be asleep. And what if he woke up while she was trying to kill him? In whatever way she was killing him. How *was* she going to kill him? And back round to the first question. Could she kill him?

Christine Frome's resolve solidified around a kernel of self preservation as she talked herself into killing the psychotic, murderous janitor currently channel surfing in her living room.

She heard a noise and froze. There was the drone of the T.V. and another more ragged intermittent noise. Yes. He was snoring. She picked up her pillow from the bed and tiptoed to the bedroom door. If he woke up she'd drop the pillow and say she was getting a glass of water. Yes. That was good. She would run the tap. If he didn't wake up for that then she'd get in front of him and try to get the gun. If he woke up at that point, she could say she was turning off the TV because of the noise. All good. She could do this.

Christine Frome gingerly put her hand into the leg pocket he'd stowed the gun in. It was already half hanging out. She tried not to look away from his face, slack-jawed in sleep he was dribbling. Christine felt nauseous. She managed to free the gun, he hadn't moved. What next? She looked around.

She put the gun to the pillow like she'd seen on the TV shows and pulled the trigger. It only went so far and

109

stuck, nothing happened. There was a massive jump of panic in her chest. She looked at the gun, her hand shaking, saw the safety catch and released it. This time.

She pulled the trigger. The gun flicked her wrist back in recoil. She dropped the gun and pillow to turn the T.V. up louder. Her ears were ringing, and the TV sounded muffled. She hoped the guard would think any noise had been on the T.V. and wouldn't knock on the door.

She found herself surprisingly calm now. She knew she'd have to destroy the gun. It was the murder weapon that killed Daniel and now her prints were all over it too. She didn't know how to do that yet so she needed a good hiding place till she did know. The pillow, she could disguise, shove it inside a cushion cover and spray it with perfume. No problem.
The body and its blood now seeping into her carpet and already in her sofa, bigger problem. She dragged the janitor's body into the bedroom, the fresh blood smelt metallic. If she could keep people out of her apartment then she had time to find solutions to all these things.

Cornelius Kutchner switched the video feed off. He couldn't have hoped for this outcome. Who knew Christine Frome had it in her? Two birds with one stone. If they could just remove any chance of Gordon Murcheson's re-election then they had at least eight years of control in the AFS to look forward to. He hardly dared to dream about the mineral rights, nevermind the tech trading and fresh food imports they'd control. The legislation they could get through while Christine was in power would never be undone. They'd have Antarctica where they had always wanted them, the same place they had the UN. And he'd be getting Doctor Canning back for the company too. He could see a very senior position opening up for him, maybe even board level.

Outside Christine Frome's door the guard took the device he'd been using away from the wall next to the door frame. He didn't know how it worked, but he'd been told it was capable of 'seeing' through walls. Not like comic book x-ray spectacles, but it might as well have been for all the sense it made to him when they'd tried to explain it. He'd marvelled at what it had shown him on his visor, pale yellow figures moving in a room outlined in hot red edges and now the evidence was safely stored in the device. He wiped his visor's temporary memory. He'd no desire to get on the wrong side of who'd told him to do this. He wondered how they'd known that Senator Frome would come back from the car park with someone, and he wondered if they had expected her to kill them too? However wondering was more than he was getting paid to do and they'd paid up front with a tidy sum. All he had to do now was put the device in the paper waste chute and carry on with Christine as if nothing had happened. He was definitely getting paid enough to do that.

Chapter Eleven - Etiquette

"You know Gordon Murcheson is dead. At least that's what Tanya says," said Anatoli as he came back out of the jet holding a wire.

"What?" exclaimed Enya. "How?"

"She says Freddie took a call from the shooter telling her. Then she and Freddie had a big argument and Freddie stormed out. I heard a bit of that."

Enya tapped on her visor which was just in range of James' back in the car.

"Get the news on, find out if it's true someone's killed the President."

"Yes, boss."

She turned back round to look at Tolli.

"Is that vital?"

"No. But I do need to do a bit of rewiring, there should be some kit at the back of the hanger. What're you going to do if it's true?"

"It's not. Gordon Murcheson isn't that careless."

She was interrupted by James coming back over her visor comms.

"There was a shooting. Daniel Ektov's dead. The senate was in lockdown till seven and they're only now announcing what happened. They don't have the shooter. I'll keep listening."

"Thanks," she said to James, repeating it for Tolli's benefit. "Depending on where Freddie went," she continued, "she might not even know."

"She left saying something about fertilising flowers in Weddell City."

"If she's going to kill the shooter, presumably she didn't order it. So who did?"

"Tanya said it was a friend of Pierre Cottrell's."

"I wonder who got him to do it then? There's a long list of people with a grievance against Gordon. Plenty of them knew Pierre too."

"I'll get to work on the jet."

She watched him disappear into the gloom at the rear of the hangar. This changed her plans, she'd been intending to drop the taxi driver off at the police station, like a good copper. Now she wasn't sure it was wise. A place like Vostok was a slippery place in more ways than one. Allegiances and vendettas would be re-shaping themselves in the wake of trouble at the top. Gordon Murcheson scared the gangs, they knew he was just as ruthless as they were. The merest hint he might be vulnerable and some would start to poke the bear. No, they had to take the taxi driver with them, there was nowhere safe to dump him here.

She called James back over the visor, wondering again why she let her principles get in the way of owning such a cool piece of kit. The stuff she used to use as standard police issue was stone age compared to this. She told him to bring the taxi into the hangar since it would be at least an hour and they weren't going anywhere else.

She saw the taxi ease through the narrow gap she'd opened between the big hangar doors. The cold air rushed inside and she shut it after them as fast as possible. She saw James pull the taxi driver out of the taxi, and Tanya get out the driver's side.

"Is it true? Freddie's flying there now. We need to warn her," said Tanya.

"You must be joking," said Enya. "We owe Freddie nothing. Me especially. Anatoli was tied up. He could have been shot dead."

"No, you don't understand, she said Gordon had taken a hit out on her, that's why she faked her own death."

Enya purposefully didn't look at James when Tanya said that. Instead she kept her eyes on Tanya.

"Uhuh, and she didn't retaliate in kind then?"

"No. She said it was Arnaud Cheung who called her to say he'd shot Gordon. Freddie got really angry with him. I should have believed her."

Enya didn't understand what it was about Frederika Tran that had clearly captivated Tanya. The woman cared for herself, first and only. Freddie wasn't charming she was deadly. She saw James looking agitated behind Tanya, still holding the taxi driver in his grip.

"We got cable ties?" she said, "seems they put up a good fight against airline cutlery. We need to secure our friend for the flight. Tanya can you go see what Anatoli can give you, he's up the back of the hangar."

It was clear that James had something to add to the story she'd pieced together so far, but they couldn't do that till the taxi driver was out of earshot. Tanya came back with something even thicker than what had been used on Anatoli. They hog-tied the taxi driver and sat him on the frozen floor. She nodded at Tanya to keep an eye on him and pulled James to follow her till they were around the other side of the jet.

"What?"

"I forgot to tell you, Santiago wanted me to scout where they were keeping Doctor Canning in Denam. He said he'd received some information and just wanted confirmation. He was lying, I'm sure of it. He had some other plan. I didn't remember till now."

"You think someone is going to spring Canning? Maybe in the confusion? What does Santiago want with Canning?"

"My guess is a reward from Global. I reckon they must be a bit pissed one of their top scientists is locked up for life here."

"Certainly feasible, they are a bunch of..." She hesitated, she'd nothing except profanities to describe Global's involvement with Canning. "Anyway" she said "we're going to be heading into this unfolding disaster soon, so I suppose we'll find out."

The sun was getting higher in the sky each day the MS Mercer steamed closer to the Tropic of Capricorn. They were nine and a half days away from Singapore where the turtles would be repatriated. Singapore had extended a welcome to the Antarctic Free State navy for this act of planetary solidarity. Dmitry was in his cabin busy trying to minimise the amount of ceremonial bullshit it was generating in an email correspondence with Elaine Tan, the UN Wildlife Protection Agent based there. The Mercer's communications had swapped over from the Antarctic satellite system to the Inmarsat system and the transmissions were much slower, he was watching the download bar stubbornly refusing to increase.

Only a few satellites had been safe in the shadow of the Earth when the solar flares that had devastated much of the technologically advanced world had hit over twenty years ago. Antarctic had been safe, but it hadn't had a satellite system back then, however it did take advantage of the situation quickly. Their Space Agency was based at Melchior on the islands at the end of Torres Peninsula as it stretched towards South America. It was where they launched their satellites from, and occasionally those for other states. He hoped they had plans for more planetary coverage.

He'd gone back to bed after the excitement of the phone call last night, and hadn't seen Senator Torres or the others at breakfast. For a moment he tried to pretend this was all just about some Loggerhead turtles, but it wouldn't stick in his head. He kept thinking about the fact someone had tried to assassinate the President. He was part of a defence force, this sort of thing was his concern. The AFS might have the navy, a constitution and a civil militia, but it was a fractious and small population spread out over a vast continental state, half of whom still had an anarchic frontier mindset only held together by The Code and a common enemy in the physical environment.

Captain Dmitry Beardmore was old enough to remember the world before and after the near eradication of most technology. He didn't want that kind of chaos to happen to his new home. He wasn't an admiral, but he'd interviewed, with Valla, all the crew for the other small inshore vessels. He mailed the captains to discuss some scenarios, and felt slightly better after that.

He arrived on the bridge just before noon, local time, and ten AM, ship time. Martin Kostov his XO was sitting in the chair. He saw Martin look round and make to stand up.

"No, no, Martin, just up for a look. Any sign of our guests yet?"

"Nobody's been on the bridge, I think they're having trouble adjusting to the time changes. I've got an AB in the radio room in case a call comes through, but it's all been very quiet."

Dmitry looked at Martin and could see he didn't like the quietness either. Both knew the danger wasn't the height of the wave crest but the depth of the hole before the crest.
The AB appeared at the door of the radio room.

"A call for the Senator."

"Put it through to her cabin," ordered Dmitry.

He turned to Martin, "Maybe I will sit. Can you go make sure the dummy ammunition is well out of the way? I don't want any confusion, later."

"Sir," said Martin, getting up from the chair.

Valla was sitting on the daybed making notes at the desk when the phone on the wall began to ring. She answered. It was Nikau. The line was bad, but eventually she had three Lomonosov names and their contact details from him in addition to the news that the Iron Prestige had been hijacked. They agreed to use email for anything non-urgent rather than have another torturous conversation like that. Then she composed an email to each of the three Lomonosov senators that while it wouldn't give anything away which wasn't already in the public domain, would hopefully get them to at least answer her. Four years of Gordon's Presidency meant most smart senators were capable of reading between the lines.

She needed some air. Stepping out of her cabin she noticed the ship's air conditioning pumping out cool air. She began to think about what the temperature would be in Singapore. Born thirty four years ago in Weddell City, all her experiences were of Antarctica. She opened a door at the end of the corridor and stepped outside. The air was as cool as inside, not cold despite it being a stiff breeze. She felt huge gaps in her knowledge open up and resolved to fill them as soon as possible with details about Singapore and weather and climate, what route they would take, and why having adjusted her watch to all the time change updates announced over the intercom, she'd felt tired at odd times of the day since they'd left.

She was standing on a deck walkway that went forward to the helideck, ahead of her she could see the Mercer's small cannon poking beyond the superstructure. There was nothing else to see except the ocean. The long slow swell caught her gaze again. She tried to imagine how deep the water was and couldn't. She would look that up too. She turned to go back inside and saw Martin the Executive Officer coming along from the helideck. She remembered something from when he'd been interviewed that had made her smile then, and she smiled again.

"Senator," he said.

"Martin, can we drop this bullshit outside of when it's absolutely necessary?"

"I could try, but it's a habit. And it's a good habit to get into."

"I suppose you're right. How's Colin fitting in?"

"Good, he's got useful skills, plus the captain has been grilling him on UN etiquette. It sounds like there's going to be some sort of event to mark the return of the Loggerhead turtles."

"Bugger, I'd hoped our visit would stay low key," said Valla. "And how long will it take to stop fiddling with the clocks? I've absolutely no idea what the real time is anymore."

He laughed. It was a nice sound, Valla thought.

"Yeah, they chose to use Weddell City for Antarctic time, and we're heading up, one fifty degrees to the other side of the world, so another two hours to catch up till ship time matches Singapore time. By the time we get there you should be acclimatised."

"Good. Talking of climate, what are we going to be wearing when we get there? I didn't pack for the Equator."

"Good point. We have tropical dress whites in store, there should be a fit for everyone. Thanks to you, Senator."

"Ah, did I tick that box? Good. To be honest Martin, I ticked all the boxes. You let me know if you're missing something and I'll make a new box to tick."

"Thank you, Senator."

"So, what *should* I call you?"

"XO," he said.

She looked at him. "Seriously?"

"Yes, I'm the Mercer's Executive Officer."

"Bugger that, Martin. XO is for brandy."

She saw him try not to smile and fail miserably, breaking into one that made her notice again how attractive he was. Well that's not happening she thought, as a brief pang of regret stung her.

"Yes Senator," he said, opening the door for her.

Chapter Twelve - Unexpected

The woman who'd collected the separated rubbish was not the usual collector nor was it the usual collection day, but nobody seemed to notice or care. The van she'd used was parked up an alley close to the apartment block it had recently visited. The woman was now in the back slowly emptying the paper waste container, item by item, examining each paper sheet or piece of torn card carefully. About half way through she found what she'd been searching for and put it in an inside pocket of her survival suit. Then she collected the emptied bits back into the container.

Once she'd taken the waste to the recycling centre she drove the van to the senate building, parking at the far end of the car park. The whole area was scrutinised by CCTV and sensors, but she was more concerned about the casual observer than the official watchers. She called the number she'd been given and let it ring three times. She waited. When she'd almost thought nothing would happen, she heard a tap on the passenger side window. She opened the door but she couldn't make out much of the figure standing there with a hood drawn over. The figure stretched out a hand, and she placed the device she'd retrieved from the waste into the hand. The figure drew back and disappeared amongst the parked cars.

Not a bit of this was a surprise to her. Sophia Wren had expected intrigue when she'd applied for the job as Gordon Murcheson's press secretary. All the stories she'd heard couldn't do justice to the truth of working for him. Every day she couldn't believe she'd actually got the job. She had began to make herself indispensable to him straight away, offering to do small errands, that had gradually changed into these clandestine meetings that

made her feel she was truly alive. She loved it. She'd
wanted to work for the Intelligence Agency but they'd
refused her application after the psychological
evaluation. She'd show them. She was determined to
make President Murcheson the greatest president the
AFS would ever have.

Wahid had finally made it to Denam Prison. It had taken
a day and a half's travelling, almost non-stop across the
whole of Antarctica. Getting to Vostok had been the easy
part. When he'd arrived there, he could feel the change
in dynamic that had been wrought by the shooting of
Daniel Ektov. Old contacts didn't want to speak to him.
Eventually he'd had to go visit one and impress upon
them that Gordon was still alive and still in charge and
was expecting the usual loyalty. That had got him a
charter jet to Denam and here he was, waiting in the
Governor's office. Waiting to find out what had really
happened here.

The Governor arrived back in her office. Her secretary
had told Wahid she was doing her daily rounds. She
came into the room with a stack of files in her arms and
dumped them on the desk, in what Wahid felt was a
pointed manner.

"We're at the arse-end of the country and nobody cares
about us till something goes wrong. You tell the President
that. In fact, you tell him I need more money. You can't
run a prison on campaign messages and bullshit jargon."

"Governor Sutar, thank you for seeing me. I'll pass on your comments personally to the President, but I'm here, as you say, because something went wrong. I'm not here to blame anyone, I'm here to find out what happened."

"Hmmm," she said, looking at him intently.

He looked right back at her. He was as open as Gordon was shut. While he owed the man his life and gave him his loyalty, he'd never understood his methods. He always felt he got more from people by openness than subterfuge.

"Amita, may I call you that?" he asked, continuing without waiting for her answer, "we're certain the woman who was shot wasn't Frederika Tran, we're concerned about the guard who's gone missing, but more than anything now, I'm worried about the security surrounding Doctor Canning."

He noticed her demeanour change slightly and that worried him. If the Governor had been compromised then the security of Canning had also been compromised and it would be only a matter of time till Global made some kind of move.

"Doctor Canning is secure. He's in an entirely different wing to the one Frederika Tran was held in. I want you to know that monster isn't going anywhere."

Wahid thought that sounded sincere, but he hadn't lived as long as he had by basing his decisions on what sounded sincere.

"I'm here to take a DNA sample from the dead body. I'm authorised by the President to order you to increase security around Doctor Canning, and if you need more resources to do that, I'm also authorised to give them to you. I hope we understand each other?"

The way the Governor was now looking at him told Wahid everything he needed to know. She was worried, he'd clearly caught her in the middle of something not quite legal. What he didn't know was whether Doctor Canning was part of it.

Freddie's jet landed at Weddell City and taxied towards the private hangars. She knew it was a risk after finding out over the radio that Gordon was still alive. Weddell City might be considered a Torres stronghold, but as the seat of the Senate it was also where Gordon held most of the strings. She'd no doubt he'd be aware of her flight. She was interested to see what he would do. She didn't think his choices included another attempt on her life, but the nice thing about tangling with Gordon was you could never tell. Freddie liked the excitement that created.

The jet door opened providing the steps down to the ground. Phil and Casey went out first. She didn't hear anything from them, which wasn't good. She appeared in the doorway, and saw them being held by similarly shaped men. There were four guys, two had Phil and Casey the others were pointing guns at her. There was a car behind them. She saw the door open and Gordon got out.

"Frederika. I trust it was a pleasant journey?"

He had begun to walk towards the bottom of the steps through the men. She smiled. She'd known Gordon for a very long time, all the way back to Kunlun and the Innonnox Mine. What was the scientist's name again? She couldn't remember. The guy with the sound laser idea. She waited till Gordon was at the foot of the steps and then stepped down them stopping on the last one, leaving her with a height advantage over Gordon.

"You're not looking too bad for someone I was told was dead," she said.

"Likewise," he replied. "I'm here to call a truce." He gestured to his car, "Join me out of the cold?"

"What about my men?" she asked.

"They can wait back in the jet if you'd prefer. With the door shut." He motioned to his men to escort Phil and Casey into the jet. She saw a bit of shoulder pushing and gave Phil and Casey the nod. She watched them go into the jet without further argument and the door close up.

"Okay," she said, satisfied with the arrangement.

Once inside the car, Gordon was the genial host. It was a spacious limousine style interior, complete with a small bar. He was pouring a whisky from a small decanter.

"Whisky?" he asked.

"No thanks. What do you want Gordon?"

"A truce. Someone's trying to kill me and I know it's not you. I might have made a miscalculation in trying to take

127

you off the board, but I don't make the same mistake twice."

"Oh. I shouldn't start trying to kill you, because you've decided to stop trying to kill me? Is that it? Bit pathetic, old man. Tell me what's really going on and I might be interested." She made to open her door, knowing this was only the preliminary negotiations and she wouldn't actually leave.

"Christine Frome is working for Global, and they want to break into Denam Prison and take Doctor Canning back to a UN territory."

Freddie let go of the handle. This wasn't like Gordon, usually there was at least one more layer obscuring the half-truth he was telling. That sounded like the whole unvarnished story. He'd either got desperate or reached some hellish depth of manipulation.

"And," she said warily, "presumably you want me to help you. Again? Like in Vostok? Where you double crossed me, and I ended up in Denam. Not happening old man. Do your own dirty work this time."

She put her hand on the door again, more determined to open it this time unless the next thing he said really surprised her.

"I needed to flush out Leon Palma. I'm sorry."

Yep, that would do it. Gordon Murcheson did not apologise. Ever. She let go of the door handle and turned to face him fully.

"I'll have that whisky."

She watched him pour a glass and took it from him. Sipping it, letting the heat of the alcohol slide down her throat, she finally remembered the scientist's name.

"Jean Mirales," she said.

"Who?"

"The man whose idea you stole, whose life you wrecked to the point he was suicidal enough to come to me for help. The sound laser guy. You just use up people, Gordon. I want guarantees before I'm going to do anything. And back up guarantees to those."

"Ah," he said, "such a long time ago. I didn't wreck his life, he managed that himself. But if you want guarantees, how about this; I guarantee I will not let Global run this country, and I guarantee Christine Frome will not be President. You can help me or you can be in the way."

Freddie recognised the change in atmosphere. He was scared she realised, really scared that Global might win. If Gordon was scared then she had something to worry about.

"What's your plan?" she said, resigning herself to the inevitable but determined to build in better safety nets this time.

Valla was asleep on the daybed. She'd been reading up on Singapore and now the information was jumbling up in a dream. The sea wall had featured, they'd gone round and round and hadn't found the opening in her dream. Everyone had been looking at her expectantly. She woke with a start. There was an alert for emails pinging.

She opened the laptop and saw an email from each of the Lomonosov senators waiting for her. She picked Dante Castillero's mail first. She knew him and he'd been a friend of her father's too. It was all very standard, but reading between the lines she could tell he was already aware of the depth of Christine Frome's involvement with Global. Good. He seemed to be intimating there was a plan too. Something Daniel had set in motion. She replied asking him to get in touch with Nikau Burns if there was anything he needed from Torres. She trusted Daniel's plan without even knowing what it was.

Daniel had been just as wily as Gordon Murcheson, yet had always managed to retain his perspective. In contrast, she felt Gordon worked from too deep within his own machinations to see the consequences of his plans. And was too egotistical to take responsibility for them when those consequences became apparent.

Then she opened the reply from Mariko Neish. She'd heard good things about Mariko, and heard good things from her too, on the few occasions she'd taken to the floor of the Senate, though she'd never managed to catch her live, only listening to recorded proceedings. It didn't surprise Valla that Daniel would have taken her into his confidence. It was very similar to Dante's mail, but also offered to keep her updated. So Mariko was to be the contact from now on. She'd no doubt that the three Lomonosov senators were in communication with each other. Finally she opened the mail from River Samson. She'd never really noticed River in the Senate, couldn't recall a single contribution he'd made in debate, or bill he'd brought forward, nothing. She could barely bring him to mind, but Nikau had passed on his details so if Daniel thought he was worthwhile then she ought to read his reply.

It was intriguing compared to the other two. He seemed to be trying to brush her off with bland platitudes. There was nothing between the lines either, no ambiguities. She wondered how much Dante and Mariko were actually telling him? Well they knew him better than she did, she had to trust them. The further she got from Antarctica the more helpless she felt and the more she'd be relying on Nikau.

There was one further email, it was from Enya. It was cryptic. Not in code, but in crossword clues. It would take a few minutes to work out. When she did she smiled. At least there was some good news about Anatoli and Tanya.

Chapter Thirteen - Lucky

Christine woke. It was still very early in the morning. For a brief second she didn't remember. Then the smell of dried blood hit her and everything came back. She ran to the en-suite toilet and started to retch. She brought up what was left of her previous day's meal and bile. She washed her face and sat on the toilet closing the door to the smell. She finally started to have some ideas. Yes, she thought, you can't keep Christine Frome down for long.

She could put the body in the bath, cover it with water, then the smell wouldn't get worse. She could clean the blood that had soaked into the sofa and carpet with what she had in the flat, she knew her cleaner kept supplies under the kitchen sink. The cleaner. She'd have to cancel the cleaner. And once she'd neutralised the smell she could leave the flat and try and find someone who was going to help her.

She knew enough not to go to Global for help. If she wanted to retain any autonomy in her political career they couldn't find out about this. Nobody could find out about this. She wondered if she knew anyone who used to be in the Resistance? She'd always been careful not to ask so she'd always be able to deny it when they'd been a proscribed organisation. She knew Valentina Torres had been, but there was no way she was calling that stuck up bitch for help. No. She needed someone who also needed her, someone down the pecking order who had some ambitions but no contacts.

All her campaign team were in the pay of Global so there was no-one there. She thought about the junior Moss senators. One name came to her almost immediately, Rafe. Rafael Dupont had barely made junior senator. She was sure he'd had no help from Global because the person he'd narrowly beaten in the election two years ago did. He must have some ambition to have managed that, she thought. But did he need her?

She had a shower in the separate cubicle and braced herself to open the en-suite door into her bedroom once more. Maybe it was her growing confidence she could handle the situation but she didn't think the smell was as bad. She took a fresh sheet from the wardrobe and rolled the body into it. Holding the two gathered ends she dragged it into the bathroom and stepping into the bath she hauled the body in the sheet into the bath. She had a fresh shower.

After two hours Christine felt the room would pass a cursory glance, but not a good look. That could be sorted later. Right now, if a guard happened to see inside, there was nothing that would shout murder scene at them. She had another shower and filled the bath, covering the body completely with cold water. She got dressed, choosing a red business suit to wear under her survival suit. She felt it would give her some confidence, a bit of a secret joke to herself. She noticed the gun was still on the coffee table. She'd dealt with the pillow already, but the gun needed to be well hid. She didn't want to keep having to move it. Where did nobody ever look for things? She thought the toilet cistern was a good idea. She didn't need the gun again. Or did she?

It was getting close to midday and she would normally have left the flat by now. She knew she'd have to appear to keep a normal schedule. But last night the Senate had been shut down. Surely, she thought, everyone would have their schedules upset? She still had the gun in her hand. Maybe the best place for it was in the car, not the flat at all? She could still get to it then. Yes, she thought, that makes good sense. A part of her wanted to have another shower. She ignored the idea and shoved the gun inside her survival suit. Then she removed it, found the safety catch and put it on, re-stowing it in her suit.

She could manage this. She wanted to manage the AFS, she should be more than capable of this. She opened the door and saw a different guard from last night sitting on the chair. She shut the door. Her heart was thumping in her chest. She'd need to calm down if she wanted to appear normal and get down to the car park. She took a deep breath and opened the door.

"Forgot my keys," she said by way of explanation, dangling them from a finger.

"Good day, Senator Frome," said the guard, "going out?"

"Yes, I'm heading to my campaign office."

"Very good. Someone'll be here when you return. Till we find the shooter, the President has ordered increased security round the clock. Do you need an escort to your car?"

"No. The security here's very good. And I have some at the campaign office. Thanks."

She walked to the lift and pressed for the underground car park. When the lift doors closed she had to fight the urge to slump to the floor. Chin up, she thought to herself. The lift reached the car park level. She got into her car and locked the doors. She opened various compartments till she found one where she could get the gun inside and some papers to cover it up with.

"Thank fuck," she said out loud.

She'd no intention of going anywhere near the campaign office. She wanted to arrange a meeting with Rafe. She'd already decided she'd offer him a position in her administration. Gordon had no junior senators in his. She could make a big deal out of showing she was investing in the younger members of Antarctica's Senate. It was a young country, it would play well, and also show she was open to change while Gordon represented the past. The protectionist past, full of suspicions. Oh yes, this would be good, and, she reckoned, an easy sell to Rafael Dupont.

Cornelius Kutchner had edited the video footage down to the salient points, encrypted it and sent it on, saving the whole file for himself to his secure backup. He'd need to get someone into the apartment to remove the surveillance devices. At some point it was possible that police or the Intelligence Agency were going to be in Christine's apartment, and finding the camera would let them know someone had footage. It wouldn't take a lot of imagination to realise it was Global who had it either. He'd no desire to put Global in the path of the Intelligence Agency or the police. Both organisations were more effective than when he'd arrived in the AFS three years ago and he couldn't rely on the inter-Family squabbling that used to go on to hide his operations under.

He'd been sent to the AFS in the wake of Doctor Canning's trial. Global's activities had been curtailed and under intense scrutiny since then, but Cornelius thought he'd been quite successful at working around them. And of course, he'd had assistance from Christine Frome in the Senate. They'd put a lot of effort into Christine, mostly because it had been harder to recruit more senators after Senator Palma's trial, but she'd seemed like a pretty solid bet.

He'd seen Christine leave the apartment, but the senate security guard was still outside. In two hours he'd shift change with one who'd been paid to remove the camera and ignore anything else he saw. It was a gambling debt the guard had so by all accounts he should be trusted to keep his mouth shut, but Cornelius had a back up plan if it turned out he had more patriotism than expected.

He was also trying to shelve the early stages of the plan to rescue Canning from Denam Prison, but he'd received no reply from his contact in Saylon for two days now. The damn country was so big, he sometimes felt Antarctica's much vaunted stable comms was inconsequential. Planning was just as susceptible to hiccups and missed messages as it was in the rest of the world. Where was Kooper?

Valla was in the conference room with Dmitry, Alison and Glenn to update them on the what she'd found out so far.

It was a lot for everyone to take in. Valla was waiting for Alison's analysis but she could see that something was up.

"I know we've all got used to my sharp mind kicking in and spilling out the probable answers but Glenn and I have been monitoring the effects it's having on my metabolism," Alison explained, "it's not good. I'm going to have to scale back how often I use it. We need to try and figure out what's going on without it. I think right now, with that amount of information we should be able to get good answers ourselves. I'm sorry to disappoint everyone."

"No, no," Valla said, "we appreciate your help and totally understand. We can make best guesses here, especially about Gordon now we know he was blackmailing James Wylie. It's no surprise to hear Cheung was involved in shooting Daniel either, but who was prompting him is another matter. What we know less about is Santiago's whereabouts in the Iron Prestige. Let's concentrate on that first. Dmitry?"

"Senator. If the Iron Prestige is behind us somewhere, we are at least 24 hours ahead of her. I'll alert the inshore vessels to do sweeps for her along the coast. I'll get the specs of the Prestige sent over and then we'll know when she'd need to refuel and what her top speed is so we can estimate where she could refuel. We should also ask for a citizen search for her AIS, see if the fishing fleet can locate her. I can't imagine Santiago or his men know too much about boats other than start, stop and steer."

Valla thanked him, and continued, "The other concern we have, is of course the President. I'm afraid it is time to call him back, Glenn. He's asked specifically for you. I understand this is a family matter for you both," she nodded at Alison, "but he's capable of petty actions just as much as deep plans. I've no desire to get an executive order to head back for Weddell City."

Alison interjected, "But the turtles, surely he wouldn't cause an international incident because Glenn didn't call back?"

Valla saw Glenn take Alison's hand.

"He would," said Glenn, "and I'm all right. I'll speak to him as soon as the sat phone is good. He's getting old, in the past we'd have been turned around as soon as he found out the Mercer had left Saylon. We've got to use these gaps to follow our own plan. Anyway, I reckon he'll have his hands full with Freddie."

Santiago Kooper was lying in his bunk. The ship rolled in the swell and he felt his head weighed twice as much as normal and that somehow these two things were related. He couldn't face standing up. He just wanted to be still. He reckoned if he could just be stationary for ten minutes somewhere impossible then he'd come back to the bunk and be fine. Trigger entered the cabin without knocking. Santiago was beyond caring at this point about the finer details of gang etiquette.

"Hey Boss, you should get up to the wheelhouse, you need a horizon."

He'd forgotten how he knew Trigger, and now that advice reminded him. He'd met him in a small fishing port to the west of Saylon, Trigger knew a bit about boats. So, he wondered, who was steering the boat now?

"Why aren't you driving?"

He'd tried to put some emphasis into his words, but they'd come out weak instead.

"Don't worry. Drink this."

He couldn't believe it of Trigger, looking out for him like this. After all the piss he'd taken out of him over the years. He narrowed his eyes, and looked at the mug Trigger was holding out to him.

"What's in the mug?"

"It'll make you feel better. I found it in the first aid kit. Said anti-sea sickness on the packet."

He took the mug and drank the liquid, swallowing the few lumps where Trigger hadn't got it all to properly dissolve.

"Thanks."
The weight of his head pulled him back, he slumped down onto the bunk again.

"We're making good time Boss, ten days till we reach Singapore. But we'll need fuel before then."

"I'll get it sorted. Need to sleep."

Chapter Fourteen - Connections

Anatoli was lying on his back under the instrument panel of his jet. The damage caused by ripping out the cockpit recorder had been bad but not insurmountable, and he'd found enough kit at the back of the hangar to get everything back up and running. He was now screwing the panel back on. The fuel tanks were full and he felt confident he'd be able to take off in amongst the flights without needing to contact the tower, giving them some much needed invisibility. Too many people would be interested in the whereabouts of Tanya or James Wylie he thought.

Knowing that James had been manipulated into taking a shot at Freddie made him worried for Enya. She looked out for James, and that meant she was close enough to be caught in the crossfire between Gordon and Freddie. While he'd been working on the wiring she'd been telling him what had been happening and also her fears for any continued career at Weddell City Police department. He could sympathise, he reckoned there wouldn't be much more charter work in Vostok coming his way.

"All back to normal, good as new," he said emerging from the cabin and walking slowly down the steps.

His back was aching and had been since being tied onto the chair, the pain renewed its presence now he wasn't lying down and concentrating. He saw Enya had noticed his stiffness. She was fishing in an inside pocket.

"Here," she said, "take these."

He took the pills and the flask of water she must have found somewhere. The water tasted stale but safe.

"Let's get going," she said.

Tanya was climbing into the taxi to get it out the way while James was hauling the taxi driver up off the ground. Anatoli moved off the steps out of the way as James dragged the guy up the stairs. Enya was over at the hangar controls. He didn't know what he'd expected but he understood the urgency.

He was ignoring the requests for identification coming from the tower as he headed for the runway. He knew the commercial schedule inside out, there was a slot in between the Saylon flight landing and the Weddell City flight taking off, because they were so often delayed by weather conditions. The one thing he didn't know was those weather conditions, the slot might be twenty minutes or five. He was also listening for the arriving Saylon flight. The tower was threatening to send a tug to block him. It was time to go.

As he got to the end of the runway he heard the Saylon flight announcing its final descent. The tower was shouting at him to get the fuck out of the way. He gunned the jet and headed down the runway pulling up hard. He could hear stuff knocking against the cabin walls behind him.

Ahead of his jet he could see the nose of the commercial liner and the pilots inside its cockpit. He knew there was nothing at this stage they could do. It was all down to him. He'd started bringing the landing gear up as soon as he'd left the runway but it was slow, especially as all the power was currently pushing his jet as hard as it would go. He hadn't heard the hatch shut and behind the screaming of his engine he could still hear the whine of the hydraulics. If the wheels didn't stow in the next few seconds they'd scrape across the top of the commercial.

The hatch clunked. The whine had stopped and the extra push gave him clearance over the top of the commercial. The tower was now a babble of swearwords, he cut the radio. He headed well away from the flight paths before banking round to head for Polar Station.

Once they were level, he heard the cockpit door open.

"Everybody okay?" he asked without turning round.

"Some tools were loose, we've got a cracked inside window and a few bruises but everybody is in one piece," said Enya as she came forward to sit in the co-pilot seat.

"It was close," he said.

"But we're free."

"Yes. For now. What's Gordon going to do with James now that Freddie is still alive?"

"Nothing. I won't let him. It's time we got some dirt on Gordon. I don't want to put you in a difficult position, Tolli, but does your dad have anything on him? Anything at all? From the old days even?"

"I don't know. I never wanted to get involved. Glencor politics is twisted loyalties, hidden agendas, nasty stuff. I'm sure my dad does have something, whether he'll give it up is another matter."

"I bet Valla knows something."

"We'll have secure comms at Polar Station when we land to refuel. But once we take off Gordon'll know we're coming. We better have a plan before we arrive in Weddell City."

"I know. And I don't think I'll be able to rely on the police either. Houten sucks up to whoever is in charge, he won't cross Gordon."

Valla sat at the desk watching the download bar. There must be something they could do about the communications? She scrolled back through senate briefings searching for Space Agency information. They had a satellite going up next month. She sighed. Then she searched for reciprocal agreements with Singapore. Nikau was on a lot of the trade missions, she was sure he'd mentioned something. There, a memorandum of support. It was worth asking if its ratification could be brought forward. Their communications wouldn't be secure, but they could encrypt anything they didn't want Singapore to know, and at least she wouldn't be spending time watching download bars. She buzzed up to the bridge. It was Martin who answered. She recognised the sudden desire to be on the bridge for what it was and put it aside. It might help if she did start calling him XO, but she couldn't bring herself to do that.

"Martin, I've found a memorandum of support between us and Singapore which includes sharing satellite coverage. Can you see if we're in range of their network?

And can you ask Dmitry to meet me when he's available today? Thanks."

"Senator. The captain's asleep just now but I'll let him know as soon as he's up."

She sat back against the bulkhead, the download bar had finally completed and there were fresh messages.

There was one from Gordon's office, from Mariko and from Nikau. She opened Nikau's first. He'd met with Mariko, the evidence against Christine was piling up, he had something good but it needed corroboration, everything else wasn't as powerful. Global lobbied everyone, and Christine had been careful to never stand out on her own in support of votes which gave Global advantages. Even after Leon Palma, she'd never appeared to be the prime mover of bills.

Damn.

Nikau had tried to find out where Arnaud Cheung had been for the last four years. Bizarrely it looked like he'd not been in the AFS. He'd confirmed it wasn't in Aotearoa either. Friendly sources in New South Wales hadn't turned up anything for him there or more generally in the supra-state of Australia, but it was hardly exhaustive. However the possibility he'd been in Tierra Del Fuego was looking strong. Global had a major base there, which meant Cheung was most likely a deep undercover Global operative. One they'd not flushed out, mostly because everyone thought he was dead. Nobody had ever thought to check Pierre's accusation, and Valla felt it was her fault she'd not checked Glenn's refutation of that accusation properly.

She opened Mariko's mail next, she mentioned meeting Nikau, reiterating the same information about Christine's voting record. They had one of the senate security guards who'd been stationed at Christine's block, he'd mentioned some unusual activity, intermittent CCTV in the car park late the same day as the shooting, he'd also mentioned another guard bragging about coming into some money. The police were working with the Intelligence Agency to investigate the shooting, and so far they'd not got further than confirming it was Cheung, finding an abandoned apartment where he'd been hiding out and noting he'd been in communication with more than a few burner phones. She could tell Mariko was not impressed. She wondered where Zhao was? And whether is was worth leaning on someone to get her put in charge of the police investigation side of things? She mentioned Zhao in her reply to Mariko.

Finally, she had only Gordon's email left to open. She felt ground down. She needed to get some air, maybe take some of her frustration out in the shooting range they'd installed. Probably, she needed exercise. She'd spent nearly four days mostly sat down in her cabin. Normally she'd be walking about the Senate and spending an hour at the gym every day. All this shit had got her out of routine. It was time to take back some control, and that meant Gordon's mail could wait.

When she got to the bridge she saw Dmitry talking with Martin. Dmitry had looked up as she'd got to the head of the stairs and he waved her over.
"I've been in touch with Elaine Tan, she's passed on our request to access the Singaporean satellite network. It's currently three satellites but it would make a big difference to the speed of communications. Elaine's going to push for it too."

"Thanks, Dmitry, that's good news. We'll still need to use encryption but I've got a feeling things are moving fast back home. I've had two emails this morning with the latest developments. But what I'm after is some warm weather clothes, I'm going to use the gym and I'm not really up for going Spartan."

They both laughed nervously, but she thought she'd seen Martin reddened slightly as he turned away towards a key cupboard next to the radio room. When he returned with the store keys he seemed to have regained his composure. It was no help to find out he was being tortured the same way she was.

They were deep in the bowels of the ship, store rooms just above the engines, the hum from them made talking difficult. Martin was unlocking a door, and then he went inside, she followed into a small room fitted out with shelves full of crisp white cotton pieces of uniform. He gestured to a set of shelves which had shorts on them, each pile marked on the shelf with its size. She felt him take her arm, felt the tension between them. He turned her round and pointed at another set of shelves with short sleeved shirts and let go.

She nodded and reading the labels picked a pair of shorts and two shirts from the piles. She headed towards the door. The air was heavy with potential, the difference between desire and duty. She made it out into the corridor. She really needed to shoot something.

Wahid had a room in the small hotel next to Denam prison. A service town had sprung up because of the prison. Visitors needed somewhere to stay, guards too, and somewhere to relax. It was a six month tour at the prison, and there was nothing to do except drink low alcohol beer and watch satellite shows. Wahid expected there to be some sort of black market in booze or porn or something, but if there was he wasn't seeing it. The hotel had a sat phone, and he called Gordon on the direct line to report his suspicions.

After the call he headed for the bar. What he'd been asked to do was pushing his loyalty to its limits. He'd been happy to look out for Glenn, though that had pushed his loyalty in a different way, but lately Gordon's focus seemed to be somewhat off from the survival of the AFS as an independent country. Wahid could usually see the pattern, or at least sense the overall cohesiveness of Gordon's plans, but this was so disjointed as to almost seem like there were several competing goals and Gordon didn't care which one won out. Wahid cared if it was the safety of the AFS that lost. His loyalty, he realised, was ultimately to the people in this harsh and unforgiving land.

Nonetheless he extended his stay at the hotel. The receptionist remarked upon it. He made up some bullshit for them and then later added the receptionist's name to a list. He passed the encrypted list on to Gordon's team to investigate. Any with connections in Saylon or Vostok were to be investigated further. The list was long because pretty much everyone involved in the prison at Denam and its servicing lived in Vostok, Saylon, or Korpur. But not much happened in Korpur, it was a town primarily involved in fish processing, people there either liked it or left.

What made Wahid uneasy was who was investigating. It wasn't the Intelligence Agency, it was Gordon's own people. People like Sophia Wren. Wahid had met Sophia shortly after she'd started working for Gordon over a year ago and didn't like her. She struck him as the sort of person who'd let you die outside: an animal in his book. Now Gordon had told him he wanted to jailbreak Canning. That wasn't right. He'd been ambivalent about the plans around Freddie because he felt she'd already been living on borrowed time after being convicted of treachery. But Canning was where he belonged, and even if Global was trying to get him out, he didn't think they were going to be so stupid as to try a jailbreak. That appeared to be a kind of stupid reserved for Gordon.

He came to a decision with the dregs of the bottle of beer, and headed back to the sat phone booth.

Chapter Fifteen - Therapy

Alison finally collared Valla in the mess room. She was sitting at a table drinking coffee when Alison walked in. She sat down opposite.

"Spill," she said, "and I promise I'll be gentle."

She saw Valla give her a wry smile.

"It's that obvious is it?"

"Valla, you've been carrying too much, I've been worried since I saw you at the lift doors back in Saylon. And more's been added. You've got to share."

"Yes. I suppose I do. Organising the navy was a big job, but it seemed like it grew arms and legs. And I was still trying to keep an eye on Gordon. I might have dropped the sled on that one. Now, now I'm fighting the snow. Soon as I clear one pile I find it's gathered in a different corner."

"We've got help, you've got contacts. You're going to have to trust them and delegate."

"It's the not knowing what's going on. Waiting on a download of email. No sat phone. But it should get better, Dmitry's in contact with Singapore, we're hoping to use their satellite system in a reciprocal agreement."

"Valla, I know there's something else. You don't have to tell me, but I can see you're in conflict. I can help you, I can teach you techniques to resolve the conflict."

"Ah Alison, it's not that kind of conflict. I've always known what to do, been able to make the right decisions quickly. This has no right decision."

Alison sat back, thinking through everything involving Valla since they'd got on board. Slowly she realised Valla had been hiding in her cabin the last day or two. She thought about who it would be from, and only one name came to mind.

"Oh," she said.

"Yes," said Valla.

Alison understood duty, understood the sacrifices and choices, but she also understood feelings. She knew how powerful they could get, and how much in the way they could get.

She saw Valla check her watch, they'd been on Singapore time for a full day already.

"Time for the gym. Join me?"

Alison was not much for the gym, she preferred walking, always difficult to do in Antarctica but not something she expected was any easier on a ship. But she knew Valla would open up more if she stayed around, and what else was there to do?

"Sure, but I'll need something to wear. What are you using?"

"Martin has the store keys, he'll get you some warm weather kit if you ask."

If she'd had any doubts about the name she'd come up with they were totally dispelled by subtle signs that accompanied this information.

"I'll go see him, meet you in there."
She got up and headed for the bridge, curious now to see how the other party was faring, and trying to work out what she could do for them without interfering.

She opened the door to the large gym. It was well fitted out. Valla was pounding an exercise bike. Alison felt vaguely self conscious about being in the room, not really sure how some of the things operated. She recognised the model of running machine and felt more confident. She stepped onto the belt and started at a brisk walking pace.

"So," she said "Martin feels the same."

Valla didn't flinch.

"It's awful. I'm trying to hide, but... I come here," she panted, "I do a bit of shooting. I stay in my cabin. Tomorrow we're going... to have a conference call... to test the satellite link. When we can bounce... the signal onto our own network... 'n' I can get in touch with Nikau and Mariko... I'm hoping... I'll be too busy to notice, and I can stop hiding."

Alison saw Valla stop pedalling as she finished speaking. Sweat was dripping down across her high cheekbones and her short blonde hair was spiky with it. Unlike Alison, Valla had brought a towel and now she was rubbing herself dry.

"I can tell you that's not a long term answer," said Alison with compassion.

Valla was looking at her, not a trace of The General remained. Alison silently cursed Gordon Murcheson and his ego, she could sense him at the bottom of all this. She wanted the old Valla back, who simply knew what to do and did it.

"I know," said Valla.

"What's the worst that could happen?"

Devil's Advocate was not a role she employed often, but it could have its uses.

"Lets go shoot something, and I'll tell you."

The room next door to the gym had been created out of some cabins during the refit. It was a long narrow space, and had targets on retractable wire. While handguns were standard issue, they were not ideal for practice on the ship. The firing range had a store of air pistols. The range was for accuracy training, everyone was expected to be familiar with their own handguns.

It was much cooler in the range, Alison shivered in her short sleeved shirt, but she could see Valla was still radiating heat. Alison had never fired a gun, of any sort. Northumberland allowed shotguns for farmers, but it hadn't been a frontier for a very long time. She looked at Valla.

"I've never shot before. You'll need to show me what to do."

At that, Alison saw the smallest hint of The General return as Valla went into teaching mode, explaining in great detail the operation of the air pistol, the safety procedures and the stance.

"The worst that can happen," said Valla, taking aim at the body target 15 metres away, "is that he loses his commission."

It was a hit to the chest, right in the heart.

"Who'd take that away from him?"

Alison approached the bar and took aim, saw Valla checking her stance but saying nothing. Her shot went ping off the back wall.

"Technically, my defence sub-committee, in reality Gordon, or whoever gets elected President, so Gordon."

Valla fired twice, this time head shots, on the edge of the bullseye.

"And how would they find out?"

Alison tried to sight better this time but holding your arm out was tiring. She fired, this time she caught the edge of the paper body target.

"Someone would make a complaint. We're not the only people here not able to be with someone they have feelings for."

Valla aimed and fired, another two shots, the previous bullseye hole ripped a bit bigger.

"And you're worried that would make them complain. You know everyone onboard Valla, you know them better than some of their families, I bet."

Alison's arm now ached with the unfamiliar position, she concentrated on holding steady and sighted. The shot actually landed inside the body line. She could see this becoming addictive.

"I know what kind of person Martin is, yes.

Valla was clearly now in the zone, the state of mind that comes once you fully focus on something, that slows time, eliminates external stimuli. Several more holes ripped the paper further at the bullseye.

Alison could understand how this helped her. Temporarily at least.

"Tell me," she said.

"He despises cruelty. He resigned his Australian naval commission over an incident with a refugee boat. Stayed for the remaining two years of it under the captain who'd ordered the vessel to come about swamping the boat. It capsized, there were sharks. Once he was free he went to the press. The navy went for him. Destroyed his reputation. I've read their report, a pile of dogshit even a school kid could see through. No wonder he emigrated to the AFS. He was skippering a fishing boat when the recruitment advert went out. I don't think he thought he had a chance. I don't want to be the one to take that away from him."

"You owe it to yourselves to at least talk. Let me mediate."

Alison took aim, forgot about the ache in her arms and fired, there was a hole not quite in the target circles but close. This was very therapeutic, she thought.

Valla was stowing her pistol away, Alison handed hers handle first to Valla, and watched as Valla expelled and then emptied the small compressed air canister from the pistol, reset the safety and put it back in the rack.

"I'll think about it. Thanks for offering."

Alison thought it was the best she could have hoped for. Valla seemed less helpless, more contemplative, strategising even. There was hope for the return of The General after all.

Christine was a big believer in carrot and stick motivation. She had the carrot, but she'd yet to find the stick for Rafe. She could entrap him, but she wanted his co-operation not simply compliance. He must become her co-conspirator, he must feel he had no option but to help her. Damsel in distress fit the bill nicely, she'd concoct a story about finding Cheung hiding in her apartment, held against her will, heroically struggling for the gun, panic after shooting him, and how it would look for the campaign. Finally she'd appeal to his loyalty to the Moss Family. Help her, and she'd help him.

She was driving while she thought this through. Her right wrist along to her elbow ached like she'd jarred her palm against something and she remembered the kick from the handgun that had been totally unexpected. She'd not realised how bad it would get while driving. It made it harder to think. Eventually she arrived at the meeting place she'd suggested to Rafael Dupont. A secluded restaurant not normally used by political staff or government officers. Out on the edge of Weddell City, near to the docks.

She'd been pleased to see he'd bought the story, desperate concern crept across his face as she continued to the denouement and her plea for help. He'd offered to drive her back straight away, see for himself and even promised to find someone to clean it up without question. She couldn't believe her luck. If he did this for her he certainly deserved a place in her cabinet. She asked him what he'd like to be in charge of. She was taken aback when he'd suggested Defence. It would be hard to wrestle that from Valentina Torres, but, she thought, once she was President what could Valentina really do.

They came out the lift at her apartment and there was indeed a fresh senate security guard sitting on the chair outside her apartment.

"Hi," she said, "This is Senator Rafael Dupont, he's come to help me with some campaign planning. Is there any news about the killer?"

"No, Senator. They've found where he was living, I heard on the news, but no sign of him."

"Oh, dear," she said, "when do you think they'll let you stand down?"

"I think there's a suggestion they regarded the threat as purely Presidential, so maybe tonight?"

"It seems such a waste of everyone's time for you to be sitting about in perfectly secure accommodation, I hope that's so."

She opened the door and let Rafe go in ahead of her. Her hand was shaking as she shut the door behind her. She could see Rafe standing at the sofa.

"Nice job," he said "you'd barely notice, unless you had one of those UV wands I suppose."

"Thanks," she said, thinking about the wands for the first time and feeling a despair settle in her bones.

"Where's the body?"

"In the bath. It can't be moved till the guards are gone."

She saw Rafe head to her bedroom and step inside.

"I can do this," he said, "Well, I can get somebody to do this. But the clean up is going to be more difficult. I know what you've offered me, but this is also going to take quite a bit of cash."

His voice was slightly muffled coming from the en-suite, she was concerned it could be heard outside, even though she knew the sound proofing in the apartment block was another reason for so many senatorial residents.

"Get a grip," she whispered to herself.

"Global bragged to me about having you in their pocket" he said, as he stepped back into the living space, "when I was running for the senate."

He sounded more confident than she expected.

"I take it they don't know about this?"

"No," she said "and it stays that way. I'm not in anybody's pocket."

She saw Rafe's concern.

"No, no, I'm not saying I believe them. Obviously, Christine, you're your own candidate. I want you to know I've always admired the way you've done things your own way."

Christine looked at him, she couldn't tell if he was being sincere. A tiny part of her, smothered under the mounting fear of being found out, felt he was being sarcastic. But she couldn't not take his comments at face value. He was going to help her, did it really matter what his motives might be?

Chapter Sixteen - Overturned Perceptions

Glenn was sitting in the radio room on the bridge of the Mercer. He didn't want to make the call from his cabin. Earlier that day they'd successfully trialled a conference call using the Singaporean satellites bounced to the AFS system. Nikau had been in on the call as had Mariko Neish the Lomonosov junior senator that Daniel had shared information with. Aware that they may be overheard the conversation was a careful dance around the details of Christine's financials and further emerging details of her involvement with Global. Nikau had divulged that he had in his possession something quite devastating if it could be corroborated, and he and Mariko were working to get DI Zhao in charge of a future investigation, once she arrived in Weddell City.

He had no more excuses not to call his grandfather. But the news about Daniel was still raw. He didn't trust himself not to lose his temper, but more worryingly he didn't trust himself not to burst out with accusations which would expose the growing picture they had about Gordon's contorted plans. He used the control techniques Alison had taught him. He felt his pulse slow, his anger seep away.

The phone was ringing.

"Hello?"

It was a woman's voice, it took him by surprise especially as it wasn't his grandfather's battle-axe of a secretary either.

"Can I speak with Gordon? This is Glenn," he said, careful to stay as neutral as possible.

"Oh, yes, of course, he's been expecting you."

Who was this woman who seemed so familiar with his grandfather?

"Glenn. I'm so sorry about Daniel. How are you? How is Alison? Daniel spoke so highly of her."

"Who was that? Before. Answering your phone?"

"That's Sophia, my press officer. She's been an absolute boon to me. Don't think I could have kept going without her."

Glenn recognised the bullshit for what it was. She was clearly still in the room.

"You wanted me to call you. So?"

"Ah, yes, things have moved on since then. I understand you're repatriating some turtles, and making some friends in Singapore. Well done. We'll make a politician of you yet."

Glenn had never, ever heard his grandfather spout such utter nonsense in all his life. He was becoming concerned. Was he in danger? For a brief moment, he actually worried the old bastard was in trouble.

"Right, she's gone now. I can't trust anyone, Glenn, only you."

He sounded properly unhinged, Glenn thought, all his paranoia finally catching up with him.

"Sack her. It's never stopped you before," he suggested, "What do you want? We're five days away from an interstate meeting that's growing in importance. I've got better things to do with my time."

"I need to keep my enemies close," said Gordon, "she's working for someone else, I'm sure of it. I have plans, they can't fail. Global are everywhere now. Don't trust anyone."

Yes, thought Glenn, well over the edge. He'd need to discuss this with Valla and Alison, because the very worse thing that could happen right now was President Gordon Murcheson losing his mind.

"I won't. Look, I've got to go. Tell me in an email, send it encrypted. Let me help you."

He thought he sounded conciliatory and supportive. He hoped that was how it had come across. Gordon Murcheson didn't believe in much but he believed in family. Though why, after the things he'd done to them, he thought it was reciprocated, Glenn didn't understand.

The line went dead.

He left the radio room in a mental state he hadn't expected to. Utter confusion was not what he thought the conversation would have left him with.

He entered the conference room to see Valla leaning over the table spread with charts, and Dmitry with dividers in his hands.

"There's no doubt they're heading where we're heading, and this is the place they'll refuel first."

Glenn saw Dmitry shut the dividers and point them at a spot on the chart showing Western Australia.

"Should we hang back and take them?" asked Valla.

"Policy is not my decision," said Dmitry, "but if you do want to take them, I'd suggest after they're well clear of Western Australian waters. It's always controversial to be taking ships near someone else's territory. Though perfectly legal for us in international waters, the Iron Prestige is AFS flagged."

"I don't expect Santiago is up on Maritime Law, but I reckon he'll keep close to shore till he has to leave it. So here…" Valla circled an area half on that chart and half on the one overlain above it, "But he could run back for shore, that would be diplomatically bad for us."

"We taking the Prestige? Good. It'll be interesting to hear what Santiago has to say," he said.

"We'll have to be smart about it. She's got two and a half knots on our top speed. If she decides to run we'll have to disable her," Valla replied.

Valla was looking at Dmitry, "What's our fuel situation?"

"We have three more days, we've booked bunkers at Cilegon in Banten, with fuel to spare."

"Ah, Banten's stayed closely aligned to the Indonesian supra-state. We've had negotiations at the supra-state level, but not at state level," said Valla, "shouldn't be any problems there if we made a request. Western Australia however, is still a basket case of old colonial attitudes. They're not going to care about the flag of a state they don't recognise. Where's the next place they'd have to refuel?"

"That's a much wider area," began Dimtry, "they don't need to empty and refill to reach Singapore after Geraldton, so they've got space. If I had to guess, I'd pick Cilegon itself. It's a big city, plenty of anonymity, he might have ties to gangs there too."

"This island," Valla said, pointing on the overlapping chart that showed West Java and its surroundings, "Panaitan. Looks like a good place to hide behind."

Glenn looked at the chart, the narrow channel between the island and peninsula that stuck out of Java would be inviting, and Panaitan had some good places to hide once it was clear what route the Prestige might take around it.

Valla said, "I'd like Martin's opinion on this, he's been in the Australian navy. If you don't mind Dmitry?"

"I would discuss it with him as a matter of course, but yes, do you want me to call him down just now?"

Glenn watched Valla. Alison had told him and he hardly believed it. The idea of Valla falling for someone she couldn't have almost made sense to him. He'd known Valla as a teenager when he'd first come to stay in Weddell City. Even then she was a rising political star, only two years older than he was, she seemed impossibly assured then. She only seemed to get stronger after the death of her father.

He'd been along on the drinking trips of course, the sons and daughters of senators had to be careful, so they socialised together, sometimes things got a bit out of hand, somewhere safe from the press. It never bothered him, he didn't care what got back to the old bastard, but he'd only seen Valla lose it once. A small resort, or what passed for that in Antarctica, near to the space base at Melchior, there'd been some of the scientists come down from the observatory based there. She'd got drunk, not unusually. The guy had apparently thought he was in with a shout. The rest of the party had been woken by his screams. Somebody talked Valla out of dunking him in the sea without his survival suit and everyone had sobered up faster than they'd wanted to. There was so much held back in Valla he wondered how she didn't explode.

He could see the hand of Alison in some of how she was coping. Now it made sense why Alison had suddenly taken up air pistol shooting.

"Yes, please," said Valla, "we need to plan this thoroughly ahead of time, my sole combat experience is McMurdo and we know there was a lot of luck involved then."

Glenn saw her nod at him and for a moment he thought she could tell which memory he'd dragged up from their party days. He smiled at her, and was pleased to see her smile back.

Dmitry was calling the bridge, so Glenn took the opportunity of filling Valla in on his recent conversation with the President. Valla's face was poker straight, which he knew was a sign she knew more about this than he did. She was up to something, something that was messing with Gordon's plans. He hoped it was a careful dismantling of cards that wouldn't leave Christine with a route to the Presidency. He decided to talk to Alison, she'd get more from Valla than he would.

Martin arrived in the conference room and Dmitry filled him in on what was known and what was being suggested. Glenn could tell there was some tension in Martin from his movements. Whether that was down to the current situation or other reasons he couldn't tell. He could sympathise though. Martin was bent over the charts with Dmitry's dividers, pacing out distances.

"We can train the cannon on the Prestige, but we'll have to board her and that'll be dangerous. We're not dealing with Patrice this time. The minute Santiago knows we're near him he'll be preparing. Do we know how many men he has?"

"City Quay CCTV show four bodies in the launch as it passed astern of the Prestige, there was no sign of anyone joining after," said Valla, using a voice Glenn recognised from many a late night poker game.

"And we want Santiago alive?"

"Yes, he's got information. We think he's trying to work with Global. The rest, not so much."

"Okay. We need to make sure we identify Santiago correctly then."

Glenn saw Valla wince slightly. He recalled the fight on Styx Street in McMurdo when they nearly lost Canning because they thought he was Pierre. He hadn't expected that to have got a write up, but then he remembered how thorough Valla could be. Always learning from her mistakes.

"We need to make sure she can't run for somewhere safe. Wouldn't shooting them out the water be our safest option?" she asked.

Glenn thought Valla was laying the hard act on a bit thick. He knew she used to have a tendency to get in pissing competitions, but he'd thought she'd outgrown that.

Martin had looked up and Glenn had seen confusion briefly dart across his face. Then he was back to being the XO.

"Once they're in the sea they're more manageable, that's true. The only problem there is the wildlife," he said, "this is shark territory. They'll be there in minutes, especially if Santiago and his men thrash about, or are bleeding at all. We might not get to them in time."

Glenn saw Valla redden. Today was just full of overturned perceptions. He thought he ought to help her out.

"So," he said, "how do we board her in a way that keeps us alive and Santiago viable?"

"We have small fast craft, the Prestige doesn't. We can use the Mercer and her manoeuvrability to keep the Prestige from running to safety shoreside. See here," Martin pointed at the south west peninsula of the island Panaitan, "that's pretty shallow, we've got seven metres draft, but the Prestige is seven point seven, we could push her into grounding herself, and there's submerged reef and rocks nearby too. The Mercer looks like it would

168

beach before the Prestige, so they might be fooled into heading to the shallows."

"I like it," said Valla.

Glenn could see her smile had returned, shades of The General were beginning to show, as Alison had mentioned to him earlier. There was no doubt the pair of them worked well together.

They continued to refine the plan, any tensions were dissipated in the single minded focus on the objective. Glenn recognised the old Valla returning. He was glad, and he hoped she'd continue. The subterfuge that she'd been involved with back in the senate clearly hadn't been healthy for her. He could see now she'd started down the second guessing path, the one that led to a mistrust of not just other people but often your own judgments. He'd been able to deal with it because he'd had his analytical skills, but also, he saw now, his deep hatred for his grandfather had given him an unshakeable core he could measure everything against.

Valla had been in the gym and the shooting range, talking with Alison, about the meeting earlier, and what was said, and how she felt. She was heading back to her cabin to take a shower and think more about what Alison had said in reply. She opened the door to her cabin and stopped. Martin was sitting on her daybed, watching her stand in the doorway. He smiled. She smiled back and shut the door.

"You've been avoiding me."

"I've been busy," she waved her hand at the mess of papers strewn across the desk.

"I know why," he said, patting the daybed cushion as invitation.

She sat on the bunk instead. People, she kept reminding herself, look after the people.

"Valla, you're not a soldier. You're a person, a good person. Cut yourself some slack."

"It's not right, Martin. I'm you're boss. Your political boss too. One of us would have to stop being what we are to make this work, and that's a lot to give up without knowing it would work."

She saw him pause from what he'd been going to say, she'd hurt him, and she felt awful as soon as she realised.

"I didn't mean that the way it sounded," she said.

"No, you did, and I know who you meant. You're trying to protect me."

He was standing up from the daybed. In two steps he was standing in front of her. He reached out to take her face in his hands and she felt an involuntary shiver down her spine.

"I'm a grown man, capable of making his own decisions. I'm on active duty and you're right, it would be wrong now. For many reasons. But what I do on my leave is nobody's business. And I know we work well together already."

She took his hands from her face and held them.

"Okay," she said, "let's try it that way."

She let go of his hands, though it was hard to do.

"And no more avoiding me. It's not conducive to the efficient functioning of the mission."

"XO," she said.

"Senator," he replied, heading for the door.

Chapter Seventeen - Twenty Five Minutes

The charges were set against the outer wall. Nobody had seen them at work because they'd had the CCTV system hacked to show nothing untoward. The seaward wall was never closely watched anyway. Who would attempt to get onto the cliff face from the broiling Southern Ocean, to then scale the ninety metre sheer face of granite, weathered into a treacherous surface that looked solid, till you tried to gain a hand or foothold when it crumbled into so much gravel?

It was still only the outer wall, two further layers of concrete and granite lay between the small task force and their quarry. This was as hard an operation as it got, they were hand picked, untraceable; with multiple layers of identities as complex as any hacker IP path.

They hung down from the edge of the cliff as they waited for the detonation. Once it went off they had thirty minutes maximum to reach and extract the target. The explosion shook the rock face. Loose chippings fell into the sea below without making a mark, the foam already violent. The three of them scrambled up and inside the wall. They wire cut through the fencing to reach the next wall, set the explosive, moved on. Two of them at all times watching for possible retaliation. They'd been promised they'd get a free run as much as possible, and so far it looked like that was true.

There was a final explosion, less dramatic but still impressive, leaving a man sized hole in the granite wall of the building. They entered carefully. Inside could be where the real danger lay. They ran to the iron bars of the corridor gate, set the plastic explosive in the lock and cowered back from it as it went off. A shower of flinty hot metal shards was followed by the main section clanging onto the lino floor. They tore open the gate and rushed towards the door marked thirty.

"Stand back from the door," he shouted to the cell inside.

He nodded to one of the black clad figures, who loaded more of the explosive which disconcertingly looked like they were gumming up the lock with blu-tac.

The explosion was the smallest yet, he wondered if it had worked at all. He tried the door, it was still fast in the doorway.

"Do it again," he ordered, looking at the watch strapped on the outside of his sleeve.

This time there was more bang, he felt sure it had worked this time.

He pushed the door open and saw the scientist huddled in the corner, with a sheaf of papers cradled in his arms.

"Doctor Michael Canning?" he asked, thinking it was always worth making sure.

Prisons could sometimes hold a surprising number of scientists, geeks and nerds he'd found. Not to mention journalists, poor saps who'd been in the wrong place at the wrong time and exchange pawns waiting for their governments to capitulate to a demand. Though he'd never had a job to rescue any of those. No, they always wanted the ones with the knowledge to build the bomb, or whatever it was that time.

"Yes?" said Canning.

"Come with us."

His two accomplices went forward and lifted Canning up from his crouching. They continued to carry him between them as they exited the cell. He tossed an incendiary into the remaining heap of papers and left, catching up with them as they were through the gate and heading for the gap in the building.

They'd reached the penultimate wall, and were again waiting for him at the wall as he stuck his head out quickly and was answered with a well aimed shot. To be expected, he thought. Behind him his accomplices were busy fighting Canning into a black survival suit. They were about to depart from the pages of the text book and descend into bloody reality. He hoped it was just the one shooter. They had ten minutes leeway across the whole operation.

He flipped his visor down, and moved the small camera attachment round the corner of the hole. The camera had a covering designed to hide its heat signature. The fact that no one shot at it was reassuring. His weapon needed line of sight, but it didn't need eyesight, camera sight was just as good. He saw the guard's infra-red heat signature, a pale yellow blob high up on a tower overlooking the courtyard. He pulled out the long barrelled gun with its flared mouth and pushed the charge button, seeing the pale blue LEDs race along from the stock to half-way up the barrel. It wasn't as long as a rifle but it was still ungainly in one hand.

They'd smeared a reflective cream around the mouth of the gun but he'd no faith in that, he'd need to be accurate with his first attempt. He checked the camera image in his visor again, calculated where to point the gun, poked it round the edge and pushed the trigger button, using all his strength to keep it level and steady.

He saw the yellow blob, disappear. He checked the perimeter of the courtyard with the camera while the gun hung down in his other hand. It looked clear, He stepped out, nothing. He waved at the others, and they jogged across the courtyard, with Canning dangling between the two and him in the lead. They were at the breached outer wall. Below the sea crashed and howled at the cliff face. He and one of his accomplices started to rig up the hoist that would carry Canning down to the froth. The other had left Canning in a fresh heap and had begun rappelling down the cliff. He caught a glimpse of him as he reached the waves and saw the small, rigid inflatable dingy now bounce into view.

He heard shouting coming from the courtyard. He nodded to the other guy to get Canning into the hoist. The guy nodded in acknowledgement. He moved back to the edge of the breach and deployed the camera again.

There were two guards, carefully combing the edges of the courtyard in concert, visors down, working their way round to the residual heat of the breach. He charged the gun again, he'd been told it had five charges in it before it would need to be re-powered. He aimed at the guard in the lead. He saw him stumble forward and then hit the ground. The guard behind him immediately flattened to the wall, and was now sighting his weapon at likely sniper points. He smiled. He rather liked this new weapon, even if it didn't have much repeatability. For a job like this it was ideal. They'd told him it would even work through heavy snowfall. He tried to recall what they'd called it, sounded like laser but not quite. He waited till the guard began moving again. They had told him the weapon had to be kept secret, no one could suspect it was being used. He still wondered how it worked, and surely without bullet holes anybody would realise it wasn't a normal gun that had been used.

He charged and fired, the second guard fell forward. He scanned again with the camera, but the area was now clear. He turned back to the cliff edge, seeing Canning halfway down to the water. His accomplice was lowering him steadily, while Canning did nothing to help, waving wildly after an escaped sheet of paper as it raced off on the wind.

"Fucking arsehole," said his accomplice.

"Yeah, supposed to be some evil genius, but hey, we've seen them all," he replied.

Eventually Canning was down into the dingy and they both rappelled down at speed to join him. The dingy had been kept off the rock face by an anchor some way out into the sea. He heard the outboard motor snap and cough into life as they drove away from the cliff face to retrieve the anchor. He looked at his watch. Twenty five minutes. Not bad.

Wahid was jerked awake by the sound of an explosion. He'd felt the vibrations through the floor of the hotel at the same time. He was dressed and heading up to the prison within five minutes. He could hear the sirens inside. It was unlikely anyone at the gatehouse was going to be there, never mind let him inside, presidential credentials or otherwise. He skirted the outer wall, at some distance because of the swampy trench that had been dug as a ramming deterrent. He heard several smaller explosions from within the prison. It sounded very like someone was being broken out of the prison. If it was Canning, he felt that Global had made a serious misjudgement. He could only get twenty metres to the cliff edge because of the fence, topped with razor wire and erected from the prison wall to a point about a mile away. He ran some way along the fence to see if he could get an angled view onto the cliff.

There was no way to see what was going on. The wind from the sea was whistling in the chain links, he tasted the salt on his lips from it. He leant against the fence straining his hearing wishing again that there was a hearing equivalent to a visor. Sound had always been an important sense in Antarctica, so often your ability to see was nil. He thought he heard an outboard motor, but he couldn't be sure.

Whoever had done this had been a seriously professional outfit. Wahid checked his visor clock. From being woken by the explosion to him maybe hearing an outboard it had been twenty six minutes. He walked back along the fence and headed to the gatehouse. It was time for him to make some explosive noises of his own.

"You call Governor Sutar now," he demanded of the guard, who'd been refusing him access, "I'm the President's personal representative, and if you want to still have a job in the morning, you'll start doing that job now."

The guard looked scared, he was clearly getting information through his earpiece about what was happening inside. Wahid reached slowly for an awkward outside pocket and pulled out his senate pass which showed his security clearance. The guard was so distracted he hardly noticed, only at the last minute as Wahid pulled the pass out did he point his handgun at Wahid.

"I have the highest level of security clearance, son. I know you're not used to what's happening but I need to get to the governor now."

Wahid saw the guard recover his composure a little and finally put a call through to the inner gatehouse for consent.

The outer gates ground open and Wahid walked into the long space between them. There was a pale blueish tinge stretched up from the golden horizon beyond the prison and the space was lit with strong LED searchlights. He walked, with his hands clearly visible, to the inner gate, almost expecting to go through the same routine of wheedle and threats to get inside. The gates, however slid open ahead of him.

Once he was inside a guard came towards him, a semi-automatic aimed at him. The guard gestured for the security pass, which Wahid was careful to hold up slowly. The guard pointed up at the CCTV camera in the corner of the wide foyer area. He showed it the pass. The guard nodded, and gestured with his gun for Wahid to follow. The more he experienced the more he was sure that he had heard an outboard motor. Everyone was heightened and jumpy but there was no sounds of active shooting.

The institution was in shock, vibrating and alert but the danger had passed.

He remembered the route to the governor's office. The guard knocked on the door and opened it. Wahid walked in on the scene. Governor Sutar was pacing while on a mobile phone, her secretary was standing hunched over the desk on the wired phone. The door was still open behind him and a guard came in.

"We have three casualties. All down in the outer courtyard. There's ropes down the cliff. I think they've got away, Ma'am."

"Who's missing? Has there been any security breaches elsewhere?"

"It's Canning," said Wahid to the room.

The governor stopped mid sentence in her phone call.

"How do you know?"

He saw a look of real fear on her face. Confirmation that whatever she'd been up to had included Canning.

"Check his cell," he said, turning to the guard who'd just entered.

He saw Sutar nod assent to the guard and heard him run back out.

"I'll have to call you back," she said into her phone. He watched her pocket it and turn to give him a searching look.

"You got here quickly" she said.

Ah, he thought, attack is not always the best form of defence, you've just given me even more reason to suspect you.

"I hear an explosion next to Denam Prison, what else am I supposed to do?" He continued, "Perhaps, Governor Sutar, you'll explain to me what you've been doing with Doctor Canning that you're now so worried will come to light?"

He saw her push at the secretary to hang up and wave her out the room.

"Nobody comes in, understand, Miriam?"

"Yes, Governor."

As the door closed the sirens became a muffled sound.

"I told you I needed money. Global were paying me to pass papers to them from Canning. What was the harm in that?"

"Money for what?"

"Do you know what salt water does to stuff? When it's twenty below to ten above, what freeze thaw does? Granite isn't indestructible. Our maintenance bill is phenomenal and the senate hasn't increased our funds, not even in line with inflation for the last five years. Coincidently the length of our President's time in office."

"I'm not going to argue, but I will ask, when did Global approach you?"

"What do you mean?," she said "I approached them. They sent a representative about a year ago, asking to meet with Canning. We let prisoners have visitors, I couldn't not let her visit, but I did suggest a few scenarios to her, hypothetically."

Wahid did some more thinking.

"What was this representative's name?"

"I can't remember now, they never came back, it all went in the mail. Someone read everything he sent just in case. I think in the beginning we even took copies. I can have a look for them."

"Please do. Was the name Sophia Wren by any chance?"

"No. No. Wasn't anything like that."

"Could you describe her?"

"Probably, though it'd be a bit vague now. Look, I've got three casualties I have to go and check on. Are we done?"

"Yes. But if there's anything else you remember, I want to know about it. First. There'll be an Agency team coming out of Saylon who'll get here in the afternoon. I'll be back before they arrive with a sketch artist."
There was a knock on the door, then it was pushed open. Her secretary was right behind the guard.

"I'm sorry…" she was saying.

"They're melted. They're all dead. Not bullets. Melted. Like they were fried from the inside."

The guard was distraught, the secretary had no trouble pulling him away from the door. Wahid was now genuinely confused, at first he'd been pretty sure it was a Global operation, then his suspicions had fallen to Sophia Wren, and to be fair some of them still lay there anyway. But now, hearing the guard describe the injuries the saser gun produced, he didn't know what to think.

Chapter Nineteen - Recovery

Anatoli was shattered, his back ached in a way it had never done before. He'd slept on floors, in drunken heaps, a few sporting muscle pulls, but nothing as deep seated or continuous as this. He tried to avoid using what was in the jet's first aid kit, sticking only to the basic anti-inflammatory that Zhao had supplied. They were going to land soon at Polar Station. His unauthorised departure from Vostok had been cleared with the Station by Nikau Burns, Valla's right hand man, who seemed to know they were coming in. His missing cockpit voice recorder had also been excused. But he wanted to get someone to look at his back before he took off again. He was worried.

The air traffic control at Polar Station was a fairly relaxed affair and he landed on the ice sheet runway, with what he thought was the minimum amount of sliding about. He tried to get up from the chair but couldn't straighten. Enya came into the cockpit.

"Tolli," she exclaimed, "here, let me help."

He leant on her small frame, tougher than she looked, she seemed to be able to take his weight.

"I want to straighten up, I'm not crawling out of my own jet."

"We'll do it in the cabin where there's more room," she said, supporting him through the cockpit door frame.

He bent down to touch his toes. Put his hands on his shins. There was a twinge. He could feel Enya supporting his lower back with her hand and her other on his stomach. He put his hands on his hips to straighten up. There was a sharp pain then it went back to the old ache. He almost felt better.

When they got inside the station proper Enya was already asking about medical staff. Anatoli eyed the plastic chairs in the waiting area with suspicion. He continued to stand despite the ache. He saw someone in a white coat appear through a doorway and head over to Enya, who was now pointing at him. He hoped they'd be able to sort it.

"Come with me, I'm the station doctor. Used to be a visiting position but you're lucky they made it permanent last month."

Anatoli followed the white coat.

Now he was lying down, on some sort of gel bed, and they'd given him something that meant he'd not be flying for at least twenty four hours till it got out of his system. He fell asleep.

"Is he going to be okay?" asked Enya, who was staring intently at the sleeping Anatoli.

Behind her the station doctor was writing on a chart. "He needs to do some exercises, ideally he needs to sit for no longer than twenty minutes at a time just now, but I understand that's a difficult ask. He's strained muscles sitting in the one posture for too long."

"It wasn't exactly his choice."

"Well, anyway," said the doctor, sounding keen not to have any more information about that revealed to him, "I can send him the exercises, some basic postural correction stuff, and give him something that'll be safe to fly with, but still cut down on the worst of it. You'll be surprised how many bad backs we get here at the Station. Some people just don't exercise out here."

Enya was silently relieved, a strain wasn't a permanent injury, it was clearly something that could be worked at. She turned to the doctor who was hanging up the chart on a tripod next to the gel bed.

"Thank you."

"No problem," said the doctor, walking on down to the next occupied bed.

Enya stood for a few more minutes just to watch him sleeping, and then headed for the canteen.

"How is he?" asked Tanya as she sat down next to her and James.

"Sleeping, doped up and apparently capable of a full recovery."

"I'm so sorry. Freddie's boys seldom expect anyone to need to stand up again after they've tied them down on a chair."

"I can imagine," said Enya,"have you tried calling her on the sat phone yet?"

187

"No answer. Probably ditched her phone already."

Enya could tell Tanya wasn't entirely convinced by her guesswork, and she felt a little bit of sympathy for her. Only a little bit because Freddie was bad, plain bad, and nobody should find that attractive, or be worried for someone like that. It was something she was still having trouble with, since Tanya appeared to be a reasonable and level headed person otherwise, with the usual amount of sympathy and empathy you'd expect in a normal human being. So why the blind spot around Freddie?

James looked tired, he wasn't saying much.

"I'm going to try and get a hold of Nikau Burns, say thanks for getting us legal again after our unconventional departure from Vostok. They've given us a guest bunk room, I think it's number ten, I'm going to go there after, to get some sleep. What about you two?"

"Oh, I'm wide awake," said Tanya "going to have a look around. I've never been this close to the Pole before. They said they're getting more adventurous tourists coming so they're trying to set up a tour. I said I'd give them some pointers, I used to do tours in Vostok. People used to still want to see the lake, back when we first arrived from Kunlun."

Enya remembered the photograph. It was worth asking a few innocuous questions while Tanya was in a reminiscent mood.

James had fallen asleep in the chair. She let him sleep, it was more important to get Tanya talking, than to worry about yet another person's spine.

"Oh, how long have you been in Vostok then? I just assumed you'd always been there."

Tanya took the bait, and Enya kept the questions general but useful. It turned out they moved within days of the accident at the Innonnox Mine. Accident was the exact word Tanya used, like she really didn't know about the saser trial. Yet, Enya remembered Tanya'd had the sound 'gun' to make the alarm noise from the empty building, where James had shot the driver from. Did she only know of the device as a safety alarm?

Then Tanya had mentioned Manny, how he'd been the mine foreman and had come with them from Kunlun, so shook up from the accident he couldn't go back down the mine. Tanya said she'd been surprised to see him at the hangar, because he'd not been in touch for a few years by then. Enya realised while Tanya spoke that she was one of life's eternal innocents, unable to see the bad in anyone for any length of time. Always willing to make excuses for them, forgive them, like she'd already forgiven Freddie. Enya wasn't sure it was sympathy she had for Tanya anymore, it was something more complex, and involved a desire to give her a good, but ultimately ineffectual, shake.

She made an obvious check on her watch, which seemed to have no effect. It was time for some direct action.

"I better go make my call," she said as the conversation paused.

"Yes. I've got to go soon for the tour. I'll try not to disturb you if you're asleep."

"Thanks, Tanya," Enya said, and meant it.

Tanya got up and Enya leant across to shake James.

"You need to find a bed, go speak to the station admin, get a bunk."

Enya called up Nikau, he'd left his number for them with the station administrator.

"Hi," she said, not entirely sure what to say beyond that.

"Hi, you must be Enya Zhao, Valla's told me so much about you."

His voice was pure Weddell City, but had some of the inflections that were creeping into those involved in the Senate, where accents from around the AFS mixed and influenced the City accent.

"I'm flattered," she said, "and we wanted to thank you for arranging the exemption so the jet's still classed as airworthy, and smoothing over our departure from Vostok."

"Well we did point out that Anatoli's jet never actually left for Denam either so they ought to really not make a fuss. They agreed, of course," he paused, then said, "We've got a job we'd like you to take on when you arrive back in Weddell City."

"We?"

"Valla, me, maybe a bit of the Intelligence Agency, though they aren't aware that they want that."

"Okay," she said warily, "doesn't sound strictly police work."

"Oh but it is, it's a murder investigation, but we can't call it that, because technically nobody is supposed to know a murder has happened. So it calls for a delicate touch and someone with a bit of experience working outside the lines. I've been told that's you."

Enya was not feeling flattered anymore. Outside the lines. What cheek! She was a good, honest cop. She'd handed the taxi driver over to the station security, along with a charge sheet, and the advice that he should be shipped back to Vostok for the attention of Chief Inspector Chapman, as soon as was convenient. It didn't matter now, he could have simply been flown back free, but it had mattered to her that he should be charged for aiding and abetting smuggling. That was entirely inside the lines. But... murder, she didn't like murderers. Who did? Yet people could still make excuses for it. Life was hard enough in Antarctica without people making it more difficult to stay alive.

"Okay," she said again, aware she was now hopelessly committed and that Nikau Burns probably knew that, "Who's our victim and who's our prime suspect?"

"I'm sorry but that'll have to wait till I meet you in person. Not safe for the airwaves," he said.

Enya was hooked.

"We'll arrive tomorrow, Anatoli's strained his back and needs a bit of rest here."

"I'll be at the airport. I'm arranging a new cockpit recorder to be fitted as soon as you've landed and the jet's back in the hangar. We can chat in the car. I'm arranging something separate for Tanya, we need to make sure she's somewhere safe. I understand you're sending the taxi driver back to Vostok?"

He sounded surprised about the taxi driver.

"Yes, with a charge sheet. There's no need to drag him further with us, he's only a liability now, before he could have raised the alarm."

She wondered what Nikau might have done with the taxi driver? She knew he'd stood by Valla when she was in the Resistance and it had been a proscribed organisation, she wondered what else he'd support her doing?

"Okay," said Nikau, "Till tomorrow, then."

"Yes," said Enya, and waited till she heard the line click dead.

"What the …" she said to herself, as she headed out the sat phone booth and towards bunk room number ten.

Santiago was in the wheelhouse and feeling much better. It had taken him nearly three days to get out of bed, but here he was, tipping about with the best of them.

He'd already arranged the refuelling at Geraldton, quieter than Perth, with less Australian police, customs or secret service. Everybody thought that Perth was easier to move stuff through, and that was true if you used a statistical approach and reckoned on one bust to every three couriers you sent at the same time. But Santiago preferred to have more control than that. He never believed in leaving anything up to Fate. His boats used Geraldton all the time, he'd built up a network of bribed officials and dockers there, so it made sense to use it himself.

They were heading up the Western Australian coast, still eight days from Singapore, but now he was feeling better, he was enjoying himself. The weather was improving, the temperature was getting hotter, hot enough for him and the boys to have raided Patrice's wardrobe for cooler clothing. He'd never pegged Patrice as a lover of Hawaiian shirts but seeing Trigger in one was almost worth all the hassle. He'd get ashore while they refuelled and get in touch with contacts back in the AFS; that Cornie guy from Global for a start, who must be wondering where he was. He was quite pleased to make anyone involved with Global sweat. He didn't like them, he'd do jobs for them because he'd get paid. But ultimately he recognised them as his direct competitor and they were certainly big enough to put him out of business, and bad enough to do it permanently.

He'd also get in touch with Kim, make arrangements in Singapore to move his operations there till the heat died down in Saylon. Maybe do a bit of sightseeing while that was getting set up. He was quite looking forward to it. She would arrange the false passports for them. Not Singaporean, that was too difficult and not worth the price of getting caught. No, they were all soon to be nationals of Sarawak, suitably far enough away for it to be difficult to check quickly, and the worst punishment for a fake Sarawak passport was to be repatriated back there.

She'd have to book them a slot through the sea wall too. The Singapore Roads, the shipping lanes that accessed Singapore and also saw inter-regional traffic were the busiest in the world, ships that wanted to access Singapore had to have everything sorted two days ahead of their arrival and were given a time slot. If you didn't make that slot, you were sent to do a big circuit in the Java Sea till you were allocated another slot. It could take a week. He remembered Patrice managed it once. Nearly lost him a big deal with an onward consignment bound for Sanya in Hainan. A week circling in an island ringed sea would make him an easy a target too.

Chapter Twenty - Greasy

Freddie had agreed to Gordon's plans, but had also decided this time she'd build in some protection. She'd contact Valla's right hand man, Nikau Burns. She remembered Nikau when he was younger and starting out working for Domingo Torres, Valla's father. Now, she recalled, there was a man who could give Gordon a run for his money. Nikau was only a few years older than her, and like her at a point halfway between the old guard that had been Gordon, Domingo, Daniel and such and their heirs, Valla and Glenn; the youngsters as she liked to put it.

Each generation seemed to be so different to the one before, and hers had been saddled with a desire for change but none of the idealism that usually went with it. It was after the cock-up at the Innonnox Mine that she gave up trying to change things and just started looking out for herself. The death of five miners had lain on her conscience for a while, but then she seemed to let them slip away. Her younger self wouldn't recognise her if they met now, she was sure.

Nikau had shown her something, she wasn't sure what it was, but he'd said he thought Global's head guy, Kutchner, might have something better on a secure server. Freddie had been interested. She thought Christine Frome was a total wet blanket, and had voted for the Larsen guy in the run-offs. If this got her in with the Torres Family and hurt Christine, then she felt sure she could weather anything Gordon could throw her way. She said as much to Nikau and he had smiled. She remembered that smile. It felt predatory somehow, at a deep instinctual level she recognised that Torres had Gordon in their sights as well as Christine Frome. It made her feel even more pleased to be allied with them now.

Not everyone in her networks had found out Freddie was still alive. When she'd got in touch with her hacker friends it had taken longer than expected to convince them it really was her and they weren't being set up. Once that was sorted, they were happy to help. They quickly located the Global guy's server in a server farm up by Melchior. Their estimates for extraction of anything recently uploaded were however vague. It was apparently 'super secure'. She left them to it.

Nikau had provided a driver and car, and accommodation for her, which she'd not yet got a look at. It was late evening, in a hardly dimmed night. It had to be just past midnight before there was a kind of dusk. Weddell City was much closer to the Pole than Denam prison where the twilight could still merit lights. She shivered when she thought about her time in Denam. It had been hard. Hard not to have seen Tanya, hard to put up with people saying she should have been shot as a traitor. She wasn't a traitor, she knew that for certain. On the whole though she'd been safe physically. Her reputation preceded her, and not everyone in Denam was there for life: most hoped to get out. Nobody wanted delayed revenge once they were free.

The driver pulled up at an anonymous apartment block and handed her a key with the apartment number on fob. She thanked him and got out. She felt very lonely all of a sudden. Her life for the past five years had been organised for her, it involved people interfering, shouting, and generally being annoying but she almost felt abandoned.

She shook herself. What a lot of bull. She was finally free, and she had plans that would keep her free. She could make more plans, she could get the gang back together in Vostok and start to make some money again. She thought about Phil and Casey, who'd been sent back to Vostok by Gordon. Like he didn't know how easy it was for her to get muscle in Weddell City. Just showing off that he was in control. She reached the apartment door and put the key in the lock. She remembered again Nikau's smile and chuckled to herself, while she opened the door.

Christine had said goodbye to Rafe at her door, as he insisted he was fine with a taxi back to where his car was. She closed the door and slumped to the floor behind it. The pain in her arm was throbbing. She thought about going to the hospital and making up a story to get it looked at, but maybe later. She didn't think she could move from where she was. She let her head hang down taking the weight on her good hand. UV wands, how could she not have realised? The whole apartment would need a forensic clean, which would, as Rafe had pointed out, cost a lot of money. Finding the cash wasn't a problem but keeping the payment secret might be more of a challenge. She could give it to Rafe, though, make it a campaign expenses thing. Maybe. Yes. That's what she'd do.

She pushed herself up against the door and stood off it. She felt dirty again. Thinking about the blood still in the sofa and carpet made her skin crawl. She went into her bedroom to undress and took a shower. She felt happier after that, and stayed in her bathrobe, typing notes on her laptop for the speech which had been sent over by the campaign team for her to look at. She heard a watery burble. It made her jump, her heart pounding in her chest, while the laptop fell to the floor, cushioned by the thick carpet. Another burble came from the en-suite. She went to have a look. The sheet wrapped body seemed to have grown in size. The sheet had billowed out, and was now occasionally releasing a bubble of something foul from under a fold. She'd been sure the water would stop that. Now she saw it wasn't true.

The sheet was a densely woven cotton. She wondered if there was a way to trap the gases inside it? But then she didn't know how much gas would be produced? And when would the sheet tear under the pressure? And, would there be a bang? She looked into the bath which now had a greasy film on the top of the water. There was no way she was putting her hands in there. She would just have to close the door, and try and ignore the noise. She desperately wanted another shower even while the towels were still damp from earlier. She settled for washing her hands instead, scrubbing them with the flannel as if she'd actually put her hands in the bath water.

She closed the en-suite door, picked up the laptop and tried to get back to reading the speech. The presidential candidates' debate had been rescheduled for tomorrow evening. This speech was for a rally in a conference hall near the airport at noon to catch the lunchtime tv audience. It would be televised live to her campaign offices in the other cities, and to smaller venues for supporters there to watch. Its tenor had been designed to provoke questions she could make the most of in the later debate.

She had to nail the speech, the rally and the debate. With the shooting of Daniel Ektov, Gordon had gained a sympathy vote from some Lomonosov quarters. Despite being a small Family, they had a big influence on the electorate in general. 'Plucky' was what the market research guys had found was most people's perception of Lomonosov. She couldn't now recall what people had said about Moss, but she remembered her feeling about it, and it wasn't a great feeling.

If it went wrong at any point tomorrow, if she didn't come out of it at least close to Gordon in the polls, then it was a lot of ground to make up. She had to make Gordon look like the weaker candidate, or what she thought was more likely, capable of making bad mistakes. They were leaning heavily on his autocratic behaviour, his funding priorities, the drop in the number of full senate sessions, the relegation of certain committees to rubber stamping already-done deals.

A news alert pinged on the laptop. She opened the notification. It was all text, no video, which was unusual. She read on. Denam Prison had been broken into. They didn't have much more on the story. Mostly speculation about who had done it and why. There was of course the UN pair, that Special Forces guy that Frederika Tran had been working with, and the doctor. She couldn't recall his name. Some of the speculation was pointing at the UN, but a lot of it…she checked the other news sites, almost all of it, was pointing at Global.

Shit, she thought. This would dominate the debate now. It would allow Gordon to hark back to the events of four and a half years ago and allow him to try and rekindle some of the feelings that saw him sweep to the

Presidency with a landslide. She tried to formulate which line of attack would be best to counter that, and failed. She was tired, and stressed. She shut the laptop and lay back on the bed. Within a few minutes she was asleep, even as a fresh burble erupted quietly behind her en-suite door.

It was early morning at Polar Station. The night hadn't existed and the golden light of the sun, dragged through a chunk of atmosphere thicker than what was stacked up above the Pole, made everything look optimistic. Enya had visited the infirmary again after she'd had a good sleep and saw that Anatoli was still sleeping. They were running thermal scans through the gel bed, to check on the inflammation on his back and the doctor had assured her it was going down. So she'd stayed up, letting Tanya have the bunk room to herself for the night. She watched some TV in the public lounge, and about two in the morning she saw the news ticker tape that ran across the bottom of every programme burst into a frenzy of newly typed text.

Denam Prison. Wow, she thought, tough to crack, but clearly not impossible. The usual suspects, UN and Global were being fingered as the culprits. By the time the rest of the AFS woke up, Enya knew their part would have solidified into an absolute certainty. Denam was far away from most places, it was how they'd managed to sit on Freddie's alleged death for nearly a day. But blowing up the jail was a different matter, there was no way to keep that quiet.

She let her detective's mind wander about the crime scene in her head. It wasn't the actual crime scene of course, but the intellectual one. The personalities involved. Who was likely to have been the target? That was easy, it was clearly Doctor Canning, he was without doubt the prison's most valuable prisoner. The news were reporting ropes left at the cliff face. So whoever it was had resources, and/or money. Gordon or Global, but on past performances not the UN. She wondered how it fitted in with the hints that Nikau had been dropping during the phone call yesterday. She was leaning heavily towards Global. Yet the other option, Gordon, would benefit immensely from this if it was true, and she had to swing back to a neutral position between the two of them. At times like this, having Alison Strang nearby would have been helpful. She thought about calling the Mercer. It was worth it to try.

The sat phone rang with an odd tone, then changed tone and someone answered with the name of the Mercer. She asked to speak to Alison and was put though to another ringing phone.

She heard Alison's voice very far away and with an echo that didn't sound like it was generated on the line but was in the room with her.

"Alison?"

"Enya. How are you? Where are you?"

"Alison, someone has broken Canning out of Denam Prison."

The line went so quiet she thought it had been disconnected, but then she heard Valla on the line.

"Do you know who it was?"

"No. It's a toss up between Gordon and Global. I can't decide. You should get the news channels up and see what Alison thinks. We're still at Polar Station, but we'll be in Weddell City by late afternoon. I'll call again then."

"Okay. We'll wait to hear from you."

The line went dead as Valla hung up. Enya felt something wasn't quite right. Not with Alison, but with Valla. She'd played enough poker with Valla back at McMurdo to recognise her bluffing voice. Perhaps there were three potential suspects not two?

Chapter Twenty-One - Gold

Christine Frome was woken by the smell coming from her en-suite. She shivered under the bedcovers as all the shitty shittiness came back to her at once. She dragged herself out of bed, and went over to the en-suite door, bracing herself. The stench was overpowering. She felt her bile rising and stumbled for the toilet, retching.

She was going to have to find a way to combat the smell. Maybe bleach would kill whatever was creating it? She wiped her face with the damp flannel, and headed out into the living space, careful to shut all the doors behind her. The smell wasn't noticeable in the living area yet, but she knew when it made its way into the corridor someone would call the building maintenance team and they'd want access. She rooted about under the sink discovering she'd used most of the bleach already. She thought about what else might work and drew a blank. She could try and look online, but she'd been avoiding that. Who knew who was able to see your browsing history? Certainly she'd not put it past Gordon Murcheson.

She'd call Rafe, ask him to bring some bleach over. She desperately wanted to take another shower, but couldn't face the en-suite and merely dragged clothes out of the bedroom, getting dressed in the living area instead. She put some towels down against the bottom of the bedroom door. She picked up her keys and opened the door.

She was dismayed to see a senate security guard still sitting on the chair outside her door.

"Good morning, Senator Frome," he said.

"Good Morning. Just heading out for some breakfast. I thought they were finished with the high level threat alert?"

"They would have been but Denam Prison got hit last night, so it's back on, with a vengeance," he replied, shrugging his shoulders.

She ought to have guessed, Gordon probably planned the whole thing. She might have a go at him in the debate for interfering with senators privacy. She could find one of the young hotheads to say something earlier in the day, so she could reference it later. She felt that she was getting to grips with her new normal of hidden decomposing body in the bath and conspiring to destroy evidence.

She drove to her favourite restaurant and ordered breakfast, having as big a meal as she could manage. If it looked like every morning she was going to lose the last night's meal then she better make up for it earlier in the day.

Anatoli stood up from the gel bed carefully, waiting to feel the dull ache, but nothing happened.

"I"m off the drugs, yeah?"

"Yes, the ones you can't fly on. We've given you something else, but you won't feel this good when you land at Weddell City, I can assure you. It's important you do the exercises, Mr. Dale."

"No worries Doctor. I don't ever want to feel this way again. Thanks."

"Good," the doctor said, moving away as Enya came forward.

"You feeling okay?"

"I can get us to Weddell City."

"That's not what I meant, but fine, you be the martyr."

"Enya..."

She was on tiptoe to kiss him, he bent just his neck to meet her.

"Let's go," she said, I have a meeting with Nikau Burns when we land, and he's arranged a new cockpit recorder to be fitted immediately too."

"Hmmm," said Anatoli as they walked towards the hangar.

"What?"

"Torres," he said, "almost as bad as Glencor."

"Tell me about it," she agreed.

Tanya and James were waiting for them at the hangar's public room.

He eased himself into the pilot seat, and breathed out slowly, waiting for a twinge of pain. Nothing. He tried to relax, keeping tense was just as bad for his back, he'd been told, as recklessness.

Five hours later they were down on the tarmac at Weddell City. The outside temperature was fifteen degrees, but the forecast was for icy rain once it was dusk. He hadn't felt anything during the flight, and had tried to keep moving position during it. He pulled the seat arm out of the way, and carefully twisted as he rose out of the seat. So far so good. He straightened, and there was the slightest memory of the pain in his lower back. He wondered how much a gel bed cost?

True to his word, Nikau was waiting for them as they came through the hangar airlock. There were two technicians with him carrying the new recorder, now passing Anatoli, heading towards his jet.

"Be careful with her," he called after them, getting a thumbs up from one of them.

"Tanya," said Nikau, "I have a car to take you to Freddie's apartment. I hope that's okay?"

Anatoli saw Tanya almost hug Nikau, pulling back only because Nikau had taken a step backwards.

"Sorry," she said, "I get too excited sometimes. Thank you."

Her driver had come forward and Tanya went off following him.

"DI Zhao, I have taken the liberty of organising a session with my own personal physio for Anatoli," Nikau said, pointing to another car, and another uniformed driver, waiting. "I was wondering if Officer Wylie would accompany him, in case he needs assistance later."

"Thanks," Anatoli said to Nikau.

He turned to Enya.

"See you at your's later?"

"Absolutely," she agreed, winking.

James was shrugging his shoulders at Enya, "Let me know when you need me."

"I'll be in touch," she replied.

"Just you and I now," said Nikau, motioning towards the final car.

"Indeed," she replied getting into the back of the limostyle car.

She waited till Nikau got in, then turned to face him.

"So, you've broken Canning out of Denam, care to divulge why? I caution you not to lie to me. What you say next determines how much I want to help you further."

Nikau laughed.

"Oh Valla wasn't wrong, you're very good."

"I don't consider this a laughing matter."

She saw him sober up instantly.

"No, I suppose not. But it helps keeps me sane. Yes, we have Canning. For his safety, and for the safety of the AFS. He's in protective custody, if you like."

"And three dead guards?"

"Trust me, both Gordon and Global had plans in action, and the death count would have been much higher. We had no choice. There's a secret civil war going on at the moment, and there will be casualties."

Enya felt her anger rising. This was Resistance nonsense all over again. She tried to stay calm, she was the professional here after all.

"It may yet be the courts who decide that."

She saw Nikau turn in his seat to face her more.

"Christine Frome has shot Arnaud Cheung dead and we think his body is still in her flat. We're pretty sure Global had a secret surveillance camera that recorded it, and the video file is in a server farm near Melchior. Gordon is slowly losing his grip on reality, he's compiling a list of people to investigate, not with Intelligence Agency or Police but with his own staff. And we strongly suspect he has a secret facility near Melchior where he was going to stash Canning, along with other scientists, to work on manufacturing novel weapons. How do you think that will play in court?"

She sat back a little, trying to take the whole lot in. She could match up suspicions she already had with some of what he was saying, but other information was brand new. A secret facility? That put Gordon well into mad dictator territory.

"So, you want me to get evidence Christine shot Arnaud then?"

"Yes. The video proof won't be enough, considering its source. We have some special footage, but it doesn't identify Christine or Arnaud, only corroborates the footage we don't yet have. We must have forensic evidence. And we think Christine is already trying to move the body. Once it's gone there's nothing concrete to say it was Arnaud. We need the body, we need his gun, and we need to eliminate Christine as a presidential candidate. Then we get Gordon."

"And what's the ultimate goal here? I don't work for politicians, I work for the AFS."

"We re-open Presidential nominations. Or we let the Senate repeal the Presidential legislation. It's up to the representatives."

"And Canning?"

"Back to a newly repaired and improved Denam Prison, with a new governor. She's been getting paid by who she thought was Global to pass on Canning's work."

"And, let me guess, that was you too?"

She had to hand it to Valla, The General certainly played a good game.

Nikau smiled, "maybe," he said.

Enya felt trapped. There was a murder. And it bordered on treachery. But there were many other crimes that were going to slide as a result of investigating this. And if she did this, she knew for certain she wouldn't remain in her job under Houten. He would make sure of it. To do this was to throw her career, such as it was, into the sea.

"We want you to head up a new unit after this too."

It was as if he'd read her mind. She scrutinised his face, searching for signs of other motives behind the offer. It seemed genuine.

"Yes?"

"An anti-corruption unit. You can hand pick your officers. You'll have powers to investigate anyone, from the President down. We don't want another Gordon Murcheson ever again."

"Or a Valentina Torres, eh?"

Nikau did a double take, then smiled at her.

"Indeed," he agreed, "I can see why Valla values you so highly."

"Okay," she started, "I need to search Christine's car. We'll leave searching the flat. Catch them moving the body instead. Difficult to say you didn't know about it when you're actually holding it in your hands. Some bullshit reason should be good enough for stopping her car, and then searching it. She's never struck me as particularly smart, so hopefully something will turn up. But at the very least we'll panic her into doing something with the body. Do you know if anyone is helping her?"

"She's suddenly started meeting Rafael Dupont, a junior Moss senator. Bit of a creep, if you ask me, reminds me of something slimy," answered Nikau, "he might well be involved. He's got a lot of ambition, even managed to beat the Global backed candidate for the junior position."

"Can you drop me at my flat? I've got a spare uniform, and the siren for the car. Makes it quite difficult for her to ignore me. I take it you have eyes on her?"

"We have two of the senate security guards reporting to us, we've been able to make sure they were allocated to her flat for the current security alert. At the moment she's out the flat."

She thought Nikau was almost hoping she'd break in. But nothing she was going to do was going to be illegal. The file on the server was clearly going to be acquired through a hack. The footages, both Nikau's special stuff and Global's video, were also not official CCTV. If this was going to stand up in court, and she was determined both Christine and Gordon were going to be tried in a court, then there needed to be some proper police work done.

"One last question,"

She saw Nikau look worried, like he knew what it was going to be.

"Freddie..." she started.

"Off the menu," he interrupted.

She didn't like it, but there were going to be other opportunities for Freddie. Freddie was just that kind of woman.

She was back in uniform, and it felt odd. Not the way she'd expected it to feel. Maybe it was because of what she'd agreed to. She was coming along Sidley Road, running parallel with Torres Boulevard, ahead she could see Christine's car. It looked like she was heading home. Ideal. She got a bit closer then put on the siren, moving to get ahead of Christine and slow her down. It said a lot for the sheer confidence of being a Senior Senator and in the pay of Global that Christine simply pulled over. Though, Enya thought, she had nowhere to run to anyway.

She got out of her car and headed to the driver's side. Christine got out. Enya knew James would have parked up a few car lengths behind them now.

"What's wrong? Officer?"

Christine's voice was slightly shaky, but it still retained an element of 'do you know who I am' about it.

"Detective Inspector Zhao, Weddell City Police, Madam Senator. You appeared to be driving somewhat erratically. I need to breathalyse you, it's a matter of procedure in these cases, but also do a vehicle check, you might have something wrong with it."

"Was I?"

Christine sounded genuinely unsure that she hadn't driving erratically. Zhao kept at the civil police routine.

"Probably something wrong in the car, ma'am. May I?"

And she was in Christine's car before Christine could speak, opening storage compartments large enough for a handgun. She struck gold, just as Christine came to her senses, and started to demand to see Zhao's ID.

Zhao, held the handgun in her gloved hand, between thumb and index finger.

"This yours?"

Christine seemed to crumble instantly. She was now a sobbing heap in the road.

Zhao called James, who drove up to be parallel with Christine's car, blocking a lane and keeping Christine's shivering mass between the cars.

Chapter Twenty-Two - Worth The Wait

Freddie looked up at the sound of knocking on the apartment door. As far as she was aware only Nikau and the driver knew she was here. And she didn't expect they would knock. She was unarmed. Gordon could have found out she was working with Nikau. They must have double agents in each other's camps. Then the knocking changed to a pattern, which she instantly recognised as one she and Tanya had used a long time ago. It couldn't be.

She opened the door and was nearly bowled over as Tanya rushed her, crushing into a bear hug.

"I was so worried about Gordon, what he might do. Enya wouldn't let me contact you, and then you didn't answer your phone, so..."

Tanya broke down, crying. Freddie knew this mercurialness was the thing she found most attractive about Tanya. Freddie had a deep dislike of mundanity, and Tanya could always provide excitement.

"There, there," she said, "I'm okay, see? And Nikau will make sure Gordon can't do anything."

"Are you sure?" said Tanya, through sobs, "he's the President."

"Not for much longer I think."

Tanya pulled back from her.

"You're going to tell me I can't know?"

"Yes. You can't, for your own safety."

She almost expected the fight to resume as if nothing had happened to them since the warehouse, but Tanya surprised her again by simply nodding her head.

The phone rang. Freddie had a new mobile, only the hacker group knew the number so far, and Nikau. Either one was going to be interesting.

She answered. It was the hacker group. They had everything Kutchner had uploaded in the past four days, all the way back to the mid-afternoon of the day Daniel Ektov was shot. There was text, but also a few videos. Freddie asked for the videos to be sent over encrypted. Then she called Nikau to let him know. For a moment she'd almost not called him. She'd thought about trying to play a more complicated game, something like she used to do back in Vostok; gang against gang, Resistance against gang, Gordon against Resistance, but her time in Denam seemed to have made her more cautious and she was also simply too tired for it now.

Tanya had headed over to the kitchen area and was busy checking cupboards.

"There's nothing here to eat. We'll have to call out."

Freddie wasn't sure.

"Okay, but tell them to meet you in the foyer, I don't want any more people knowing I'm here."

"Ooh," said Tanya, "just like the old days."

No, thought Freddie, not at all like the old days.

The files took nearly half an hour in total to download onto the laptop. Nikau had left her the new laptop in the flat. First thing she'd done was scrub the hard drive and re-install everything from scratch.

Tanya had disappeared downstairs to meet the takeaway food delivery guy.

There were three files, plus the de-encryption software. They'd agree a key for it when they'd met in person. She looked for the earliest time stamp.

Kutchner was a dirty old bugger, what Christine got up to in the privacy of her own bedroom was none of anyone's business. She stopped the file as soon as she realised what was going on and deleted it. The second file was what she was after. She sat in silence as the events unfolded. Well, she thought, I'd never have thought you'd manage that Christine. The final file was Christine moving the body to the bath. Freddie, who'd had experience in matters of body disposal couldn't imagine what Christine thought she would achieve doing that. It was clear Christine was beginning to behave irrationally, three showers was a bit excessive, even give the circumstances.

Tanya came back inside with the pizza boxes.

"Look who I met at the door?"

Freddie looked up instantly, but was relieved to only see Nikau. Tanya could be so naive sometimes.

"You need to see this," she said to him.

"Do you want some pizza?" said Tanya.

"Just a slice," said Nikau.

They all sat down to watch the two files.

She saw Nikau put his pizza slice down as Christine was hauling the body to the bath.

"What's she doing?"

"I don't know, but there's no way she should be anywhere near presidential powers," said Freddie.

"Oh, don't worry, I have good news on that front. Enya Zhao has just found the gun Arnaud used, in Christine's car. Christine is in custody at the moment. It's time to nail Gordon now."

Freddie gave Nikau a warning look, but realised it was too late anyway. Tanya, seeing the footage, now knew too much to be safe in Weddell City.

She saw he'd brought a thumb drive and was busy copying the files. Faster than they'd taken to download.

"Nikau, I need you to find somewhere safe for Tanya to stay. If we're going after Gordon I don't want her anywhere near me, or Weddell City."

"What?" protested Tanya, "No, Freddie no, not now we've just got back together. You can't send me away."

"I can," said Nikau.

He was getting up, pizza slice in one hand, thumb drive in the other.

"but maybe you'd like some time to talk. Give me a call," he said, heading for the door.

Freddie waited till the door was closed behind him then took Tanya into her arms. "You can stay till tomorrow morning, but then you have to go, you have to trust me, Tanya."

"Okay, Freddie."

They kissed. Something that Freddie had dreamt about for the last five years, and it was worth the wait.

Gordon got the call from his contact in the Weddell City Police Department. He couldn't believe his luck, and didn't. Christine Frome getting arrested wasn't in his plan. If she genuinely did have the gun that had killed Daniel in her car, then she wasn't going to be his presidential opposition, and that was a big crevasse of uncertainty he needed to plan for straight away.

Shortly afterwards, the TV company called cancelling the debate, citing unforeseen circumstances and promising to reschedule it. This whole thing was going to start reflecting badly on his current presidency if he wasn't careful. He called Sophia. He didn't trust her, but she had her uses. There was something odd about her, she was too keen, and much too enthusiastic about his list she'd taken on.

Gordon had started it two years ago so he had tabs on his political rivals' support, to get some feeling for the groundswell. So far he'd uncovered that she'd appeared to have expanded the list and redesignated those on it as enemies of the state. He felt things were getting away from him and he didn't know how to rein Sophia in without it coming back to bite him. Instead he'd decided to give her enough rope to hang herself and was merely waiting for the moment to pull the steps from under her.

"Sophia," he said, "I'd like you *personally* to keep an eye on Christine Frome. She's got money to post bail, so she won't be in custody long."

That would keep Sophia out of his way, while he figured out how to play the Senate. He was already sure he was going to call an emergency session. Was he going to push for fresh nominations? Say that Christine's arrest was a mere hiccup in the democratic process? He knew her campaign had been saying he was autocratic. Letting the Senate decide would play well, and he could almost guarantee the outcome went whatever way he wanted. If he could decide what suited him best.

"Yes Mr. President," said Sophia as she wheeled around and headed out of his office.

He had to get a hold of that list and go through it himself. If that got out, it would be difficult to explain. He went into the secretary's office and picked up Sophia's laptop. He didn't expect to get inside it himself, but he knew a girl who could.

He informed the Senate admin that an emergency session would be called for tomorrow afternoon. Video participation would be accepted with the usual certification. Most senators were not currently in Weddell City, the senate having been closed for the last few days, first due to the shooting and then because of the time period called purdah before the election. The original televised debate was to be the opener for that, voting would take place for the whole three weeks during which he'd expected to slowly grind Christine into a paste.

He'd not yet opened the polls. There'd been articles about that in the press, some not so subtle. Once again he felt pressurised into decisions ahead of their time. But at least he had a valid excuse now one of the two candidates was in police custody.

Finally there was Wahid. He'd not heard from him. Not even after the dust had settled from the break-out. He had no idea where his right hand man was. And Wahid didn't do that. He thought he could trust him. Maybe his order to break Canning out of Denam had sounded like an over-reaction but, surely by now Wahid would see the danger was real. And that Global had already made their move.

He moved away from his desk towards the bookcase and the decanters. Before he poured a whisky he caressed the blacked spine of the Frobius Turbine technical manual. Wahid had brought it back with Glenn from the burnt out geothermal station. The manual and Glenn were the only things left of his son, Bruce. Lately he'd been thinking about the past. It wasn't helpful, but it had started intruding whether he liked it or not. He poured the whisky and told himself he was getting soft. It was a weakness, and weakness got you killed. You had to be hard. Antarctica was a place only the hard survived in.

Look at Christine, he said to himself. And continued to think about her.

There's no way she arranged the shooting, but somehow she's ended up being stuck with the gun. Who arranged that? Was Global really behind the break-in? Maybe it was time to call in Freddie and see how she'd been getting on. Not that his plan was important now, but it was a convenient excuse. He could use Freddie elsewhere.

He sat down in the leather armchair, his hand stroking along the arm. The alcohol burned down his throat, reminding him there was no pleasure without a bit of pain.

There was a knock at the outer office door, and he got up to open the door.

"You called?"

"I did."

"This it?"

"Yes, I want a complete mirror copy. Can you make it so the mirror updates when something is created or updated."

"Yes. How savvy is the owner?"

"Basic, I think. Her skills lie in other directions."

"All right, old man. Too much information."

He scowled at the hooded figure crouched over Sophia's laptop.

"Here's the address," she said, "don't access it at the same time the laptop is being used."

"Why?"

"Too Long: Didn't Read, 'cos' I said so."

He disliked the girl's brusqueness but she was good, and didn't care who she worked for as long as she got paid well. Gordon reckoned he was her best customer in that regard.

She shut down the laptop, brought it back up and then closed the lid.

"All done."

"I'll transfer now," he said pressing a few keys on the mobile and sending a considerable sum into a secret bank account, similar to the two he himself had.

"Anytime, old man," she said as she slid out of the office.

Gordon still had no idea how she got into the building. He'd never caught more than a final glimpse of her on the CCTV as she entered and left his office. He'd thought before about asking, but had always decided that might put her off. Though now, it might be worthwhile knowing for himself how to get in and out without being seen.

He opened his laptop and typed in the url, found the list file and started to read it. The more he read the more worried about Sophia he became. This wouldn't just bite him, this could knock him out and leave the door wide open to Global. How many people had she already 'interviewed'? And what had she done with the three who had stars against their names?

Chapter Twenty-Three - Clean up

Rafael Dupont had a friend who worked for the Weddell City Police. They'd known each other back in Progress at high school. They'd moved to Weddell City about the same time, and had kept in touch even as they made new connections in the 'big city'. It was now a mutually profitable friendship and little to do with their common background. His friend had called him and told him Christine Frome had been brought in. She'd been booked for the murder of Arnaud Cheung and for obstructing an ongoing murder investigation. His friend also said there were rumours she might be charged with treason. He thanked him and hung up.

Treason. Fuck. He'd be done for aiding and abetting. He'd met her and been to the apartment, all witnessed and easily verified. How could she have been so fucking stupid to have kept the gun in her car?

He had only one chance now and that was to remove every single trace of Arnaud Cheung from Christine's flat before the police got anywhere near it. And that meant a cleaner right now, one who could get down to a molecular level. He called the number he'd sourced earlier for Christine.

"I need it now."

"I bet," said the cleaner, "price has doubled."

"Done. Get there now and get started. Half up front, half when I've checked it."

"All up front. You're in no position to bargain and I'll be carrying all the risk till it's done."

"Okay," Rafe said "but I'm coming too."

"Oh no. No sightseers, no amateurs."

"Fine," said Rafe and hung up.

He transferred the eye watering amount into the cleaner's account. If only Christine had already paid him the 'expenses'. He sat back on his sofa and made some secondary plans. If this came off, he could go for Christine's senior position. One step closer to being President. If it didn't he'd need a fast escape route. You didn't get shot for *unknowingly* helping traitors but he felt Gordon might swing the Senate to consider it for him. Gordon could be quite vindictive when he wanted to and Daniel Ektov had been his campaign manager.

Nikau was meeting Mariko Neish, temporary Senior Lomonosov Senator, at her Senate office. The Senate building was eerily quiet but he was used to it since Valla always preferred to be there when it was like that to get work done. He wondered how she was doing on the Mercer. He had brief sat phone calls with her now the Singapore satellites were available, but he was feeling the distance today. Things were happening fast. He doubted she'd want to take part in the emergency debate over a foreign satellite link, but it was yet another thing she wasn't here for. The distance was good for other things in the plan, but it didn't help fast reactions to unforeseen events.

"Mariko," he said proffering a hand, "nice to meet you in the flesh."

"Nikau," she replied shaking his hand.

"Christine's arrest brings a few things forward faster than we'd anticipated. Have you been able to get Enya Zhao in charge of the investigation in to Daniel's shooting?"

"Tomorrow. That Houten guy's a real jerk, I needed Dante to have a word with him."

"We think Rafael Dupont might do something tonight, he's implicated otherwise, and I've heard Christine is having a full breakdown. If he's involved, he'll know she won't protect him."

"Indeed," said Mariko "he's a slime ball of the first order. He'll sell her out if he can. We have the flat being watched discreetly, but I've been thinking Nikau, should we save him for another day?"

"Why?"

"Well, despite most people thinking he's a slime ball, he's got presidential ambitions, I've heard him talk. If we don't nail him properly this time then he's only going to get smarter and therefore more difficult to catch in future. Maybe, we store up what we can get, till we have a mountain of shit to bury him completely."

Nikau pondered the scenario. Rafael Dupont wasn't stupid enough to be caught at Christine's flat now. If he was trying to clear the path he'd trod with Christine he'd be scratching CCTV right away. Nikau had no footage of them together yet. He was relying on Zhao to get that as part of the investigation. Zhao had said anything collected from now on must be done legally. He'd acquiesced against his better judgment.

"Okay," he paused, "I see what you're saying. Hang on a minute then…"

He took out his mobile and rang his contact at the apartment block.

"I need the CCTV footage for the week… everything you've got. Usual price… Thanks."

"Glad you agree," said Mariko once he'd put the phone away. "let him think he's got away. He'll relax, and it'll be easier to watch him for mistakes."

It was Mariko's turn to dig out her mobile, but this was because it was ringing.

"Hi… Are they now? Can you get some video footage of them? Good. Stay with them when they leave. We'd like to know who they are and what they do with the body. Stay safe though."

Nikau looked at her with open curiosity.

"Two people have turned up at Christine's apartment block in biohazard suits, presumably fake IDs, and are hulking some pretty heavy duty chemicals through the place."

"Wow, that must be costing him a fortune. We could use that to our advantage. Get someone into his support network with the lure of fresh donations."

"Yours or mine?"

"Whoever makes the most sense, I'll leave it up to you, just let me know."

"How's Valla?" she said, catching him off guard with the change of topic. Mariko was like that, she simply jumped to the next thing on her agenda once she'd got every piece of information she'd wanted.

"Frustrated," he answered, though he felt between himself and Valla, he was possibly the more frustrated.

"I can sympathise," said Mariko and almost like she was saying it to him and not for Valla.

The Senate chamber was the fullest it had been for a long while, maybe thirty in the chamber and another five on the large monitors. Gordon noted Valentina Torres wasn't there. He reckoned others would also notice her absence. Although it was common knowledge, thanks to a press article a few days ago, that she was heading to Singapore to repatriate the turtles. Not everyone was going to think that was appropriate. Gordon knew it wouldn't be many, but it was still a place he could start from. Valla was far too popular in the Senate for his comfort.

The chamber was called to order and the single point of business was read out. The debate was scheduled to take two hours and then there'd be a vote. The business was the re-opening of presidential nominations in the light of Christine's arrest and charges.

The justice system in Antarctica had borrowed from quite a few of its colonial masters. It boiled down to a complicated mix of Napoleonic and Roman based jurisprudence. One wasn't quite considered innocent until guilt was proved, and they'd adopted a not proven option to add to those of guilty and not guilty. The idea was borne out of the knowledge that isolated, local, populations tended to hold to the concept of 'no smoke without fire', and so early legislation had tried to encourage well evidenced cases for both the defence and the prosecution. This was primarily because they'd also had to have judges act as prosectors at a low level, enshrined in the position called Sheriff. Nowadays the newspapers called it mob rule when a verdict looked unpopular, and nuanced when it was popular. Who it was popular with entirely depended on the newspaper owners and their readership.

The judicial system was not Gordon's priority, and never had been. People like Dante Castillero were always banging on about reforms, and he was always fobbing them off. He didn't think many in the chamber thought Christine was innocent, so there wasn't even a discussion about the merit of waiting till a trial was over. They went straight to a discussion about whether Gordon should re-run too. He was happy, this was going just the way he wanted it to.

Nikau got a call while he was watching the debate from Valla's office. He checked the phone and saw it was Mariko. He'd not noticed her in the chamber but had assumed she was there.

"You're not in the chamber?" he asked.

"Not yet, just going in, wanted to let you know, I've told Zhao the biohazard guys from last night dumped the body in the harbour. She should be on the case now. Got to go."

He saw Mariko come into the chamber, through one of the doors at the top. She headed down a few rows and sat with Dante Castillero. Nikau was getting bored with the debate. They were all standing up and saying, more or less, one of two things. One group wanted to scrap the Presidential position entirely and the others wanted the Presidential vote to be a full reset. He knew which group Gordon had been influencing. He knew which group would win out too. They'd have to move against Gordon soon, before the opposition to him disintegrated into so many competing Presidential candidates.

Valla had wanted to know the outcome of the debate, it didn't seem worth his time to wait now, it was painfully clear what the outcome was going to be. It was two o'clock in the afternoon in Weddell City, he checked the time in Singapore and saw it was one o'clock in tomorrow's morning. It was better now than later, he thought.

He was used to the ringtone changes now, and the phone was picked up quickly.

"I'd like to speak to Senator Torres, please. I'll wait."

A minute later he heard a sleepy Valla.

"Nikau, is everything okay, I didn't expect to hear from you... ah, till four. I take it everyone has sifted to one of two corners?"

"Pretty much. It looks like Gordon will get to stand amongst the other candidates again, right back to the beginning. Giving him even more time to build a campaign. There's Christine, though."

"I heard before I went to bed. Will the Larsen guy win this time? Who was it again?"

"Felix Maine, elected senior to replace Leon, straight up guy, just not a complicated thinker. Gordon will run rings round him if he does get selected again. And he doesn't even have Global's money behind him."

"So far," said Valla.

"I don't see him taking it," he paused, "On other matters, I spoke to Mariko, Zhao is in charge now."

"Good. Make sure the breadcrumbs are laid."

"Valla?"

"Yes?"

"Are we sure this is the right thing to do?"

"No. I'm not sure, but I can't see any way round it. Gordon will consolidate his hold. He'll either change the legislation or he'll be the power behind a future

President. Then he dies, and the AFS falls on itself like a pack of huskies who've not been fed. While the UN and Global sweep in to nick the tasty bits."

"You can be so graphic sometimes," he said.

"Don't call me at one in the morning if you want subtlety."

"Night," he said hanging up.

His mobile rang.

"Freddie, what's up?"

"My friends sent me some of the text files they downloaded along with the video. I think you need to see them. Do you have somewhere secure I can send them to?"

"I'll come over. Did Tanya leave with the driver okay?"

"Eventually. Don't come over. Gordon's been in touch, he wants me to come to the Senate after hours tonight. I think he's cooking up a fresh plan. You know how paranoid he can get when he's doing that."

"I'll text where you can send the files to. Be safe Freddie. We're in the end game."

"Safety's for whimps. That's what they used to say in Kunlun, back in the beginning. You know that. You remember?"

He thought Freddie was sounding a bit depressed, but now he was concerned she was going to do something reckless to get out of it.

"Stick to the plan, Freddie," and under his breath he added, "please, stick to the plan."

"See you Nikau."

The line went dead and Nikau was torn. Freddie wasn't crucial to their plan but she could cock it up. She could mess with Gordon to the extent he'd start to look for reasons why. The plan relied on Gordon looking in the wrong place. His attention must be kept squarely in Weddell City and not be allowed to roam anywhere else. Not to Progress or Melchior in particular. The MS Alvarez was due into Progress in two and a half days time. The extraction team would depart, with their healthy bank balances, and Canning would be kept aboard the Alvarez until it was safe to take him back to Denam.
This would allow Zhao time to have a reason to go to the base at Melchior where Gordon's stash of dodgy scientists would furnish the final nail in his political coffin. Or at least, that was the plan.

Chapter Twenty-four - Extra Deep

Detective Inspector Enya Zhao surveyed the apartment. She could smell nothing. It was oppressive in its nothingness. No food smells, no sweat, no perfume, no smell of new carpet, and no smell of a new sofa: an absolute absence of odours. Yet the carpet looked newly laid, the sofa just out its wrapper. As a person who liked a clean environment she had a grudging respect for whoever had been here. Their expertise was obviously in limited demand amongst a legitimate clientele, however she herself would have paid for this level of cleanliness. But, she thought, maybe not what had been charged here.

She had all the details Senator Mariko had sent about what had happened last night. Even now they were trawling the west dock area for the body, and a team had been sent to round up the cleaners.

There was only one clue here, and it was of the hole variety, not the sort of thing you could stick in evidence or attach a tag to for the court room.

"Let's go to the dock," she said to the forensic officer she'd brought along, "if you're finished?"

"Ive got some close ups of the sofa and carpet, and some fibres collected. We'll run them for solvents, and fibre stress. You'd be amazed what can be discovered."

"Not DNA though?"

"No," said the officer, looking a bit crestfallen, "that's been totally obliterated."

"Christine could just claim to have had a bit of a wild party then? One that needed an extra-deep clean."

"Is that what she's saying?" enquired the officer, zipping up their bag and standing.

"She's not saying much now her lawyer has managed to stop her babbling incoherently."

Zhao and the officer drove to the dockside where James Wylie was overseeing the trawling operation.

"James," said Zhao as he came towards the car, "find it yet?"

"No. The information you gave me said they'd attached weights to the body. It's nearly 40 metres deep here. Temperature's determining no-one can stay in the water for longer than twenty minutes, and they spend nearly ten of those minutes getting there and back. We need a bathyscaphe to do a proper search."

"I'll arrange it. The faster we find the body the better. We need to confirm it's Arnaud Cheung."

She called her logistics officer and told him to sort it out and liaise with James. She knew there were a few companies with something approximating to a bathyscaphe. They used them for checking pipelines, cables and bits of research for the universities. She'd had to deal with a domestic once that involved two researchers. Turned out the fight had started as an argument in a bathyscaphe and got violent back on land. They'd been using something which had been modified to use pressured air tanks and the mix had been wrong.

The company got sued and went bust. Zhao was of the opinion lax legislation was at the root of the problem coupled with a hard-man attitude to safety that even now pervaded the AFS.

She headed back to the Police Department. She didn't like working from there. Houten had made the atmosphere toxic. The department had fallen into two groups, those supporting him and those who thought silence was the better part of valour and while not actually supporting her, were at least not actively getting in her way.

She'd been able to secure an office, with a door she could lock. The forensic officer had disappeared to their lab when they'd arrived. She didn't expect to see them again just read their report.

She got to work on her questions. Where had Arnaud Cheung been hiding for the last five years? And what had he hoped to gain by shooting Gordon? Because it was pretty clear he'd tried to shoot Gordon from Gordon's affidavit. While it was always worth getting independent verification of anything Gordon claimed and he'd said Daniel Ektov had pushed him out the way, it had been corroborated by forensics.

She was waiting to interview the cleaners that Mariko's people had spotted, videoed and tailed last night. She'd have preferred if they'd also contacted her at the time, but then she'd been quite adamant about procedures, and it wasn't till this morning she'd officially taken over. Inside the lines was proving to be an irritation and she was wondering about relaxing her need to stay quite so clearly within them.

She had some background research on Arnaud Cheung, Senator Rafael Dupont and Christine Frome. It looked from the files that Arnaud had been hiding out mostly in Tierra Del Fuego, a state practically run by Global.

So Global wanted Gordon out the way. That meant Christine must be their's, as Valla had suggested. They must be flapping about now she'd been arrested. Which horse would they hang their hat on next? She looked at Christine's information.

The first thing to hit her was the newest file on Christine, it showed the financial transactions Valla had alluded to in an encrypted mail a few days ago. She added Cornelius Kutchner of Global Corporation to her list and decided Rafael could wait. Global was too juicy not to try and pop.

Kutchner split his time between Weddell City and Vostok where Global had their main office. The frequency of hyperplanes back to UN states had meant a few big UN based companies used Vostok, but they all had an office at Weddell City too. You couldn't lobby a senator from Vostok. That had to be done in person apparently. It had resulted in a wide range of dining opportunities and cuisines to try in Weddell City, which she felt did not outweigh the potential for corruption.

Her mind wandered to the job Nikau Burns had offered her. An anti-corruption unit, free of Police and Intelligence, her's to staff. She started to make side notes on what she was digging up. Might as well build up some information bases. Who knew what might suddenly become *edited* once the unit was up and running. She inserted the thumb drive and began saving files to it.

Kutchner had been successful in negotiating an easing to the restrictions placed on Global after McMurdo. The lifting of the restrictions had been rubber-stamped by a committee. A Gordon Murcheson executive decision, she thought. Most of them had covered a facility called ACRYD.

She looked to find an explanation for the acronym. Antarctic Combined Research - Yellow Department, that suggested other colours She did a search. She found a Blue Department and a Red Department. All based out at Melchior. Close to Tierra Del Fuego, she noted.

It was also where Nikau had said Kutchner had his secure server. When she was running the anti-corruption show, those servers wouldn't be as secure as they were now and she promised herself a good look through them. Then, thinking about lines, decided that look would be just ahead of any formal announcement about the unit.

There was a knock at the door.

"We have the cleaners. Got one at the airport, another down the docks, both trying to do a runner."

"Good," she said, "Give them the warm interview room. Leave them for an hour, no drinks."

"Yes, Ma'am."

Enya smiled at the recollection of Chief Chapman's comment on Ma'ams.

She returned to the files. She couldn't now find a reference to ACRRD. Someone had edited the Red

Department off the system. There was no trace of it, anywhere. She tried searching for A C R R D instead, then with full stops between letters, and finally the whole title. The references repopulated. Something done in a hurry with plausible deniability built in. Nice, but not terribly effective. It would have only put off the casual search. What did the Red Department do that meant someone was trying to hide it?

She looked, and found only Gordon Murcheson, in the form of Presidential security clearance at every step. When she was done here, she thought, it would be time to take a trip to Melchior. Maybe take Anatoli, stay at the fancy resort near there, pretend they were having a break. She tried to recall the name: Hielo Cabana, that was it, Ice Cabin. And thinking about Anatoli reminded her, he had agreed to ask his father about dirt on Gordon. It hadn't been on their minds last night. It was worth asking now.

Freddie found herself on Gordon's private jet heading to Melchior. It had been an unusual meeting with Gordon. She knew him well, or at least she thought she did, because the meeting she'd just had didn't fit with the Gordon Murcheson she had in her mind. He'd always sounded like he had a grasp of all the threads, and it only sounded like paranoia to those without the full compliment of threads themselves. However when she'd met him earlier, after the Senate voted to fully re-open the nominations for President, in his stone clad office, he had just sounded plain paranoid.

That office, she thought. Freddie had never been in Gordon's office before and when she saw the huge slabs of stone she'd wondered why the room didn't echo. Despite its brightness she had felt she was back down a mine. The proximity of Gordon had only heightened that feeling. The disastrous trial of the saser mining tool, where five miners had been fried to death within its beam. The strange smell it made, like there was a static charge in the air, all the sensations she'd buried from that day had come flooding back.

So now she was heading out to Gordon's secret facility. He'd told her his fears about Sophia's list too. She sounded like a real charmer. Freddie's job was to find out what Sophia had going on at the facility that Gordon wasn't hearing about. She had full security clearance but was not officially working for him. He'd set her up with an Intelligence Agency pass. Freddie thought Glenn Murcheson would find that amusing. Possibly, she concluded, just before hauling her ass back to Denam.

She hadn't heard from Nikau Burns. Surely by now he'd have read the text files? Checked out at least some of the payments Gordon had made to Global. She realised she also now had the perfect opportunity to snoop around and see what tech these mad scientists were using. Some of it might still be banned, though the list was getting smaller, but biotech enhancements were still on the list.

She'd not even had time to pack. The northernmost tip of Antarctica could get unpleasantly warm if you continued to wear a survival suit, and Freddie's basics were not exactly socially acceptable. She still called them basics, a Kunlun mining term.

She'd been born in the Progress Massif. And when people said, 'in the Massif' they weren't exaggerating, Kunlun was mostly hollowed out of the bedrock. A city not underground but within the mountain. The rock was warm, the mines were warmer, basics were what you stripped down to when you were deep in the mine.

The riches within the Massif area made it worthwhile tunnelling deep into the mountains. Rare earth metals and radioactive minerals were in high demand by the UN states as they tried to rebuild their technologies. The UN had curtailed mining elsewhere in the world through its ecological legislation and Global had fought hard to retain what little mining operations it had left. The rumour was they cost the company in environmental damage offset charges, almost as much as it made out of them.

Global's need to expand into the AFS, where the charges didn't apply, was what had brought Alison Strang to Antarctica in the first place when she'd been one of the elite negotiators known as Special Strangers. Freddie had heard about Glenn's partner, and her biotech enhancement. She wondered again what she'd find at Melchior amongst the scientists?

Six hours later they landed at Melchior. The Torres Peninsula petered out into a string of islands with Melchior, the city, spread across two. Sparse habitation covered almost all the surface of the one in the line of the string and also the inshore edge of a larger one, still known as James Ross Island. This was the island the Space Agency launched their satellites from. The airport was on the western side of the string island now simply called Melchior after the city. It wasn't large enough to really be called a city, but there was the expectation it would end up as one. Like small babies called Maximillian, it was waiting till it grew into its name.

The science bases were all on James Ross Island, and the houses, business district, and the fun, such as it was, were all located on Melchior.

It was midnight and this far north the twilight was close enough to be referred to as night, the base sat fifty nine degrees south and had begun to enjoy a very similar climate to the early twenty-first century climate at a similar latitude north. Twenty two degrees in high summer had become an unremarked if occasional temperature. Freddie, had been told there were clothes shops within the airport complex for those visitors who hadn't managed to pack appropriately. Both those coming and going. She found the Temperate Store next to the one selling the most popular brand of survival suit in the AFS. She loaded a few things into her basket and used the currency card Gordon had given her for expenses.

Freddie found the cashier's accent unusual, and they had to both slow down to be understood during the transaction. Clearly not many folk from Kunlun made it out here. She had a room booked in a hotel already waiting for her. She strolled out of the airport in a tee shirt and jeans, her survival suit in a large bag. The warm breeze ruffled her short black hair. It was something she thought she could get used to.

Chapter Twenty-five - Fight

The Mercer had anchored across the strait from Panaitan, behind a small island off the peninsula. Dmitry had switched the AIS transmitter off. They'd okayed the operation with the local Banten police and the Indonesian supra-state navy. They'd agreed marine damage fees in case there was shooting or worse, a fuel spill. The small boats were ready. The radar at its maximum limit. All they needed was the Iron Prestige.

She must be only a few hours behind them even though she'd refuelled as expected in Geraldton. It was tense waiting for her, waiting for something to happen. Captain Dmitry Beardmore realised he'd never experienced this particular kind of waiting before. There was a lot of waiting involved in being at sea. Waiting for slots in busy straits, fuel bunkers to become available, pilots. But this wasn't at all like that kind of waiting.

He watched Martin, his XO, who seemed to be unaffected. He'd decided to ask about it at the debrief afterwards. Martin was sitting in the chair, Dmitry could see him from the sofa at the back of the bridge.

"Got her," said Martin calmly.

"They left the AIS on again?"

"Stop, start and steer, like you said," answered Martin.

"Well, let's do this."

"Yes Sir."

The engines kicked up a notch as Martin took them out of their hiding place. One of the best things about the ex-survey vessel was it's supreme manoeuvrability. Its acceleration was, however, another matter. Originally built for fuel efficiency at 5 knots, it was no cheetah.

Dmitry headed for the bridge windows with his binoculars. He sighted the Prestige. It was still heading into the strait between Panaitan and the peninsula.

"Doesn't look like they spotted us yet. Get up to six knots and if she's still on course we'll have to encourage her."

"Yes Sir."

The engines ramped up their hum, sending vibrations through everything. Dmitry could feel it through his feet. The Mercer swung out into the middle of the strait and turned to head for the Prestige.

"She's slowing… looks like she's spotted us."

"About time," said Dmitry, whose patience for unobservant skippers was nil in general. He put down the binoculars.

"She's turning to port."

"Good, she'll try to skirt close to the island. Are the small boats ready?"

"Sir, signal sent."

"Then let's get up to speed."

Santiago was in the wheelhouse. The windows were all open, being the highest point of the Prestige it was where there was the most breeze. He checked the thermometer on the instrument panel, thirty three degrees was not a real temperature, it couldn't be. But it certainly felt like it. Jack was sitting in the chair while Santiago stood at the open window. The island on their left looked lush as did the mainland to the right. So much greenery. Santiago had flown once to Singapore, there were trees and plants there but it was still mostly concrete. This was overwhelming compared to that.

"What the fuck?" he said turning back from gazing at the tropical forest and seeing the ship ahead for the first time.

"There's no ID, might be a smuggler?" said Jack.

"Fancy. Didn't know you could avoid ID. Pretty big for a smuggler. Let's take the other route. I'm not sure I want to meet it, if it is."

"Okay Boss, we'll need to slow a bit to turn."

"We've got time, I've built in five hours leeway to the slot at Singapore."

After a few minutes of slowing, Santiago felt the Prestige heave to port against the low swell created in the strait.

"Stick to the shore. They look too big for shallows."

"Sure Boss. Do you want me to get Trigger up?"

247

"You telling me you can't do this Jack?"

He turned to look at him, trying to recall where he'd picked Jack up from. He had a bit of a Vostok accent, must be from a visit to the Bud gang. But Jack had been in Saylon for a while.

Jack was looking back at him, there was no fear in his face.

"No, I just thought…"

Santiago interrupted, "I do the thinking around here, is that understood?"

"Yes Boss."

The Prestige picked up speed again after their turn and headed for the edge of the second headland now dead ahead.

Whoever they were, Santiago thought, they looked too big to follow or catch the Prestige, so they were inconsequential. He continued gazing at the island as they now closed in on the first headland.

"Sir," said Martin, "there's another vessel in the area, just showing up on the radar, posting AIS as a Banten police vessel, they're coming up quick from the south east."

"Oh," said Dmitry, "wanting to join in the fun. Call them on the agreed channel, make sure they stay to the south of the Prestige."

"Yes Sir."

"Boss, there's another vessel, says police here."

"Fuck. Maybe they are smugglers. We have to get gone. Give it all we've got and get as close to shore as you can."

"Boss."

Santiago felt the ship pull forward as Jack pushed the engines all out. He looked astern out of the window at the following ship, it started to drop behind. But he could see the police ship too. She was shadowing them, almost level.

"Boss, the police vessel hasn't turned, they're staying with us."

"I can fucking see that. How long till we can get round the headland?"

"Five minutes, maybe less."

"Make it less."

"Boss."

Santiago saw the second headland grow ahead of them. He saw the police vessel was making no attempt to close in on them, or hail them or anything. Maybe they were just buzzing an unusual vessel. After all the Prestige was AFS flagged and a long way from home. This might be nothing at all.

"Boss?"

"What? What the fuck now?"

"There's two fast approaching boats, coming round the headland."

"Why the fuck aren't there any binoculars in here?" Santiago swept his hands along the ledge of the wheelhouse windows sweeping fag ends and dust to the floor.

"What d'you want me to do?"

"Just get us round the corner, we can beat them on the straight."

Santiago peered ahead looking for these two boats. He could see white spray but not the boats. Must be inshore inflatables. No match for the Prestige.

All of a sudden the Prestige shuddered violently to a hard stop. A horrible grinding sound vibrated up from the keel as it did. Santiago was thrown into the wheelhouse window ledge. Jack seemed to leap out of his chair with the force of whatever they'd hit, he was now spreadeagled on the deck.

"What the fuck have you done," said Trigger.

Santiago saw him standing grasping the wheelhouse doorframe. He had never heard Trigger swear in his presence. He watched as Trigger bend down to pick Jack up off the floor and then punch him back onto it.

"What's happened?" asked Santiago.

"We're grounded," said Trigger getting into the seat. Santiago could see him wrestling with a lever.

"We're fucking stuck. He's rammed the sand bar and its got reef in it too. It looks like we're caught on it."

"We won't sink?"

Like most AFS natives, Santiago couldn't swim. There'd been nowhere to learn. Certainly not in the early days anyway.

He saw Trigger checking some instrument panels.

"We're taking on water. But we can't sink, we're stuck on the reef. We need to get off the boat."

"I can't swim."

"There's life rafts."

Santiago had never seen anything that looked like another boat on the Prestige. He'd also become aware that Trigger had stopped calling him Boss. A groan made them both look down. Jack was coming to.

"Is Vann in the engine room?" Santiago had used his Boss voice, it was worth reminding Trigger who was in charge.

"I think so, Boss."

That's better, he thought.

"Jack, go get Vann, get him on deck, we'll head for the island in these life rafts that Trigger says we have."

He could see Jack throwing Trigger an evil look as he went past.

"Right," he said to Trigger, "show me these life rafts."

Dmitry watched the Prestige ram the sandbar. He could see the line of breaking water on the edge of the reef within it. They were now receiving updates from the two rigid inflatables. He ordered one to board the Prestige and the other to stand by and wait for the signal. The Mercer was now slowing on its approach to the sandbar and the Banten police vessel was also close to the Prestige. Through his binoculars Dmitry could see a policeman filming the Prestige. He reckoned they'd clocked up a few thousand in marine damage fees already.

"Martin, tell the police vessel the men onboard are armed and dangerous, and they ought to be careful not to get shot."

"Yes Sir."

The three man team in the first rigid inflatable heard the order to board, and moved alongside the stricken Prestige. The first guy tossed the boarding rope over, as the other two aimed their short barrel sub-machine guns at the edge of the hull. They saw movement and froze, but whoever it'd been hadn't spotted the rope and had disappeared. The leader gestured to the rope guy to start climbing.

They were onboard, crouched down at the stern where the winding gear for the trawler nets gave them good cover. The leader looked ahead up to the wheelhouse and saw two figures leave and move toward the bow. He waved the team to follow him. They all knew what the target, Santiago Kooper, looked like and recognised him as one of the figures.

As they approached the two figures, the rear guy peeled off downstairs into the ship, looking for the movement they'd spotted before.

"Hands up," the leader announced to Santiago and his man.

Santiago was turning around putting his hands up but his man's hand was going for the gun stowed in his waistband as he was turning. The leader shot him. They had orders specifically for Santiago, but he'd still tried to incapacitate rather than kill the man. He motioned his guy forward to secure Santiago and moved forward himself to kick the gun out of reach. He saw Santiago looking beyond him but wasn't going to fall for that. His 'Hands Up' signal had been relayed over the radio to the other inflatable team and they were boarding now. Anyone who was trying to sneak up on him wouldn't last long.

Once Santiago was secure, his guy had bent down to check on Santiago's man.

"Still got a pulse," he said.

The leader saw him look astern.

"Where's the other one?" said the guy.

The team leader turned to see his third guy returned from the interior of the Prestige, with one of Santiago's men in tow.

"Dead. Knocked his head in the engine room, must have been when they hit the reef."

"Mercer, we are ready to return, all hostiles accounted for," said the leader.

"Well," said Dmitry "that went as cheaply as we could manage. I hope Senator Torres is proud of us. Martin, get our environmental team out to secure the Prestige from contamination leaks, and arrange salvage. Let's try to keep our invoice at its current total."

"Yes Sir. I've also moved Patrice to a locked cabin with a guard. I didn't think it would be wise to let Santiago know he was onboard."

"Good idea, XO. Once the contamination team returns, start for Cilegon. Let the Senator and the State Negotiator know to meet me in the conference room. We'll have a full debrief with the teams after that."

"Sir."

Dmitry left the bridge feeling relieved. So far it had gone very smoothly. He had Martin to thank for much of that too. He caught a passing AB and ordered refreshments for the conference room. Nobody had stood down for lunch yet, but the Mercer would shortly be getting back to normal. He entered the conference room and was surprised to find that Valla and Alison were already there.

"Have you been here all the time?" he asked, watching Valla in particular. He knew she played poker and he'd found it difficult early on to know what she was thinking, but now he thought he was beginning to know her tells. Alison, the state negotiator, was completely different though. Her emotions didn't give you any clues about her thoughts. She'd appeared, somehow, to have managed to divorce the two things. The only thing he could tell was that Alison was relieved, but then so was everybody.

"We have. We've been working on the interrogation of Santiago."

"Oh," said Dmitry, "we're doing that now?"

"As soon as practicable," said Alison, clearly inferring she was going to be doing it. He thought he'd check that inference.

"And you're going to do it?"

"Well, we've just been discussing that. If it's a woman asking the questions it's not going to be so effective on Santiago," said Alison, "we aren't sure who else to give the questions to. Glenn would be ideal under normal circumstances, but maybe not with Santiago right now. So who do you think?"

Dmitry considered. There was a knock at the door, and two ABs appeared with coffee flasks, cups and sandwiches.

"Colin," he said, as the ABs left, "Ideal. Cool, level headed, and he's got marine training, knows a bit about getting answers already."

"So Captain, fill us in on the operation?" said Valla, smiling at him.

Dmitry reported a brief outline of what had happened, and showed Valla the current marine damages fine invoice, having received an estimated bill from the police vessel by fax, before they'd headed off.

Before he could stop her, he heard Valla whistle she read the total. It was his one superstition.

"Please don't do that again," he asked.

"Whistle?" asked Valla, "Dmitry, are you superstitious?"

It had been a half mocking tone, but he knew every native of AFS took superstitions seriously.

"I'm sorry, of course I won't," she said, "provided you don't find a way to increase this bill."

Chapter Twenty Six - Disposable

Detective Inspector Enya Zhao was feeling frustrated. It was nearly six in the evening. James Wylie who was in charge of finding the body of Arnaud Cheung hadn't yet found it. The bathyscaphe had only been in operation for an hour but she'd been hopeful that it would have found the body in a relatively short time. She'd double checked the statements from Senator Mariko Neish's people, and they were quite clear where they'd seen the cleaners' van stop, and where they'd seen the cleaners dump a sheet wrapped body, wrapped round with chains.

Chains. Of course. She called James and told him to find a big magnet to drag the water with. In the meantime she was about to interrogate the cleaners who'd been stewing, literally, for nearly two hours now. She could hold them for another twenty six, so she was quite sure she'd have enough to charge them with before that ran out. She reviewed the CCTV footage from Christine's apartment block. The bio hazard suits meant they weren't identifiable but the van was, and it was registered to one of the cleaners in custody, a Dennis Taylor, presumably the boss. They'd lifted the van. Unlike their work environment the van was relatively contaminated. Both cleaners' prints were found on it and on equipment inside it.

She opened the door and felt the heat hit her. The two cleaners had got out of their survival suits as much as had been possible while handcuffed to the desk. They looked soggy.

"Gentlemen, would you like some water?"

One looked up at her, but the other scowled at him before saying something expletive riddled that had long ago failed to have an impact on Zhao. She took the water bottle out of a cool bag she'd brought in with her. The ice inside created a foggy mist immediately above the bag's square opening. She twisted the top, condensation glistening on the outside of the bottle, and took a long drink. It wasn't just for effect, the room was that hot.

The one who'd looked up, the junior cleaner she reckoned, glanced at the bottle. She put it down on the table, out of reach, and went back to the interview room door, opening it. She called Officer Eric Jordan over. He'd just come on shift and was one of the few officers who'd done more for her so far than just stay clear of Houten.

"Jordan, can you move one of our suspects to another interview room, this one seems a bit hot?"

"Yes, Ma'am," he said coming over with keys. She pointed at the boss, and watched Jordan unlock the cuff chain from the table.

"The end room if it's free, please," she said, knowing it had an intermittent flickering bulb and had done for years.

"Yes Ma'am," said Jordan, pulling Dennis to his feet and moving him to the end interview room, to experience a fresh irritant, which couldn't quite be called torture, because who hadn't experienced a room that was too hot or an annoying light bulb? And while it was annoying, was it really torture?

"Now," said Zhao, "What's your name?"

The other cleaner, Bertold Owens, looked up, clearly now quite frightened. He stammered his name out, providing his middle name of Christian, which his file had been missing. She was impressed.

"Listen Bertold," she said "I like what you do. It's just a pity you do it for the wrong people. I'd like to help. Perhaps, we can come to some arrangement?"

She could see him looking at the slick water drops on the side of the bottle.

"Would you like a drink?"

"Yes."

It seemed he couldn't deny his thirst any longer.

"Was that a yes to helping me too?" she said, putting the water bottle close to his hands, but not yet close enough that he could get it.

"Yes. Yes, I'll tell you what you want. Dennis doesn't pay me enough to put up with this."

She pushed the bottle within reach and watched him bend close to the table to get enough free play to get the bottle to his mouth.

"Take it easy," she said, "don't gulp it fast or you'll be sick."

She saw him slow down, he finished what was left and she took the bottle back out of reach.

"Good. So, I suppose it was Dennis who took the call, and you've no idea who paid you?"

This was the point at which she would find out which interview room she needed to be in.

"I know who's apartment it was," admitted Bertold.

"Do you?" asked Zhao, intrigued. "Whose?"

"It was Senator Frome's. The one that got arrested. Dennis said Dupont had called him already, just inquiring like, and now the pigs had her, no offence, Inspector, that he'd get double for the job."

"Ah," she said, "Dennis not a big fan of the police, then?"

"Not really, said something about not getting paid enough for jobs he did on the quiet for some. Reckoned they were just another gang, with a more high profile boss."

"And how do you feel about the police?"

Bertold had been looking at his hands while he'd relayed most of this, like he was trying to pretend he wasn't chained to a table. Now he looked Zhao straight in the eye.

"I'm wanting a decent income. I don't want no stress. The chemicals make me cough even through the filter masks. He's giving me the used crap. Keeps the new stuff for himself. I'm not fucking disposable."

"Well, if you just write down, on this sheet," she said sliding a pad of paper and a pen within reach, "everything you know about what happened last night, everything you did, and as much as you can remember about what was said. We can definitely make that happen."

There was a knock on the door. She left Bertold busy writing and opened it. It was Officer Jordan.

"James Wylie has the body, they're taking it to Pathology now."

"Excellent. Dump Dennis back in a holding cell. He'll keep till I get back. Let Bertold finish and treat him nice, but keep him separate now, from anybody. If you can, don't let Houten's guys near either. Let me know even if someone shows an interest. I'll be back as soon as I can, maybe not till morning."

"Ma'am."

Officer Eric Jordan was someone she was considering asking for in this new anti-corruption unit. If it came to pass. He was too good and too straight to waste away under Houten. She headed towards the Pathology Department.

Enya Zhao wasn't very familiar with the Pathology Department. She'd been there three times in her whole time at Weddell City Police. Once as a cadet, because that's just what they do with the cadets. Usually while running a book on the side for who'll vomit the most. The other two times were a suicide and a domestic argument with an undiagnosed heart condition. Both times she was there purely to get the report and be assured there was no foul play. The domestic was worse, as it had been purely a verbal argument, they were pretty broken up about it, and it didn't help everyone assuming it had got violent till the heart condition had been found.

She'd never seen a body which had been submerged, or smelt one that'd been in lukewarm water for forty eight hours before being dumped in the freezing sea.

She hung back in the room staying close to the door. She'd won someone a lot of money when she'd been a cadet, and nothing had changed about her constitution.

"Well? Is it Arnaud Cheung?"

"We've matched finger prints and dental with what's on record. Waiting on DNA, but unless someone's hacked the records then its your man Cheung."

"Good. I understand due to the two stage disposal of the body it's going to be difficult but any idea on time of death?"

The pathologist was talking over the body on the table. Enya had studiously kept her eyes on her. It seemed finally the pathologist had noticed, and she had come round to the other side near to Enya, and was removing her gloves, tipping them with practiced ease into a biohazard bin.

"Not keen on bodies?"

"No."

"Fair enough. We can continue this in my office."

"Thank you."

"Too many of my colleagues seem to get a kick out of making folk hang about here. Never saw the point of it myself. I can show you close ups on screen of anywhere on the body if I need to."

The office temperature was cool like the rest of the department, but comfortable enough, with a big screen on one wall. The first thing the pathologist had put up on the screen was a graph of how they'd estimated time of death, working backwards from when it had been fished out of Weddell City Dock. The time window was large but included the period they had evidence for. Christine had mentioned the late evening news. She'd probably exaggerated how long things had taken given the other time stamped video evidence they had, but it was all stacking up.

"I don't suppose you found anyone else's DNA?"

It was a wild hope.

"Not on the body."

Oh well, thought Enya, maybe forensics would be luckier with the sheet or his survival suit.

"He was killed with a single shot to the head at near contact, possibly through a cushion or pillow, the bullet made it through his head, there's an exit wound. He was probably lying down when it happened."

Enya noted that. Just how thorough had the cleaners been? The sofa looked new, but if it wasn't, perhaps deep within it now lay the bullet, while the cleaners had simply fixed the upholstery.

"Excuse me, I'm just going to make a quick call."

She got a hold of James who was in the canteen and told him to get over to Christine's with forensics and check the interior of the sofa. She felt rotten to ask him after he'd spent most of the day frozen at the dockside but it was him or Jordan, and Jordan was looking after the cleaners.

"Thanks. That's been really helpful," she said to the pathologist.

"Oh, I'm not finished. There's one more thing, quite odd really."

The screen flicked and there was a close up of his right eye. It was very creepy. But Enya could see a tiny scar, well that's what it looked like, but it was on the iris. Was that even possible?

"You see it?"

"Yes. Is it a scar?"

"Yes. We removed the eye after this, there's been surgery, looks like a lens replacement, but then we saw stuff on the retina too, and the optical nerve."

"Bio-tech?"

"Possibly."

"Thanks. Can you prioritise the report, include this too, nothing is too weird to put in."

"Late tonight, with pictures."

"Thanks."

Enya left the pathologist's office wondering where Arnaud Cheung had got his surgery, who had performed it, but more importantly what did it do for him when he was alive?

She called Forensics, asking to speak to the officer who'd been with her earlier. She discovered he'd gone home for the day, but upon checking her email, without sending her the report. She'd go down in person in the morning. They could all play silly buggers taking sides with Houten or whoever, but this was a presidential assassination attempt she was investigating and there ought to be a bit more professionalism on show.

Next she got a hold of Jordan. Bertold's statement had been full and frank. He was typing it up for her, he said. She thanked him and said once he'd done that to charge Dennis and Bertold, and get someone he trusted to keep an eye on Bertold when his shift finished.

She checked her watch. It was nearly time for Anatoli to pick her up. They were having dinner tonight at his parents. His father had agreed to give them an insight, as he had put it, into Gordon Murcheson. She liked Arne Dale. He was tall like his son, but a completely different complexion; pale, blond and ginger with blue eyes. Anatoli had taken after his mother, with his sallow skin, dark curls and brown eyes.

She'd been apprehensive when she'd first met them. Senior senators, especially Torres and Glencor, were the AFS equivalent of aristocracy or old money, most having been founders of the Free State, including Arne Dale. He was younger than Gordon Murcheson or Daniel Ektov by nearly twenty years. But the Dales had made her feel at ease and she'd began to consider them practically family. Her parents had died soon after they'd arrived in the AFS and she'd been brought up in various institutions: in Saylon till she was five then in a new establishment in Weddell City. They'd been safe places, but not exactly overflowing with family atmosphere.

Anatoli appeared in her office door.

"Ready?"

"Yes," she said switching everything off and pocketing the thumb drive which had all the sensitive information on it. "Hows the back?"

"Fine. I'm going to see Nikau's physio next week, but the exercises seem to be working."

"Good," she said, standing on tiptoe to kiss him, "I need you in peak physical condition."

"How can you make a promise sound like a threat?" he asked.

"Police training," she replied, as they left the police department and got in Anatoli's car.

Chapter Twenty Seven - Diplomacy

Freddie woke up to the sound of sea birds. It was an impossible cacophony. She checked her watch it said six. She'd hoped for a longer lie in. She got up and put on the clothes she'd bought last night. Today she was going to see the sights. Get a feel for Melchior. Locate the Antarctic Combined Research facility where Gordon's Red Department did whatever it did. She'd get the personnel list later and then pay a visit to each scientist individually. She might have no networking up here, but she could manage intimidation perfectly well on her own. Especially with a Gordon generated Intelligence pass.

She asked hotel reception for a taxi who was willing to give up their day for a fixed rate and went off to have breakfast. The range of food on offer would have cost a fortune back in Vostok, but this far north and only a thousand kilometres from Tierra Del Fuego it was considerably cheaper. She was getting a better understanding of how the nearness of a UN state impacted on the AFS.

The taxi was waiting when she'd finished. She asked him to go up the mountain on Melchior first. She'd heard you got a great view from the streets at the top: several snaked their way up and had individual houses built on them. Freddie wanted to see what a house looked like.

How weird would it be to live that apart from someone else? Kunlun was one the densest habitats in the AFS, but pretty much everyone, everywhere else, lived in an apartment. Even senators in Weddell City lived in apartments. The taxi drove up and quite soon it was twisting and turning as the road climbed higher. Having now seen what a house was, she suspected a few senators had houses out here on the quiet.

Freddie felt pressure building in her ears and wiggled her fingers in them to relieve it. They levelled out and took a sharp right, climbing again till there was no more road. The view was short to the north with the summit of the mountain obscuring everything. But to the south it was spectacular. The rest of the Torres Archipelago was laid out, a series of peaks set in the sparkling water, all the way to the beginning of the peninsula proper. Looking east she could see how near James Ross Island was too. She could see the ferry leaving the harbour to head back to Melchior Island.

She asked to go across to James Ross, and saw the taxi driver look at her oddly. Apparently only the scientists went across, tourists weren't interested in the Space Agency he said. She informed him this one was and he shrugged his shoulders. Her accent being so strange was clearly getting her a lot of leeway in behaviour.

She chatted general stuff with him on the way back down to the harbour. Finding out how little Families meant to the locals. They mostly seemed to be Larsen or Torres but without much enthusiasm for either. She asked what the locals thought went on over on James Ross. He included some pretty lurid outlines which he then refused to elaborate on. Freddie wondered if, at their heart, they might have a grain of truth.

There was a queue of cars waiting to get on the small ferry and they had to get the next crossing. A round trip was apparently an hour or so, depending on how quick cars unloaded themselves. Freddie noticed there weren't many tracked vehicles around, and the taxi driver explained that the snow had been getting less and less each year. They now relied on the second hand clearing vehicles the AFS had snapped up from various sub-arctic states who no longer required them. It seemed from the taxi driver at least, that Melchior was one of the strongest areas of support for the position of President. He had a lot of good things to say about Gordon in that role too. She smiled to herself.

They disembarked from the ferry onto James Ross, and he pulled over out of the way in the harbour area.

"What'd you want to see then?" he asked.

"Everything. Show me everything. What's to the south? Is there a good place to take photographs of the islands?"

"I've only taken someone down that way once, the road ends at a research facility, but I think I remember a few places to stop for pictures."

"Let's go then."

The taxi driver had asked at every headland if Freddie wanted to get out, she'd let him stop, made a show of getting out, looking at the view and then saying it wasn't quite right. Which was technically true, because she'd not yet seen the ACR facility. When she could, then she'd take her photographs. The third headland showed her what she wanted to see. She took her photographs, zooming in, to see the small landing jetty, noting the spread of buildings away from what would be the fourth headland. Then she took some photographs of the islands too. They were very picturesque, stacked behind each other slightly and then stringing out to her right heading south.

Tomorrow, she thought, I'll arrive here officially, in a hire car. But for today she carried on with her sight seeing, asking the taxi driver to take them up to the observatory on the mountain. Another good place, she hoped, to get shots of the ACR buildings.

Later on, back in her hotel room, she enlarged the photographs on the laptop, trying to keep the detail. Trying to figure out what each building was for. She was tired. The heat, even in her temperate clothing, was getting to her. She'd been sweating in the afternoon sun while they'd waited for the ferry back across to Melchior. The last time she remembered sweating was in the Innonnox Mine. It did not bring back good memories.

The MS Mercer berthed at the bunker station in Cilegon. No one was allowed to go ashore, but the bunker station didn't exactly look inviting anyway. Valla was leaning on the handrail watching the small dark men running about. How could anybody run in this heat she thought? The bunker station smelt of oil and fuel and rust. Behind that she could smell hot wet earth, the same smell she remembered from a school visit to a commercial greenhouse growing fruit and tropical vegetables. But the lights in that greenhouse couldn't match the intensity of the sun here. It was just as well the sun was almost directly overhead, because she'd have been worried for her eyesight if it had been at a height you'd accidentally glimpse it at.

Martin was coming along the walkway, he stopped and leant on the rail next to her. His uniform was crisp and unsullied. She wondered how he managed it, her's was creased, and had remained so since its first wear despite her best efforts.

"Who does your ironing? And do they take commissions?"

He laughed, and she felt a familiar shiver run up her spine.

"I do my own. They teach you in the navy, you know."

She risked a gentle flirt, something she wouldn't have done days ago, but they'd settled into something pleasant, if slightly frustrating since then.

"I like a man with hidden talents."

He smiled, and she saw a twinkle in his eyes as he did so. She changed the topic of conversation swiftly.

"What're they doing?"

"Securing the ship, and connecting the fuel line. We have a fire team on stand by throughout the whole refuel. It's going to take five hours," he said, "the Captain was asking for you."

"Oh. Where?"

"The conference room. He wants to go over the ceremony for the turtles."

"Yes, of course. Thanks."

She leant off the rail and started to walk towards the door. Martin followed.

"You've never left the AFS?" he asked.

"No. Never. Never been much more than sixty degrees north to tell the truth."

"What do you think?"

"It's green. Very, very green. And it smells. Not bad, well, not all bad. But so many different smells. And the sun. I just never grasped how much more concentrated it is. You can read stuff, but it's not the same."

"No, I suppose it's not. I've been to Singapore twice, been here in Cilegon a few times too. I'd be honoured to escort you in Singapore. The Captain says you'll need to get formal wear."

"Well, that's very gallant of you. I'm now properly worried about this ceremony."

She smiled and was rewarded with one of his heartbreakers in return.

"Senator," he said.

"XO," she replied, closing the door behind her.

She arrived in the conference room more composed than when she'd left the outside. Dmitry, Alison and Glenn were already there. There was an itinerary on the screen.

"Sorry I'm late," she said, realising she probably didn't look in the slightest contrite about it.

"I'd just started,' said Dmitry, "this is the agreed timeline for the ceremony. Elaine Tan has been working hard to try and keep it minimal, but in Singapore everyone must be accorded their rightful place at such events. So you can see here…"

Dmitry used the pointer to point to the first item, which was labelled, 'Introductions'. That made sense she thought. Then saw it was scheduled to take twenty minutes. Her eyes went to the end of the event and she saw it was an entire evening, from five in the afternoon all the way through to eleven o'clock at night. Six hours of formalities. She scanned back up the list, seeing an hour and a half given over to dinner. Okay, not so bad as she first assumed.

Dmitry had been talking, "… and the President of Singapore, Rita Hussain."

"Can I have the list? I'll need to study it. Is there background on everyone, even just a bit?" she said covering up the fact she hadn't heard who it would take twenty minutes to be introduced to.

Alison had spotted it however, and had winked at her. God, it was like being back at school, Valla thought. She felt the urge to kick against it begin and tried to submerge it.

"I'm sorry, Dmitry, I'm just not a formal kind of politician. I understand we're to get kitted out too?"

Dmitry nodded, "Yes, Martin has offered to take the three of you into Singapore the day we arrive to buy formal wear."

"It's the four of us attending, is that correct?"

"Yes. Alison can field anything awkward, Glenn's security and you and I are the formal representatives of the AFS."

"Right. What's not a topic of conversation? What neighbours don't we mention? Anything odd going on in-state?"

She realised Dmitry had gone into cruise ship mode, with his emphasis on itinerary, positions and event timeline. And she'd gone to war, obviously in a very political way, but nonetheless, she was in General mode. She saw Alison and Glenn share a smile between themselves.

She saw Dmitry shuffle some pages.

"Okay, here's the political landscape in-state just now. We don't talk about the housing, it's a big topic of conflict in their parliament right now. The population is still growing, and the housing needs renewing. The Greens are strong here and fighting any new development. Talk about the turtles, talk about ecology. Do not mention our invoice for marine environmental damage."

Glenn piped up, "Don't mention leather, fur or burning wood."

Alison was scowling at him, then caught sight of Valla.

"Old joke," she said by way of explanation but without elaborating further.

"I get the picture, the AFS is not compliant with the UN's rigid ecological laws. So we should perhaps only make soft noises about changing the AFS slowly," said Valla, "Out of curiosity, Dmitry, what's your opinion of Elaine Tan?"

"She's struck me as very rational, intelligent, and understanding. She's a UN representative but also Singaporean, she knows how to balance the two. She's mentioned Global Corp a few times. They're here in pharmaceuticals, but they're also backing an expansive new development that would bite into the national park here."

"I'd like to sit near to her if that's at all possible," said Alison.

Dmitry shuffled a sheet to the top of his pile and checked it.

"You're either side of the director of the aquarium where the turtles will be quarantined before they're released back into the wild.

"Good."

"How many are sitting down for dinner?"

"Just ten. The pre-dinner drinks reception is eighty. It's the best Elaine and I could do without diplomatic incident."

Valla took a deep breath in. Diplomacy was something she had to work at.

Chapter Twenty Eight - Stars

Anatoli and Enya were invited by Arne into his office. The Dale apartment was spacious: with guest rooms, Arne's office, a large catering kitchen and even a TV snug. Zhao wondered how many rooms you could justify, but the office was surely the one room a senator could. It was wood lined, with bookcases on three sides, and a large wood burner stove on the fourth wall. A fire was roaring inside it. It was the ultimate luxury nowadays. Since the AFS had been recognised by the UN, there had been a slow move towards adopting some of the more sensible ecological legislation, much of the time as part of a trade deal with a UN state. Some states were keener than others, usually those at danger of being drowned by rising sea levels or of turning into a desert.

Arne had closed the door behind them and was gesturing to seats arranged around the fireplace stove. Zhao sat near to the stove, the dancing flames were utterly fascinating.

"Cognac?" asked Arne.

Zhao looked at the bottle, inside the liquid looked like whisky, which she didn't like, she declined.

Arne smiled at her, "We can have wine with dinner."

She saw him pour two decent measures for Anatoli and himself and after passing a balloon shaped glass to Tolli he sat opposite them.

"So, now I have fortification, let me tell you about Gordon Murcheson. He's not a man whose actions can be discussed while sober."

Zhao wondered how much of this was going to be admissible in a court, technically she expected it to be hearsay, but even at that, there would hopefully be some thread they could pull that would unravel Gordon Murcheson.

"He has a list," said Arne taking a large sip, "his press secretary, Sophia Wren, maintains it. People have disappeared who were on that list. Not enough that anyone has noticed. It's probably about two and a half years old, they're the supporters of political rivals, mostly in Moss and Larsen. He's not stupid, Torres is too socially proactive, and Daniel Ektov in Lomonosov was too clever. I've heard rumours there are Glencor names on it now. Find that list and you'll have Gordon. Just be careful, Sophia Wren is dangerous, she'd strip you and leave you in the snow."

Enya understood why Arne would know this but not want to do anything. Till now, Gordon seemed unassailable.

Nikau Burns sat at his desk. He'd got up early, had made some coffee, and was still sitting in his dressing gown looking at the closed laptop. To open it was to dive into a place so murky and complicated it was getting harder and harder to retain a sense of the right thing to do. Valla was right, they couldn't let Gordon or Christine succeed as President, but who would become the next president? The Senate vote had been decisive, even though many of them voted that way purely to get Gordon re-elected. The AFS clearly wanted a president. If they were working to remove candidates, he felt they ought to be working to put the right one into place. But who would that be?

He sipped the coffee, thinking about the email that had arrived late last night from the Mercer. It was encrypted but its contents had been devastating for Gordon. Santiago Kooper had given up the details of who had contacted him to kill Freddie. Santiago had identified Sophia Wren, which pointed back to Gordon and confirmed James Wylie's testimony. It was at that point Nikau erased all the evidence of contact between himself and Sophia. She was the tool with which Gordon's downfall would be completed and nobody should find a Torres hand on the handle.

Santiago had also spilled on his interactions with Global, mentioning their interest in Dr. Canning and the fact Global had asked him to break him out. It was clear he didn't know that Canning had already been broken out of Denam. But Santiago had mentioned a confusing phone call with Cornelius Kutchner when he'd refuelled at Geraldton, which explained why Global were now on the defensive about the break out, they still didn't know whether Santiago had Canning.

Freddie had been in touch too, now she was at Melchior City, she'd explained what Gordon has asked her to do. Nikau was wary, Freddie was suggesting Gordon had no control over Sophia, and he wondered if that was going to be Gordon's get out? Was he setting Sophia up? He needed DI Zhao to find out what was going on in the Red Department soon. Ideally before Freddie had a chance to report back to Gordon. Freddie'd said she'd try to draw it out, but he didn't fully trust her either.

And then there was Mariko Neish, the Lomonosov junior senator who was acting as a senior to replace Daniel. She was as sharp as an ice pick. Her plan for Rafael Dupont showed a wily long term view that Daniel would have appreciated, he was sure. An idea began to form while he drank the last of the coffee.

He composed an email to DI Zhao, outlining Sophia Wren as a person of interest in the death of Daniel Ektov, specifically as the person who gave the senate security guard the infrared device from which Zhao already had the footage, and as the person who collected it from the paper recycling, actions still available on CCTV. He passed on the name of the guard. Once Zhao started looking at Sophia, hopefully she'd get access to the list. Then he emailed Mariko asking for a meeting. Finally he sent an encrypted email to Valla, with the latest news and exhorting her to fly back as soon as possible from Singapore.

Martin Kostov was on the back shift, midnight to four in the morning. He liked the shift. So quiet just sitting on the bridge, not quite alone, with an AB on watch, and one in the radio room now, but almost everyone else was asleep. Night time here was properly dark too, they were very close to the Equator now. Around nine in the morning they would dock in Singapore and in the afternoon he would take their VIPs out to buy formal outfits for the evening ceremony. He didn't envy Dmitry his role in that. He was perfectly happy to stay onboard and keep an eye on things.

Patrice had been reluctant to divulge Kim's contact details so far, but the plan was to let him make contact the following day. With Santiago in custody, the need to protect anyone associated with Patrice had receded.

He had called ahead to the tailor shop he had recommended to Dmitry that they use and organised an exclusive appointment there at two, the garments would arrive by four after any alterations, and that would be plenty of time as the ceremony was taking place in the port-side conference centre. The turtles were to be unloaded immediately upon arrival, but that wouldn't be his problem, he'd be asleep by then.

At least he hoped he'd be asleep by then. He'd been having trouble sleeping since she'd returned and ordered the vessel to head to Singapore. It hadn't dawned on him the unspoken current he'd felt between them during the interview process would ever come to anything. He hardly expected to see her again. It had been easy when it was a daytime press event, but then it had turned into twelve days at sea, at close quarters. And now there was some sort of commitment between them. He hardly believed it.

He'd exercised earlier, hoping to tire himself out, any worries about the ceremony weren't his, and he was quite happy to be escort for the afternoon, but… He stopped himself there. He was thirty nine, he had a new country and a new job. Things he hadn't thought would be his when the navy had gone to town on his reputation closing ranks around the captain, known throughout the fleet as an utter arsehole, but a well connected one. Why shouldn't he be lucky enough to find someone now? Even someone with added complications.

The radar was starting to get busy, lots of small dots, some moving, some stopped, now showing up. He could see some of the ships lights through the windows. The traffic in the Roads had always been busy but these days, as the world's economy picked up its pace, it seemed more like a current of steel and goods flowing with the water. He concentrated on what was nearest and how fast it was moving.

He was up at midday, having his breakfast when the three of them came into the mess room for lunch. All identically dressed in the white tropical uniform from the ship's stores. There would be time, he thought, to pick up some off-the-peg clothes on the way back, then perhaps they wouldn't look so self conscious. Valla seemed to be growing into her uniform, however Glenn still looked mildly uncomfortable in one, which had surprised him initially. But he was beginning to spot an AFS native easily these days. Something in their core was non-conformable, their first instinct was always to push back, and rank held very little sway over them.

They sat down with him, and he sensed their excited anticipation, even Alison Strang, despite having been a recent UN state resident, looked keen.

"Singapore is a busy city, and mostly pedestrian," he said, "you'll need to stick close or we risk getting separated. I've got some maps made up. The phone network is very intermittent because of a tower shortage at the moment. Everyone needs to carry a water bottle too. It's forecast to be thirty seven degrees today and the humidity is almost as bad."

"You wouldn't think we were just going shopping for dresses, the way you describe it," said Alison laughing.

Kim Button, as she was known, because no one had ever bothered to properly learn her last name, hunched down behind the large crate at the dock side. There was a Singaporean security point at a temporary barrier set up in front of the ship's gangway. The ship was smaller than Kim expected, but still, it was a warship. There'd be trained personnel onboard. Rescuing him was not going to be easy. She'd heard about what had happened to the Prestige, and about the repatriation of the turtles and put two and two together, realising he would have to be on the Mercer when it arrived in Singapore. Santiago Kooper wasn't her boss, in the same way that Patrice Reilly wasn't her lover. Neither of them had a legitimate claim on her loyalty, but Santiago knew too much about her, while Patrice knew nothing.

Tonight when most of the attention would be on the delegation at the ceremony, that's when they'd hit the Mercer. She had a small team, they knew the docks and they knew hand to hand in the tight corridors of ships. She felt confident she could get Santiago free and create enough confusion on the dock side to escape into the city.

She watched the group of white uniforms descend. Two women and two men. But only one looked like they usually wore the uniform. She wondered if she should follow them, but discounted it. Some crew going shopping or sight seeing. This was a diplomatic mission, no one was expecting trouble, why invite it by tailing them and risk being discovered.

She checked her watch, recalling that the ceremony would begin at five and glanced over to the massive Singapore Port Conference Centre building less than five hundred metres away. The building's white eco-concrete shone in the sun, and they were unfurling banners and flags across its front. She didn't recognise the flag, till she realised it must be the AFS flag. Five black rippled lines on a white background, and a red starred Southern Cross constellation laid across them in the left, the flag fluttered alongside another of red and white, with the crescent moon and stars of Singapore.

Kim had little time for flags, but the sight of so much preparation made her hopeful about the evening's plans. All the security would surely be surrounding the President and other politicians attending? No one was going to notice some dock workers going about their business.

Chapter Twenty Nine - Lovelorn Idiocy

Martin would normally have been off shift at eight but he wasn't going anywhere until everyone was back onboard and the gangway was up. He had a feeling between his shoulder blades and had done since they'd got back from the shopping expedition. Something at the docks had set him off and he still didn't know what it was, but he trusted his instincts.

There hadn't just been refugees during the post Carrington years, there'd been pirate activity everywhere. He knew the story behind Glenn Murcheson's change of Family, it was an integral part of the citizenship test, but the north coast of Australia had been attacked by pirates too. Early on in his naval career he'd seen combat. The pirates' small fast craft weaving in and out with their machine guns mounted on the prows. Sometimes even in port it hadn't been safe. Tonight Martin had fallen back on the old routines from those times and had set up repel teams. He'd moved Patrice out of his cabin, freeing up a guard, while Santiago and his men were safe in the brig, deep in the ship.

He still didn't feel happy. He wondered if some of it was now to do with Valla. She'd looked stunning in the dress and it had hit home to him how much he wanted a relationship with her to work, however it had to fit around their positions. She was out in the conference centre and there was only Glenn Murcheson with training to protect them. Dmitry was a fine captain, and a capable military thinker, but he didn't have combat experience. What Martin knew of the Singaporean security was that it could control a crowd, but seldom came across a determined individual.

Santiago wouldn't be heading for Singapore if he didn't have contacts here. And they'd know about the Prestige from the newspapers. Their five thousand AFS dollar environmental damage fine had made the headlines around the whole of South East Asia.

He looked ahead from the captain's chair, watching Patrice at the window. He'd agreed to say if he spotted anyone he recognised. Martin didn't trust him, but right now he had limited information and little choice.

"There's Kim. What's she doing here?" said Patrice.

Martin got up, and headed for the window, the bridge was on low lighting so no one outside could see movements. He looked through the binoculars at where Patrice was pointing. He could just make out a shadowy figure. Some movement caught his eye, and he saw two more figures. He recognised the stances, the guarded movements, the furtive runs between cover.

"You're quite sure that's Kim? Your girlfriend? Hiding down there with two other black clad guys. Looking like they're going to try and storm my ship."

"It was her, I swear. I don't know about the others. Maybe she thinks I'm being held prisoner. Which, you know, like, I sort of am. Though," he said giving Martin a big smile, "I am cool about it."

Martin radioed his teams and put them on alert.

"How well do you know this woman?" he asked Patrice.

"I know nothing and she knows nothing about me. That's our agreement."

Martin shook his head.

"Don't judge me. I needed something pure."

Martin picked up the binoculars again and saw the trio start to creep up the gangway.

"Well it looks like your purity is about to get a bit tarnished."

He headed back to the chair, calling the first repel team up on the radio.

"Three hostiles on gangway, engage."

"What?" shouted Patrice, "No, you can't shoot her. Let me go and talk to her. Please?"

"You must be mad. Not a chance. Stay here."

But Patrice had already been moving as he was pleading, and now Martin saw he had a surprising turn of speed as he hurtled down the stairs. Fuck.

Patrice had spotted Kim hiding amongst the random crates on the dockside. Inside he already knew that she wasn't here for him. The dream was crashing down round his ears, and all he wanted to do was try and save her. Not himself. Martin was a nice guy and all, but he was going to defend his boat. Patrice understood that kind of thing. He ran for the door, expecting Martin to catch him. But he was lucky. Of all the times to be lucky, he thought. He half fell down the stairs and headed down the next set, that put him on the main deck where the gangway went down. Outside might be easier if Martin's teams were waiting inside. He opened the door to the walkway that ran along the side of the ship, and ran towards the gangway.

"Kim," he shouted, "Go back."

The bullets peppered along the side of the ship, ricocheting at a wide angle, as the three on the gangway opened fire on him. On him. Kim was shooting at him. The thought paralysed him. He stood stunned as the gunfire got more accurate and he felt the bullets hit him, till he had to fall. He heard the other guns fire now. Single shots. As he lay on the deck, he saw the two on the gangway try to retreat back down over the heap of a fallen comrade. There was Kim trying to climb over the body. He saw her get hit. He couldn't watch anymore. He let his head rest on the cooling steel deck. He heard shouting coming from near to the Conference Centre building, and suddenly there was bright light illuminating the dock side. He could sense the brightness through his closed eyes.

"Team One, Secure the gangway," Martin was rattling off orders now he had reports of what had happened. "Team Two, secure any of the attackers still alive and transfer them to the sick bay."

One of the members of Team Two turned up at the bridge.

"Sir, all attackers are dead. We've moved them to the dockside. The Singaporean security have taken control of the dock."

"Right. Any sign of Patrice?"

"No Sir. But they were firing along the main deck initially. I'll go check."

"Let's hope he's still alive. Stupid fucker."

Martin was angry with himself. He should have handcuffed Patrice to something.

The brig alarm went off. Damn, not over yet. He punched the ship's alarm automatically in response, and flicked the exterior lighting to floodlit.

"Intruders aboard. Team One to the brig. Team Two small boat."

Whoever this was hadn't come up the gangway. Valla still needed Santiago alive as far as he was aware, more so than Patrice. They'd have to choose their moment to take out these rescuers. Martin went out to the water side bridge wing. He scanned the water for what the rescuers must have arrived in. He couldn't see a boat, but he did make out a rope dangling in the breeze. Had they swam over?

Santiago had admitted he couldn't swim. It didn't look like his rescuers knew this, if this was how they expected to get away. He radioed Team Two with the information.

He heard back from Team One, only the cell holding Santiago had been shot open. He sent them to the main deck on the water side. His operator was now at the forward floodlight and had it trained on the dangling rope. A figure appeared at the rail, with another, looking like Santiago with his hands cuffed. The floodlight moved to focus on them. Cuffed. Did they mean to kill him? He could see Santiago shaking his head, trying to push the man off him. Then the other figure lifted Santiago and pushed him over the railing.

Martin drew his hand gun and took aim at the figure. Santiago fell, there was a splash as he hit the water. He hit the figure in the chest as soon as there was a clear shot. The figure crumpled. Martin looked down to where Santiago had entered the water. Team Two were already there, and someone was diving off into water.

Team One arrived on the main deck walkway, edging up to the fallen figure Martin had shot. He saw one check the figure for a pulse, then give a thumbs up to him. Martin went back inside the bridge.

The time was half past nine, the dinner would be half way through. He wondered if those inside the Conference Centre knew anything about what was happening at the docks. They'd not made any plans to be in emergency contact. It had been expected that on Singaporean soil, security was out of their hands anyway. And the idea someone would board the Mercer and chuck Santiago in the drink was low on the list of probable events.

He got the report from sick bay. Patrice was alive, but shot up, they'd stabilised him but he'd need surgery soon. Martin radioed the Singaporean security down on the dockside, requesting an ambulance and detailing the injuries. The captain in charge seemed efficient and willing to wait till the immediate emergency was over before asking for details. The guy who'd chucked Santiago over was also being patched up in sick bay, under guard.

Santiago had been pulled from the water and was now being hauled out of the small boat and onto the dockside. Sick bay would manage fine with him. He gave a brief report to the security captain and offered a fuller debrief once they were convinced there were no more intruders lurking onboard. It had been agreed between them that it served no purpose to interrupt proceedings in the Conference Centre.

It was quarter to eleven, apart from a few stubborn blood stains on wooden parts of the gangway you'd never have known what had gone on an hour and a half ago. Martin had even had time to show the security captain around the Mercer a bit before they'd shook hands at the bottom of the gangway. But the sick bay told another story.

Valla could sense something was up the minute they stepped out of the car. She looked over at Alison, who was looking back at her and gave a quick nod. Alison nodded back. Martin was waiting at the foot of the gangway, he looked guilty. She could see Glenn had already hung back and was scouring the dockside.

"Can we meet in the conference room, now?" said Martin.

"Lead on, XO," said Dmitry.

Suddenly the night had changed and Valla felt more at home. Sometimes it felt that crisis was where she worked best, although the evening with the President, 'call me Rita', and the other officials had gone well. Singaporeans had the sea to contend with, a mixed population and a continued drip drip of immigration, not so very different from the AFS, if on a tiny scale in comparison. They had found lots of common ground to talk about, not least Global Corporation's somewhat cavalier attitude to democracy.

"There was an attempt to rescue Santiago. Three assailants came up the gangway, and one approached on the water side," began Martin.

"We've still got Santiago?" said Valla, thinking of how many threads hung off him that led back to Gordon.

"Yes. He was pushed overboard. What I don't understand is that he was still hand cuffed. They had access to the keys when they reached the brig."

"They weren't part of the same team. They were taking advantage of the rescue attempt," said Alison.

"Ah," said Martin, "That makes sense. We've got the pusher, but the others on the gangway are dead. And it's my fault. I had Patrice loose on the bridge, acting as a look out. He tried to warn them, they opened fire on him. We could have taken them alive without that."

"Patrice knew them?" asked Dmitry.

"Yes, one of them was this Kim woman. As soon as he shouted they opened up on him. He's in surgery just now, but they said he'd make it, nothing vital."

"That was lucky," said Glenn.

"He's not seeing it that way at the moment," said Martin.

Valla had been thinking, who benefited from Santiago's death? Gordon certainly, but did his tentacles stretch as far as Singapore? Or was it Global, still unsure of the whereabouts of Canning, and happy to eradicate any suggestion they were involved in even planning a break out?

"Alison, do you think it was Global?"

"Probably, even without using my sharp mind, they're here, and they're interfering. We heard that tonight," replied Alison. Valla saw her turn to Martin, "We're handing the guy over to Singaporean security tomorrow?"

"Yes. I spoke with the captain on duty tonight."

Valla saw Alison was keen to interview him, she nodded, "Maybe it would be better to use Colin again?" she said pointing to her evening dress.

"Yes. Yes, you're right. I'll get a list of questions worked out. Is Colin up?"

"He can be," said Martin.

Valla had heard the careful tone throughout and wondered what Martin was worried about.

"XO," said Dmitry.

"Captain."

"Patrice was aiding our investigations. I am given to understand," Dmitry was looking at Valla, "that charges of smuggling had been dropped in return for information."

"That is correct," she agreed, wondering where this was going.

"Therefore what Patrice chose to do was not your responsibility. Though, more security on the bridge would perhaps have been helpful. What set you off anyway? It was quiet when we left."

Ah, she thought, people died and it could have been prevented. But Dmitry was right, you can't be responsible for other people's stupidity, or lovelorn idiocy.

"Sir, it was just a hunch. Something when we came back from the shopping expedition. I set up standard repel teams and waited."

"Well then, you did everything you could."

She didn't think Martin believed that. But they had Santiago, slightly soggy by the sounds of it, Patrice with extra ventilation and now someone to question, who could point to Global interference both in AFS and Singaporean affairs. They were winning as far as she was concerned.

"I have the questions. Like before, ask in this order," said Alison, pushing a hand written note across the table.

"Read it all right?" asked Alison.

"Yes fine, said Martin.

"Good," said Alison getting up and nudging Glenn who had his eyes closed.

Valla watched them go. She thought Martin looked tired too.

"XO, you're relieved. I think you need to go get some sleep. I'll sort this." Dmitry had his hand out for Alison's note, but he was looking at Valla.

Valla took a moment to figure out why. Did everyone onboard realise? She supposed it would be quite hard to keep a secret on a ship. It would be more like something everyone chose not to mention.

Martin was standing, she stood up too. Tomorrow she, Alison and Glenn were on the hyperplane out of Singapore back to Weddell City. Martin still had four weeks of his tour left.

Valla took his hand as the conference door shut behind them. He squeezed it and didn't let go. Two doors down he opened the cabin door. His cabin was very similar to Valla's maybe a bit larger. The door shut.

"I wanted to tell you how beautiful you looked tonight."

Valla wasn't used to receiving this type of compliment. Of course she was aware of her looks. Most of her life had been spent trying to get people to see beyond them, and she'd been quite successful at it too.

"Thank you," she said, feeling out of her depth suddenly. They had become so used to not giving in, she wasn't clear on how to now proceed.

His hand stroked her cheek and followed round to the nape of her neck. She did the same bringing his face close to hers. They kissed. She could smell him, soap and paper and a trace of gun oil. More intoxicating than anything she'd drank that evening.

She pulled back to look him in the eye.

"You shot someone?"

"The maybe-Global guy, yes. Tell me this isn't how it's going to be?"

"Sorry. I could smell the gun oil. It won't happen again."

She took hold of his face in both hands and gave him a longer, more intimate kiss.

"I shall wash in gun oil if that's what it takes, " he said, smiling.

Oh that smile, she thought, I've lived on that smile for twelve days.

"I don't expect that'll be necessary, your smile is enough."

They were standing in the middle of the cabin. She kicked her shoes off to the side, and they were eye to eye now. She still had her hands around his neck, now she let them caress his shoulders and slide down his arms, which he still had around her waist. She pulled his shirt out of his shorts, and started unbuttoning it.

"I would retaliate, but I don't think I'd know where to start on your dress."

"The wise warrior avoids the battle," she said smiling and pushing the open shirt down over the tops of his arms.

She heard him laugh, so genuine and disarming.

"Allow me to assist," she said twisting her arm behind to catch the dress zip and pulling it down so she could shrug the dress off like the top of a survival suit. It pooled at her feet.

"Appear weak when you are strong," he said, "gets them every time."

"Them?" she said, poking his bare chest, then running her hands up across it, "How many have you had?"

She pulled him close again, while he shrugged off his short sleeved shirt to the floor.

"A gentleman does not tell tales. It's enough to say, no one to match you."

"Martin?"

"Yes?"

"Take me to bed."

Chapter Thirty - Jet Lag

DI Enya Zhao was writing up the report on Christine Frome's murder of Arnaud Cheung, while she waited on a cross referenced list of Moss and Larsen family activists who had gone missing in the last two and a half years. She was also waiting on clearance to access the file that Intelligence held on Sophia Wren. Some parts of her life would be easier when Glenn Murcheson returned from Singapore tomorrow. She wanted him to look over the evidence too, having already mentally added him to her anti-corruption wish list.

There was enough to charge Christine with the murder, and so they had. She'd been denied bail, considered a flight risk and put on a suicide watch based on the video footage alone. But Enya wanted Alison Strang to look over the evidence to find the patterns that she might have missed. This case had to be water tight.

James Wylie knocked on the glass door. She waved at him to come in.

"I've got the cross reference list, it's only three names. they all went missing in Weddell City, about six months apart from each other. Timing would suggest another one is due."

"Interesting."

"I did some digging, looked at the missing person reports. They were all invited to attend a meeting about Antarctic Combined Research, something apparently they had been trying to find out about on behalf of Moss in one case, and Larsen in the other two. I couldn't find out much about it myself. It's based in Melchior apparently."

"Did it say who with?"

"No." replied James.

"I've come across this ACR place already, red, blue and yellow departments, couldn't get anywhere further on them. Isn't that where Nikau said Freddie was?"

"Did he?" said James, "I don't always get to hear the full story."

He was grinning at her, which she was happy about because that was how James Wylie was supposed to be; a good copper, keen, if a bit sleepy in the morning, and still wasted working in traffic, which was how she'd got him seconded back to her.

"I'll see what Nikau will admit to on Freddie's behalf. I think we might be joining her shortly. Pack for the temperate isles, James."

"I'll have to shop for that. Never been myself. Heard some wild stories about Hielo Cabana though."

"Maybe next time."

"Boss."

She watched Wylie disappear and thought about a trip to Melchior. She'd need more than James. Eric Jordan if she could prise him from Houten, Glenn if he was up for it, and her sergeant from the time out at Wilkes Enterprise Zone, Chris Saraband. Tolli could fly them out for the going rate. And then he could stay well out of it this time. She dialled for Nikau Burns.

"DI Zhao, how's the investigation going?"

"Which one Nikau?" she asked, well aware that much of what she was looking into was somehow suiting Valla's right hand man and therefore the Torres Family.

"Enya, I only have the best interests of the AFS here."

"Well, I had a source corroborate the list story, and I've found three names of missing activists, from Moss and Larsen, who've all been looking into something called Antarctic Combined Research, based in Melchior, where Freddie is. I thought you might have some more information as I'm being stalled without Intelligence clearance at the moment. Same for Sophia Wren. Can't wait till Glenn gets back with his heavy-weight surname."

"If we want it to stand up in court, it's the way we have to do this, as you've said. But I can tell you Freddie is out there to find out what's going on at the ACR too. There's three departments, Yellow, Blue and Red. We think the illegal research goes on in Red, Global seems to be legitimately involved in Yellow. Red needs presidential clearance but Freddie has other ways. You know…"

"Did you send her?"

"No, Gordon did. I think he's trying to pin anything happening out there on Sophia Wren. Are you going up there?"

"It's a plan. I need Glenn first."

"The Singapore flight gets in late tonight, but they'll have jet lag."

"What now? I thought they were leaving tomorrow morning."

"They're moving back through twelve hours worth of time zones and the flight is only five hours. Look don't worry about it, but don't expect anyone to be very focussed."

"So still tomorrow morning?"

"Maybe. I've had jet lag, sleep can just hit you in the middle of the day, or it can keep you wide awake at three in the morning. Just be glad we're all in the one time zone here."

"And Alison?"

"Who knows," Nikau conceded.

"Well tell them I need Glenn and the flight will be Victor Oscar nine seventy, leaving at ten in the morning."

"I will."

There was a quiet hum of activity on the MS Mercer even though it was five in the morning. Valla slipped back to her cabin and packed after a quick shower. The hyperplane flight was at seven and they were to be afforded an official escort through to the airport cutting the travel time down from two hours in the early morning rush hour to thirty minutes. Singapore had taught her a few things about privilege and the power of official flags. Not that she wanted to emulate that in the AFS. People needed to be better organised and plan their journeys, not push others out the way. It was the difference in population she told herself, feeling slightly guilty about the escort.

Martin had got up with her to relieve Dmitry and find out what Colin had found out from their mystery assailant. She expected something in an email. But when they got to the gangway he was there, crisp and cool, looking like he'd had an eight hour sleep. She didn't feel the same given it was closer to two hours. They had their survival suits in hand luggage and were wearing the temperate clothes they'd bought on the way back yesterday.

"Some reading for the journey," he said handing her the interview transcript.

"Thank you, XO."

"Senator."

The car pulled up, the Singaporean and AFS flags fluttering on either side of the car hood.

Glenn had opened the door before the driver could, and was now apologising to him. They got inside and it set off with motorbike outriders. Valla skim read the transcript.

"Wow."

"What?" said Alison and Glenn together.

"He's dumped Global fully in the shit. Names and everything. Cornelius Kutchner, head of Global Corporation, AFS section. He'll have a hard time wriggling out of this."

"We need to get a meeting arrange immediately between the miner representatives and Global, this could be the thing to ease the block in negotiations," said Alison.

Straight back to work, thought Valla.

"More importantly, do we not have something from Freddie's hacker guys, showing Gordon making payments to Kutchner?" asked Glenn.

"We do, but we didn't know what they were for. Do you think he's been using Global as assassins?"

"It's Gordon, anything is possible," said Glenn, "we need to see how much Kutchner thinks Gordon will protect him, and how much he believes Global will dump him like a pyroclast mid eruption."

"Kutchner has to be key now," said Alison.

"Agreed. Nikau will meet us when we land. We should debrief before we go home."

She saw Alison looking at her.

"What?"

"You remember being crotchety about the time changes when we were coming here? This will be worse. Much worse. Trust me, a debrief will be the last thing on your mind when we land."

She saw Glenn nodding.

"Oh. Well he's going to be there anyway."

Valla's internal body clock said it was midday, but her watch, the clock in the airport, the dial on Nikau's car all said midnight. It was hardly different from the daytime so her body was fine with it, but everything in her head said no to the time. She was definitely up for a debrief but Alison and Glenn declined. Especially after Nikau said Glenn was flying again in ten hours time.

They arrived back at Valla's apartment. It smelt slightly stale and she kicked on the air conditioning to give it a flush through.

"Coffee?" asked Nikau.

"Yes. Thanks. So, we've got a full and frank confession that Kutchner paid our guy to kill Santiago. We passed it on to the Singaporean authorities, and they're charging him with attempted murder and throwing in conspiring with pirates, given he was using Kim's boarding attempt as cover. They're happy to give us a video feed when we need him."

"We're close. But we still need more evidence directly tied to Gordon. Not Sophia. He's using her to take the blame."

"There's time," she said, looking at him, "Isn't there?"

"They've re-opened nominations. We've got to get him soon, or at least off the election list."

"Did you say Mariko is going to stand?"

"I actually said it would be good if she did. I took the liberty of meeting with her yesterday. She agreed."

"Good. We don't have a candidate do we?"

"No. No one else would stand. It's your right to stand for us. If you don't then the general consensus is we're free to choose. Though I expect your endorsement would carry a lot of weight."

"I stayed out of it the last time, I don't think I will this time."

"I didn't think you would."

She saw him smile, it was the smile her father used to call the wolf grin.

Glenn wasn't tired but knew he needed to sleep to get back to Antarctic time. He'd experienced this once before on the way to and from Northumbria with Alison and Gary. He'd not enjoyed the process. They had blackout curtains for Alison in the summer, and he was glad of them now.

"Come to bed, it'll help," she said, winking at him.

"A double bed, what luxury."

"I kind of liked the bunk, it was cosy."

"Hmmm," he said getting under the covers.

The alarm went off. He'd dozed on and off for most of the seven hours. He didn't feel too bad, but then he remembered it was still only mid evening Singapore time. The real problems wouldn't begin till later today. He kissed her forehead, wondering how she'd managed to stay asleep through the alarm, and found she hadn't.

He was dressed, packed with the few temperate clothes he owned and heading in a taxi to the private hangars at Weddell City airport, to once again fly with Anatoli Dale, Zhao and Wylie. The whole thing felt like unfinished business as a result. Only, more people had died since. Daniel Ektov for one. He'd tried not to think about Daniel, but back here in Weddell City, with the constant election news it was difficult to avoid.

He paid the taxi at the barrier, recalling the night when he'd stood there and watched Valla's jet disappear into the sky with a half frozen Alison onboard.

Today the morning was cool, but the ground was dry, the sun was shining, he could see James Wylie standing at the foot of the steps to Anatoli's jet, talking to someone he didn't recognise. He strolled over.

"Glenn," James greeted him with a grin, and a surprising amount of alertness for the time of day.

"James, you're sounding awake, what's happened, intravenous caffeine now available?"

"Ha. I think they've finally got the supplement amounts right. This is Sergeant Chris Saraband. Chris, this is Agent Glenn Murcheson."

"Hi," said Glenn, "you one of Zhao's proteges?"

"I have that dubious pleasure, yes. I was at Wilkes Enterprise Zone, and yet here I am again."

"Good to have you onboard, where is the Detective Inspector?"

"Glenn, where's your tan? Go all the way to the Equator and don't change colour? What were you doing? On second thoughts don't answer that."

He turned to see Anatoli descending the steps.

"Anatoli, they still letting you fly?"

"I am forgiven. Come on, Enya's onboard and tapping at her watch."

Glenn let James and Chris go ahead of him and climbed up the steps with Anatoli behind bringing the steps up to form the door of his jet.

He watched Anatoli disappear into the cockpit and headed into the cabin to find a seat and stow his bag.

They were airborne and two hours into the four hour journey. Enya had laid out everything; evidence and conjecture, both officially and unofficially. He felt his temper rise to a level he'd thought belonged in the past.

His body was telling him it was midnight and it was becoming difficult to keep control of his temper as a result. He was staying quiet till he could be sure of himself. He knew Enya at least had noticed. He was pleased Valla had been in touch to give Enya an update on Kutchner's role, and glad that Enya'd had time to put out an arrest warrant for him before they'd taken off.

"Go have a lie down," Enya ordered, "I don't need you awake now, I need you when we land."

Two hours was, he thought, better than nothing, but when he was awoken by Anatoli's landing announcement he was less sure.

Chapter Thirty One - Niceties

"What do you mean she checked out?"

The receptionist pushed the guest book at Enya, and pointed at the entry two days ago. The signature didn't look right. If Freddie had signed it, then it looked like she was in no state to. She took a photograph of it and sent it to Archives for a check.

"I need a hire car, please, in half an hour."

They headed upstairs to the rooms, agreeing to meet in her room as soon as they'd freshened up. She reckoned in Glenn's case that would mean drinking many coffees and a lot of cold water on his face.

"I called Nikau," she said "he hadn't heard from Freddie since she sent the photographs in the evening. The day after she'd arrived."

She showed the photos to the rest. The small jetty, the three anonymous buildings making up the ACR facility, and the view of them from the observatory.

"Should we not be hiring a small boat?" asked Glenn, pointing at the jetty in the photograph.

"Get me a search warrant and I'll hire a boat. But I'm getting nowhere on my Police ID."

"I'll see what I can do."

She saw Glenn get up and walk over to the window with his phone.

"I propose we simply arrive and ask to look around. The level of hostility and or obstacles to that will give us a good idea of how deep in the proverbial they are."

"What do we think has happened to Freddie?" asked Chris.

"Nikau sounded worried," she said, "he mentioned Sophia Wren hasn't been seen in the last two days either, at a time when she should be shadowing Gordon's every interaction."

"Who is she again?" asked Chris.

"Officially Gordon's press secretary, however all the evidence points to her maintaining this list. Three people have disappeared from it after showing an interest in this ACR place. Nikau thinks she's Gordon's fall guy, I'm not so sure."

"Do we think Freddie has been disappeared?" Anatoli asked, sounding like he had mixed feelings about it.

"Possibly. She'd have put up a good fight, but I'm guessing alone, with a strange accent versus the local large employer, she wasn't going to find many friends."

"You think they have Freddie in the facility?" asked James.

"I do. Though I'm about to try and get a hold of Alison and see if we can get some probabilities."

She looked around at Glenn still on the phone, the conversation animated. She'd wait and let him call.

"Do we know which room Freddie was in?" Chris asked.

"The book said seventy eight."

She saw Chris get up.

"I'll just go have a look, shall I?" He was jangling some skeleton keys.

"I did not hear that, Sergeant Saraband."

The door closed and Glenn came back from the window.

"Kairns said he'd get a warrant, but maybe an hour or two. He has a favour he's cashing in."

"Could you ask Alison for her thoughts on the situation?"

Glenn looked reluctant. She knew they were concerned now about the metabolic demands of what Alison called her 'sharp mind', which had been increasing since she'd first controlled it five years ago.

"This is a one shot. Are you sure you want to use it now?"

"We need to know the probability that Freddie is there and in danger. Timing could be everything."

"Okay."

Glenn returned to the window.

The room door reopened. Enya looked up expectantly at Chris.

"As clean as a whistle. Nothing out of place. Except, an old mining trick. Freddie's in trouble, she's left a help sign on the edge of the door frame."

"Shit," said Enya, and got worried faces from all in the room. "Wylie?"

"Yes?"

"Did you bring your vanta-black toy?"

"I never travel *with* you and *without* it," he said with a grin.

She looked at Anatoli, who'd been sitting on the edge of the bed. She'd told him she didn't want him at risk in anything they got up to. She could tell he was unhappy at being left out.

"I have ten years militia experience," he said, "I never missed a training session. Enya, let me help."

It seemed pointless to argue, if Freddie had been removed from the hotel then they couldn't rely on anyone local for help.

The room phone rang. It was reception, the hire car had arrived. She sent Chris down to sort it out.

Glenn sat down and put his head in his hands. This looked bad. She waited. She saw him take a deep breath in and out.

"Alison says they're probably doing biotech experiments at the facility. She said there's an eighty five percent probability Arnaud got his eye thing there and not at Tierra Del Fuego. She doesn't believe Gordon doesn't know anything, sixty percent probability he's aware of what Sophia is up to. The facility also worked on the saser to weaponise it. But they've been working with Global on the bio-tech. She arranging to question Kutchner, they arrested him at Vostok airport trying to leave."

"Six months," James said, reminding her of the frequency of the disappeared.

"Some sort of recovery or testing process? Maybe Freddie will be their next candidate?" she said.

"We have to get there before they start," said Glenn.

"They could have done it already, Freddie's been gone two days," she countered.

"Sophia arrived yesterday evening," said James, showing the passenger manifest on his phone, "I put in a request when you'd said she was missing from Weddell City," he said by way of explanation.

The room phone rang again, this time it was Chris, asking where they were.

There were five of them and the car was small. Only Enya was under a metre seventy eight. She sat in the back squashed between the next two smallest, Chris and Glenn, while James and Anatoli sat up front.

"Someone's taking the piss," she said.

315

She heard James unable to stop his giggle and shook her head.

"Let's get across there now."

There was a queue of cars waiting on the ferry, which hadn't moved from the opposite harbour for forty minutes so far. They were standing out of the car to wait. Enya was eyeing up the boats in the harbour.

"Let's go commandeer a boat. I think they know we're here."

Glenn and Chris headed over while the other three walked more sedately towards the nearest fishing vessel. It was a small shellfish boat, there were stacks of creels next to it on the quayside. She saw Glenn jump down from the quayside, followed by Chris. She quickened her pace and the other two strode on ahead. When she made the edge of the quay, she could see Glen helping the skipper up off the deck, presumably he'd tried to resist the requisitioning physically.

"You'll get your vessel back in good order, and all damage will be paid by the state. Please let my officers get on with their work," she shouted down, motioning that Glenn needed to get him off the vessel.

"He's got the key and won't give it up."

"Okay, let him stay onboard, we'll finally find out what exactly goes on across there in the Combined Research Facility."

She saw the skipper reach for an inside pocket slowly, with his other hand up in the air, taking out the ignition key. Thought so, she said to herself, they'd rather turn a blind eye to what's happening than find out. Cowards.

They were all onboard and cast off. Glenn was in the wheelhouse manoeuvring out of the harbour while a small crowd had began to coalesce around the skipper on the quayside.

The small boat rocked on the waves once they were in the channel between the islands. They were standing holding onto whatever they could as it bounced along.

"Presumably there'll be security at this place, and they're going to know we're coming," she was nearly shouting over the engine "I think we need to split up into two groups. One to try the front door and one to try sneaking in."

She looked up to see Glenn waving to her to come over to the wheelhouse. What now? she thought.

"Did you tell Valla we were here?" he asked.

"No, but Nikau knows so it's the same thing. Why?"

"One of her inshore navy boats is just south of the facility, the MS Bozhinov. Should we hail them?"

"I think so," she said, "They've got guns, more than we have."

"Okay."

The Bozhinov replied and there was some back and forth till Zhao took the radio and asked for the captain. Captain McIlroy came on.

"Captain, can I ask if you're able to assist us in securing access to this facility?"

"Detective Inspector, can I ask if you are in receipt of a search warrant?"

Zhao looked at Glenn who checked his phone. There was a moment while he tapped the screen a few times. It looked hopeful, considering nothing would be an easy thing to see. Glenn gave her a thumbs up.

"Captain, I can confirm this, and a copy will be with you shortly. We believe the security forces present either do not recognise the authority of the AFS or are unaware of the potentially illegal acts taking place inside. We may need to use lethal force to gain entry. We believe there are hostages inside the buildings as well as civilians, some of whom may be innocent in all this."

"I can provide you with a team of four commandos. And we'll maintain cover on the facility."

"We're especially interested in the building with the jetty."

"I understand."

Zhao could see the Bozhinov hauling up the AFS flag to make it quite clear whose authority was being questioned. It was she realised an almost opposite situation to that they'd encountered at McMurdo. She was determined not to make the same mistakes the UN marines had made. Firstly, she'd not be underestimating the forces at the facility. They would have body armour, better guns and more ammunition. However the Bozhinov's commandos would have the kit, so they should lead the assault. Her team needed to be behind them and be able to break out once the facility was breached.

"Everybody brought their visors, yes?"

There was a chorus of assent.

"How are we for ammunition? Just the basics?"

There was a nodding of heads, it was clear they were also thinking the odds through.

She got in touch again with the Bozhinov suggesting they would follow the commandos, both parties aware the entire radio spectrum was unsafe for detailed planning. Glenn got a text message.

"She says commandos will bring some spare ammo, and five extra vests. They've identified a landing spot with cover if we can make it to this spot we can move together."

Glenn showed the map image from his phone.

Enya looked through the binoculars as they approached the southern edge of James Ross where the ACR buildings were.

"I see it. I don't know how we're going to get to it, but it does have cover."

"What if we beach the boat?" suggested Anatoli, "it would provide cover. It's an expensive option but I rather like spending money instead of my life chances."

"Agreed. Glenn let them know we'll be beaching the vessel as soon as Bozhinov's commandos are ready to launch."

She was watching the Bozhinov through the binoculars, she could see activity on the deck. It looked like it was time. Glenn's phone pinged with a text to confirm.

"Glenn, get us beached, firmly but gently if that's at all possible." She turned to the rest, "Gentlemen brace for impact."

She felt the boat run up the shingle, they'd had plenty of momentum and she felt it pushing her forward as she pushed back against the door frame of the wheelhouse. Nothing was coming from the facility yet. There was open ground to cover before the glass frontage and protruding canopy where the doors were located. She looked back to see the small boat coming from the Bozhinov heading their way.

"Lets get off this thing. Without getting shot," she said.

They moved, to the side of the wheelhouse and crouching down, to behind the gunwales, waiting to slide and drop over the side to where the commandos would be landing. It was a small bite of pebble beach taken out of the two metres of sediment that crumbled and leaked ground water. James had his sniper rifle out and was scoping the facility from behind the wheelhouse.

"I'm not sure," said James, "I think there's someone on the roof."

She nodded at Glenn who had picked up an oily rag from within a coil of rope. He threw it up towards the edge of the boat.

"Yes," said James, "they're good, but I'm better."

She heard his shot sing out.

"Got him."

"Nobody else?" she asked.

"No."

They were down on the shingle as the commandos jumped ashore to meet them. The leader approached her while the other three were unloading the small rigid inflatable.

"Jan," he said holding out a protective vest.

"Thanks. Enya," she said.

They'd got the vests on and stashed as much ammo as they could about them. James was checking to see if the sniper had been replaced.

"I don't see anyone else on the roof."

They'd agreed a plan for covering the expanse between them and the door. It was simply not to cross it. They'd leave one shooter here, but move to the side where the edge of the building came closer to the shore and try the fire exit in that side.

"Do you see any CCTV? Think you could take it out?" she asked James.

"I'll see."

She watched him move the rifle slowly across.

"I could shoot the likely places, but I don't see anything particularly obvious."

"You stay here. We'll move round to the side," she looked at Jan, who nodded, "Then Glenn will text, you shoot those lovely plate glass doors and anyone that comes out armed, okay?"

"Boss"

"I'm afraid that's it. There's no point planning further since we have no idea what we're up against or the layout inside. We expect there's an operating theatre inside somewhere and holding cells of some kind. Those are our priorities. If they're armed and stay armed shoot them. I've no time for niceties, they saw the flag."

"Oh, and if you see this woman, don't trust her," said Glenn showing them all a picture of Sophia Wren.

Chapter Thirty Two - Talisman

They squeezed past the bow of the beached shell fish boat, brown dirt falling on them from the sediment. The commando leader, Jan was ahead. He was pulling his visor down and moved his head above the edge, having scrambled up its base.

"Nothing," he said as he slid back down.

Glenn didn't like this. It could be that the facility didn't have a lot of security. They'd had a sniper though, so what they did have sounded experienced. It was looking like they would be allowed to reach the facility and maybe be ambushed inside. He went to test the comms on his visor and was greeted by a wash of white noise. He switched it off, and checked his phone, there was no signal.

"They're blocking all comms," he said, "I've no phone signal either. No way to let James know we're on the move now."

"Don't you worry about that," said Enya.

"Well," said Jan, "are we doing this?"

"Yes," said Enya and put two fingers in her mouth to let out an ear piercing whistle.

There was the sound of breaking glass, as they ran towards the side of the building. They flattened out in a line against the wall. Glenn could see Chris at the end watching the rear corner. He listened for shots from James but it looked like no one was willing to use the front door.

They shuffled along to a fire escape door and he watched the commandos placing plastic explosive on the hinge side, roughly where the top and bottom hinges would be. Two of them moved to the other side of the door and he saw the nearest guy put his fingers in his ears. He did the same.

It was still loud.

The nearest commando kicked the door inwards and hastily took cover again. The door creaked and now sat at an angle in the doorway but it hadn't fallen in. The guy now jumped behind the door. A shot rang out, hitting the side of the door. Glenn tapped Enya on the shoulder, and waved his hand in a forward motion.

Maybe the front door wasn't such a bad option after all. He saw her nod and point to Chris. He shuffled past to tap Chris, leaving Anatoli watching the rear corner. They ran past the door to the front corner of the building. The commandos took the opportunity to get their eye on where the shots were coming from down the corridor as Glenn and Chris' movement triggered shots.

With his visor down he could see James occasionally checking the door. But they still had the glass frontage to get across. If there was a way of getting James to shoot that out too?

He flicked a coin forward in the air. It caught James' attention, thankfully not his trigger finger. He pointed round the corner at the windows.. The glass was made to withstand severe gale force strength, as a spread load, but not high velocity, small impacts in very specific corner areas. There was the sound of more smashing glass as

James shot the windows out. He waited to hear if there would be any answering gun fire. There was nothing. The more nothing he came across the more the knot between his shoulders bunched.

He moved round, scanning the interior, crunching on the glass fragments. It was a reception foyer the length of the windows and door. There were posters on the wall, comfy leather chairs, low coffee tables. He could see the opening of a wide corridor down near the reception desk. He moved inside. Chris joined him. They edged along to the side of the corridor opening. He tested the comms again, still static. It'd be good to try and sort that, he thought.

His mind was working on what was possibly round the corner when he realised Alison had said this was where they'd weaponised the saser. The sound gun that Wahid had brought to the geothermal station at McMurdo. He shivered. It worked on line of sight, that was all he knew about it, other than it fried your insides.

He turned back to Chris and explained what he'd have to watch out for. This could be why there was so much nothing happening. They'd be lured into a trap and hit with the guns. He hoped Enya or Anatoli would also realise soon. He was wondering about making a run for the reception desk when something caught the corner of his eye. It was James Wylie making a low run across the plaza in front of the building.

James had arrived panting behind Chris, getting a thumbs up from both of them.

"I think they might have sound guns," he said to James.

"It crossed my mind," James agreed.

"So, what's the next move?" asked Chris.

"I don't know, mirrors?" he said.

Glenn was grasping at straws, his tiredness was beginning to affect his ability to plan, then he saw James pointing back at the leather chairs.

"What?"

"Armour," said James.

Glenn thought anything was worth a try. They lashed the four cushions together with webbing strips from the chairs. It would mean lying behind it and belly crawling and it might not even be enough.

They moved the remaining furniture up to the edge of the opening and then pushed it out into the corridor to narrow the opening. Glenn's need to see what was down the corridor was overpowering, and he knew his lack of sleep was also going to make him take risks. He pushed the bundle of cushions beyond the furniture and belly crawled behind it, shuffling it across the opening till he was on the reception desk side. He stood up, had a quick check of the room door behind him, which opened on an empty kitchenette, then headed to the desk. He found the public address system.

"This is Glenn Murcheson of the AFS Intelligence Agency, we have a search warrant for this facility. We are backed by AFS police and navy forces. Lower your weapons and surrender. Repeat, lower your weapons and surrender. We have orders to shoot armed individuals on sight for treason."

It was worth a try, and saved all that 'stop or I'll shoot' nonsense that usually saw you get shot yourself.

He couldn't resist any longer and took a quick look round the corner. It seemed clear. He heard gunfire from somewhere to the right. He gestured to James to take a look through the scope, watching him disconnect it from the rifle and poke it round the edge. It seemed like minutes till James gave him the thumbs up and slid his scope back onto the rifle.

Now he had to decide about the cushion barrier, it was awkward and bulky and might not work, but like a talisman he couldn't let go of it. He dragged it behind him as they skulked down the corridor to the place where it became a T-junction. To the left ought to be where Zhao and the others were at the fire exit.

He checked round the edge. The door was now lying down against the internal wall, there was a cluster of metal made up of a trolley and a table, also pushed to the side. He could see empty casings at his feet with a trail of blood leading off to the right. So they'd been shooting from here, but there were no bodies. This meant they'd either surrendered or retreated.

He wanted the rooms in the left hand corridor checked. Carefully. He was sure James and Chris knew how to do that, but he emphasised the words 'booby trap' before he let them go down the corridor.

They came back, with all limbs intact. It was the right hand corridor then. He was about to turn when he noticed the skirting board across from him. The flooring was lino, it went up to skirting height but opposite him was some wooden skirting. He pointed to it and James and Chris both shrugged their shoulders. He moved to the right hand side of the area of wall with the wooden skirting. He saw James and Chris take cover to the left.

He pushed. The wall wavered. He pushed harder, felt the wall move to the left as if it was on wheels above. He looked through the thin gap. It looked like another reception area. From what he could make out it was empty. He dragged his cushion bundle closer in front of the gap and lay down behind it, pushing the wall to the left with some effort. It squeaked with the unusual directional strain on the wheels. There was the smell of static. Glenn instantly remembered it from McMurdo. Now they'd find out how worthwhile the cushions were.

At the same time as he smelt burning protein he heard a shot. James had turned, aimed and got out of the way while the saser had been fired.

The acrid smell threatened to take him back to a memory, till something synthetic started melting and overpowered it. Glenn rolled to the side as a hissing sound approached through the cushions and a wisp of smoke broke through the leather, like a cigarette burn in reverse.

He had to hope there weren't many of these guns around because the cushions had been a one act play.

He let James check out the room for conventional shooters. Then they pushed the wall completely across and entered the area. James went over to the guy who'd had the saser. He picked it up and passed it to Glenn. It was shorter than the one Wahid had used, lighter too. There were four out of five lights lit on the stock, presumably a record of shots left. They stripped the guy of anything useful. James had shot him through the forehead, and he looked oddly peaceful.

There was another plate glass window and door. A rear entrance or a secret entrance. Whatever, he thought, one half of the building was clearly kept in the dark about the other half.

There was only a corridor leading to the right from this area. Glenn stowed his hand gun and held the saser. Despite a lot of effort, he was not ambidextrous with a firearm. Holding one in his left hand was only going to result in trouble. He let James lead the way. They moved down the corridor. It had no doors on it. He checked again for the comms, clicking on and off almost instantaneously when he heard the white noise.

They stopped. James had come to the end of the corridor. It looked like a dead end. They all looked down at the floor. There were black marks like a trolley wheel would make and they went right up to the wall. This time there was no skirting to give the game away, but Glenn thought instead of sliding, this particular wall was a hinged door. The black marks favoured the right hand side of the corridor ending. He gestured to James and Chris to take cover in the left corner. He pushed against the right side near to the lines. It did indeed shift. He pushed hard and the door swung open. A volley of machine gun fire erupted through it. Glenn felt his adrenaline surge. He pressed the charge on the saser and smelt the static. He saw James get ready. He swung the gun out into the opening and fired, mid height and central. He might get lucky, but he thought the worry of getting fried would be enough to cause a pause in the flow of bullets. James had fired almost simultaneously. There was no further shooting from the room. They waited a moment.

Glenn ducked around and back. The room was an operating theatre, or something like it. The sub machine gun lay on the floor ahead of a guy in blue uniform. Behind him was an operating table. From his briefest of glances Glenn thought there was a body on it. Whether alive or dead was not clear. There was a dark corner to the room which he wasn't happy about, he pulled his visor down. He was about to charge the saser when James waved at him.

He saw James crouch down and fire up into the darkness. Of course: he recalled the scope had filters on it, similar to those on a visor. It was right to save the saser for those shots where they couldn't make a visual.

They entered the room. Glenn went to the body on the table. It was dead, and had been for a while, pale and stiff, but it wasn't Freddie. However it looked like they were in the right part of the building anyway. He wondered where Enya had got to.

Chapter Thirty Three - On The Count Of Three

Enya heard the shattering of more glass, and saw Jan fire down the corridor through the gap. There was no answering fire. She saw him push the door and heard it clang down into the corridor. Whoever had been there, had fled at the sound of the windows shattering. They scrambled over the barrier that had been put behind the door, and headed down. There was a trail of blood leading down the corridor. They paused momentarily to cross the wide opening on the right to the reception area.

Beyond the wide opening, the corridor had two doors on the right hand side, the commandos went ahead and checked them out. One was a broom cupboard the other was medical supplies. They reached the end of the corridor which now turned right. One of the commando's looked round quickly. She recognised the smell of static in the air. She pulled on the side of Jan vest. He turned to her.

"You smell that?" she asked, "That's a sound gun firing up."

He nodded, "What's it do?"

"Fries your insides, only needs line of sight, but the shooter doesn't need to see you."

"We're stuck then?"

They heard Glenn's announcement over the public address system. She wondered if it would have any effect.

There was the sound of arguing coming from the right. It looked like some of the security were having second thoughts at least. There was the clatter of what sounded like a weapon hitting the floor. The commando moved enough round the corner to fire. There was a hissing noise in the wall and wisps of smoke from a hole in it. Enya moved behind him to see around his arm. A fight was in full force between two security guys. The sound gun was flailing in one guard's hand having just been discharged. The commando took further aim at him and fired. He went down. The other guard ran.

She turned and saw Jan standing at the wall looking at the deep hole made by the sound gun.

"Fucking hell," he exclaimed.

She saw Anatoli nudge him and nod at her.

"Sorry, Ma'am."

They moved warily down the corridor to where the fight had taken place. There was no sign of the weapon that she'd heard drop. Must have been picked up by the running guard, she thought. She prised the sound gun from the other guy's hand and checked the stock, four lights lit out of five. The corridor now turned left. She could hear shots. It was difficult to tell where they were coming from, somewhere behind walls to where they were at least.

She was trying to keep count for a rough guess of what might be left to encounter. She still felt outnumbered. The commando as before checked round the corner. He held up two fingers. She saw Jan make a gun sign with his hand, the commando tilted his hand back and forth. A maybe. It seemed that Glenn's announcement had got some of the security rattled. Before she could decide what to do, she saw Jan step out into the corridor.

"Drop your weapons. This is the navy."

She could hear a gun drop, but it only sounded like one, almost at the same time she heard Jan fire. The singing in her ears peaked and then abated slowly. She'd be living with that for days now. The three commandos ran past Jan and grabbed at the guy who'd dropped his weapon.

She looked round at Anatoli. He shrugged his shoulders. The security guard who'd surrendered was dragged back into their part of the corridor.

"Where does that go?" asked Jan.

"Offices."

"Where's the operating theatre? Where d'they keep the people?" she shouted, unable to properly hear herself.

"What people?"

She was very tempted to smack him across the face, then realised, the ones not giving themselves up, were the ones who knew exactly what shit they'd been protecting.

"He doesn't know," she said more quietly, "Tie him up, try and put him somewhere safe."

They all heard more shooting, it sounded like it was far away from them. They turned into the corridor and moved quickly to the next corner. It was a side corridor to the left. The lead commando waved them on, and they headed into it.

There were two doors each side of the corridor. They'd left a commando at the top of the corridor. The first two rooms checked out as offices, as did the third on the right. The commando who'd entered the fourth room did not re-appear. The doors were double doors unlike the rest. Nearby was the door to a stairwell. She saw Jan signal a guy to head down the stairs and watched the door close quietly behind him.

She saw Jan push one of the swing double doors open slowly. There was the smell of static. They all sprang back from the doors as a now familiar hissing sound heralded the effect of a highly coherent terahetrz sound burst, hitting matter. Providing it was one gun, they were now equally matched thought Enya, four charges left. The trick would be to get them to waste theirs. She pushed her door hard with her foot, making it swing inwards. Another burst of static and smoke. Whoever had the gun didn't fully understand it, she thought. She nodded at Jan to kick his door. This time there was nothing. She pushed at hers gently. Still nothing. The interior of the room was pitch black. She flicked her visor down and onto thermal. The room looked empty except for a crumpled heap in the corner. The commando she guessed. There were footprints in the carpet leading to a wall, another door?

The other two entered the room, visors down, and they moved, keeping close to the right hand wall, working round to where the footsteps disappeared. It felt like a door to her, but it had hermetic sealing, there was no thermal leakage from it at all. She felt Jan pass her and saw his thermal signature on the other side of the door. It was wider than normal, or it might be another set of double doors. She pushed and felt strong resistance, but not like it was locked. The shooter had to be inside. She gestured with hand signals they should push together on a count of three.

There was the smell of static as she charged the gun. They pushed and the doors gave. She could see several figures inside all hot red, and one with a hot stick. There was the smell of static, but Enya had already fired at the figure holding the hot stick. She saw the rest put their hands up. She flicked up her visor and blinked her eyes a few times, the room was very brightly lit. She saw four people in white coats, and now she could see there was someone in a chair. Strapped down in something resembling a dentist's chair.

She watched Jan secure the four white coats, while Anatoli went forward to see who was strapped down on the chair. She could see him start to release the straps, whoever it was they were out cold.

"Not Freddie," he said.

Well, she thought, these guys know exactly what goes on here. She picked the tallest white coat and went over to him. She grabbed his balls and squeezed tightly, seeing him grimace and try not to double up.

"I could injure you badly, in places it would be hard to find evidence of," she said to him, "Where is Freddie Tran, the woman brought in two days ago?"

He was shaking his head from side to side. She saw Jan pick up the sound gun from the floor.

"How does this work again?" he said, grinning at her, and pointing it at the doubled up white coat.

Another white coat spoke up.

"We're unarmed. I thought you said…"

The white coat shut up as she saw Jan swing the sound gun round to almost point blank range of him.

"The woman brought in two days ago, where would she be?"

"Ehhr…downstairs. Probably. Maybe."

They left the white coats, one per room, tied up and gagged. Jan had pulled his dead commando out of the room and left him in the corridor. Enya knew it was hard to lose someone on an operation, there was a part of her screaming inside to send Anatoli back to somewhere safe, but they had to keep going.

They entered the stairwell having pulled back the commando guarding the top of the corridor to now watch the room doors and the stairwell door.

The air grew staler as they descended. Natives of the AFS were sensitive to the various moulds and fungii that could grow in certain habitats. They knew which ones were bad, which was most of them. She knew these were all bad ones, and she saw Anatoli wrinkle his nose too. The commando had gone down here a while ago. That there was no sign of him made her feel uncomfortable. She could see he'd started to check the cells, and there was no other word for the small lockable rooms, all so far open and empty.

They moved slowly, Enya pulled her visor down but couldn't see any clues on the cold concrete. There seemed to be nobody down here as they approached the back of the space, then she saw through an open cell door, the commando. She stopped, and saw Anatoli and Jan who'd been looking at the other side's cells, look over.

Jan put his hand up to stop. She understood, this could easily be a booby trap. The commando looked alive, but out of it, he'd be no help to them. She watched Jan go over towards the cell entrance. He was feeling round the frame for a trigger. She saw his hand stop and his other hand follow something. She saw him look round at her. He was unmistakably sizing her up. He nodded his head towards the cell interior and she understood.

She handed Anatoli the saser and took off the protective vest dropping it on the floor. She squeezed through the opening clear of the door and the door frame and saw where the wire had been set to the trigger of a sub machine gun, the change in tension would set it flailing around in the confined space, enough to do serious damage. It was crude. She grasped the trigger taking up the tension and then dropped the clip out from the gun. She pushed the wire off the trigger as Jan came inside and picked the commando up onto his shoulder.

Anatoli gave her back the vest and helped her put it on. She was shaking now. She felt him squeeze her shoulders. She tried to calm down. Where the fuck was Freddie?

They didn't find Freddie, but they did find a second set of stairs. There was a half landing and they turned to the right, at the top of the flight was a door. She gestured to Jan to go first. Her hearing was now shit from the gunfire. She'd already spotted all the commandos had frequency filter plugs in their ears. Another piece of tech she promised herself.

She saw him put his hand up for stop, then she saw him press a finger to his lips. Clearly there was someone on the other side of the door. She was watching Jan, waiting for a signal. He showed three fingers and tapped his chest, then two fingers. Three of us, she thought; must be Glenn, James and Chris, and two hostiles. If there was talking then there must be some sort of impasse.

She saw Jan tap his watch and then hold up three fingers. She nodded, on the count of three.

They burst into the room. There was a shot, and one of the people with their back to the stair doorway fell. The other one dropped something and put their hands up.

Beyond them she could see James bringing down his rifle, and Glenn and Chris rushing over towards them. She saw Glenn stoop to the person who'd fallen. She could see now, it was a woman, in a smart business suit. There was something familiar about her. She realised it was Sophia Wren. She looked down at Glenn and he shook his head, then she noticed there was a handgun in Sophia's outstretched hand.

She saw Glenn stand up and check the pulse of the prone figure on another dentist chair. She'd hardly noticed it till now. It was Freddie. Thank god for that.

Anatoli and Chris had Freddie between them, Jan had his dead commando and the other one was helping his injured comrade as they made their way out of the building. Enya agreed to stay with the wounded while the rest went back in to round up the prisoners, and find a way to shut the jammer off. She knew they'd been successful when she heard Anatoli over the visor comms.

"Marry me," he said.

She didn't know what to say. Only Tolli could think that was appropriate right now. He did know everyone else could hear?

"I'll think about it," she replied, hearing a burst of laughter that was quite obviously James Wylie.

She saw them come through the shattered doorway, the four white coats, the guard who'd surrendered and the guy who'd been with Sophia. Chris was carrying the person they'd found in the first dentist's chair and laid them down next to Freddie. She could hear Jan calling the Bozhinov.

"You're all as bad as each other," she said to the line of expectant faces, Glenn looked away, but James and Chris were laughing.

"Don't string him out Enya," said Chris, "give the boy your answer."

She looked at Chris and saw him nod towards Anatoli with a straight face.

She went over to Tolli, taking the visor off so there'd be no accidental transmission. She looked at his face. He didn't look like it was the adrenaline talking. She'd seen similar sorts of things before. He looked calm.

"Yes," she said.

She felt him grab her round the waist and swing her round. It could be adrenaline now, she conceded.

"This isn't very professional, Tolli, put me down."

"Sorry. But I thought, of all the things I've been afraid of today, asking you wasn't going to become one of them."

"I see," she said, smiling.

Chapter Thirty Four - Drawing Teeth

It had been a long session. Cornelius Kutchner was a tough nut to crack, Alison had to admit. Her first session had to be cut short as she realised he'd had some training in Special Stranger techniques. It was hardly surprising, Global had plenty of money to hire them, and smart enough people to analyse them while they were working. The days of the Special Stranger were probably numbered anyway, especially since the program had been cancelled fifteen years ago.

Her sharp mind gave her an edge, but it came at a price. She was ravenous as she sat down to a large plate of pasta and sauce. This was the third session she'd just finished. He was giving the information up, but it was shrapnel, it needed a team of people to help put the shards back together into a narrative that would stand up in court. Luckily she and Valla had instigated a university course which incorporated a lot of Special Stranger techniques along with negotiator and mediator training. She'd been able to get three students to work on the answers before she'd even asked the first question.

She scraped the plate clean and pushed it to the side. The door opened and she expected to see someone coming to take it away, instead it was Valla, with a plate of cake and ice cream.

"Hello, and thank you," she said, scooping up a mouthful immediately the plate went down.

"I hear it's been hard going. I wanted to let you know I heard from the MS Bozhinov, she was up at Melchior doing a bit of training when she had to help someone execute a search warrant. We lost a commando but everyone else is okay."

"Oh. Nobody tells me anything."

She continued to spoon the cake up.

"I find that hard to believe," said Valla with a broad smile.

She laughed. It was true, she only ever had to ask. Very specific and slightly odd questions most of the time.

"What happened?"

There was one last piece of cake and spoonful of ice cream, she almost felt sated.

"They shot the place up, as you'd expect. Rescued Freddie, killed Sophia, which I'm kind of pissed off about, but apparently they had no choice. Oh, and Anatoli asked Enya to marry him."

"He did what? When? Before or after it all?"

"After. She said it had appeared to put asking her into perspective for him."

"Poor Anatoli." she said, "Anything specific I can use with Kutchner. It's like drawing teeth."

She saw Valla looking at her oddly.

"Pulling teeth. It's an old saying."

"Ah, that makes more sense," said Valla, "Well, from the first report, there were Global employees present at the facility, a Doctor Long, eye specialist and a Doctor Gray who's worked with Doctor Canning in the past."

"That confirms my suspicions about Arnaud's eye surgery. Thanks."

"The Bozhinov is bringing the suspects in, but I heard that Anatoli will be flying back with the team and Freddie tomorrow. Enya's arrested Freddie for kidnapping Anatoli."

"You have a problem with that?"

"We need Freddie to get Gordon. He's going to try and say it was all Sophia."

"I can show you what I have from Kutchner so far. He's never met Sophia. It's quite clear all his dealings were with Gordon, and it does include the attempted murder of Santiago Kooper in Singapore. I think you might be all right. Or have you promised Freddie something?"

"Not in so many words."

"Valla."

Gordon heard the news from contacts in Melchior. Some of what they reported was in the late night news too. A navy boat was called on to assist with Police and Intelligence Agency carrying out a search warrant at a secret facility. Secret, that was the word they were using, despite it not being secret at all. This was the tone that was being set. He sensed Nikau Burns behind some of this. Domingo's man always came across as easy going, he had the press in the palm of his hand most of the time. He'd also heard it was Nikau's idea to back Mariko Neish.

Gordon needed Wahid, but he'd gone to ground. He needed Freddie but she'd also stopped answering calls. He did not need Sophia Wren. Not least because she was dead, but primarily because a lot of this shit was her fault, and he needed to make sure it all became her fault.

The news had been quiet on the details of what had been found at the ACR buildings. But Nikau had made sure they mentioned Sophia Wren. He could work with that. He'd fenced with Nikau before, it would be a close fight this time. He had other people, less reliable, but he made some calls before turning in for the night.

He woke earlier than usual, a rare bad dream. Bruce was in it. He was damned by his old mistakes but he refused to regret anything, even that. He made coffee and switched on the TV to hear some sensationalist bullshit about experiments at the ACR Red Department 'sanctioned by Presidential order'. He put the cup down and called up his lawyer.
"Nancy?" he said, "You hear this bullshit they're saying about me. Get it stopped, I don't want to hear it by the lunchtime news. I'll be putting out a press statement as soon as I write it. But you nail those Torres loving hacks' balls to their grubby little desks."

"Gordon, good morning to you too. What exactly do you want me to stop?"

Gordon calmed down, Nancy was impeccably straight, and her client confidentiality was legendary.

"It was not a Presidential order, it went through the relevant committees, there was no details on what collaborative work would be done with Global. Isn't it Global guys they found there?"

"I can get them to change the presidential order part, Gordon, but your press secretary was shot dead on the premises. Rumour has it she wasn't caught in cross fire either."

"How bad is this, Nancy?"

"Gordon, you tell me. From what I can see so far, you look like you couldn't control a young keen employee, that's not good when you want to run the AFS."

"I'll pass you the press statement for a check over. Thanks Nancy."

"See you soon, Gordon."

Never in his life had he felt this out of control of a situation. Even when they were taking control of Antarctica from the colonial states during the chaos created by the Carrington events, he had known which actions to take and what those actions would produce. He'd had Domingo, Daniel, Leon Palma and Arne to help, even Clarissa Roth had had her uses. Now he felt alone. Well, fuck them, he thought, I can do this without help.

He sat down with his coffee and started on the press release.

Valla was in her senate office. It had been her father's and she hadn't changed anything. He'd commissioned a ceramic frieze for one wall showing a map of Antarctica, it had distances marked on it between the cities, and little relief volcanoes, the ice sheet even had a relief aspect to it. Valla had loved it since she saw it freshly installed in the then empty room, she had named all the volcanoes touching each one, and remembered her father's pride. The other two walls had bookcases against them now, there was a full set of the laws and constitution for the AFS in leather bound volumes, plus a stack of ring binders with the latest amendments waiting to be published.

As a precocious seventeen year old she'd decided to read them. She made it through the constitution and about ten pages into the first volume. He father had laughed and told her it was further than he'd ever got. That was when she realised politics wasn't about making laws, and running a country wasn't about having those laws enforced. It was about people. You could use people, you could try and protect people, but the main point of good politics was to lead people in the direction that good people already wanted to go in. And it required an understanding that good people weren't always people like yourself, they came in a number of guises. She even thought once upon a time Gordon Murcheson had been a good person.

What had happened to him? Had he really begun to lose his grip on reality as Glenn and Freddie had already suggested? She'd prefer if he did stand trial he did so as someone with full capacity. He had some fancy lawyers. Nancy Carter was one of the best, if Nancy thought it would stand scrutiny she'd make that case. Thankfully Nancy wasn't Christine Frome's lawyer. They'd set the date for Christine's trial. It would start before the run off elections finished. She wondered how much Gordon had tried to alter that? Some things were going to come out during this trial that would damage him too. Perhaps he didn't expected them to, till after the run-offs finished?

She wasn't usually in her office during the day, so it had remained quiet, and her secretary always fielded calls. The knock on the door was unexpected as a result. The door opened and Nikau Burns slid into the room.

"I sent Tricia out to get some lunch, she said you've not had breakfast."

"I'm not hungry. What's up?"

"Mariko would like you to back the return of the senate for an emergency debate, I said yes. But she wants you to share a platform at a press conference with her after she formally asks for it."

"I'm not comfortable with that. What does she think she'll gain? She's going to get most of the Torres vote already."

"Gravitas?'

"More like the illusion of navy backing. No. That's a dangerous precedent to set. I thought you said she knew what she was doing?"

"I think she does. I didn't expect you to say yes. I told her that. She's testing you maybe? Seeing how power hungry you might be."

"Fuck's sake Nikau, we don't want another Gordon on our hands. Tell her to rein in that paranoia of hers or I'll come over there and do it for her."

She slammed a drawer in her desk shut. Why couldn't anyone get it through their thick heads all she wanted was the Defence Portfolio and to make sure the AFS stayed a free, and vaguely democratic country.

"Calm down Valla. She's still young, finding her feet. Did you know she wants the emergency debate to discuss barring Gordon from standing in this election?"

"Ambitious. I'd have gone for a simple delay. We're not ready to attack Gordon so openly. I think we need to have a meeting with Mariko before she wrecks things."

"Agreed. In an hour?"

She looked across at Nikau, he'd planned this, she could tell. She didn't want Mariko to be a Torres puppet, it was important to her whoever was president was capable of doing it on their own, without needing direction. Did Nikau not think the same?

Valla was just finishing the salad lunch that Tricia had brought to her, when Tricia announced Mariko Neish and Nikau Burns had arrived. They came in and she watched Mariko. So far it had been Nikau who'd been meeting her in person. She was quite different to the mental picture the emails and his reports had built up in her mind. She was taller than Valla had expected. Something about the name Mariko had made her think small and fine featured, a bit like Enya Zhao in fact. Mariko's build seemed to owe more to the Neish part of her name, maybe a strapping Highlander. She reminded Valla more of Glenn Murcheson than anyone else.

"Come in, come in, take a seat."

She'd pulled her desk chair round and set it with the two armchairs around a low coffee table. Tricia and her had shifted the desk back against the window to make the space. The chairs were equidistant from each other. She didn't want Mariko to feel interrogated or intimidated in any way. Even if that would be what occurred.

Mariko took the armchair nearest the door, Nikau moved to the other, leaving Valla with her desk chair sank to its lowest setting. It still left her taller than them.

"I want to say," began Mariko, "I meant nothing untoward when I asked for you to share the platform with me."

"I understand," said Valla, "it's just the navy is the only standing force we have and the Defence Portfolio needs to be ultra-neutral. I'm backing your bid in my role as head of Torres, but I can't promote or go against senate votes. For what it's worth I agree with the recall."

"I had planned on asking other senators."

"I think you should still do that."

"I will."

"About your reason for the recall, though," said Valla, looking directly at Mariko, trying to suss her motives out, as if Mariko was sitting there with a Royal Flush and not bluffing. She saw Mariko looking straight back, giving nothing away. The kid was good.

Valla continued, "There will be things coming out during the trial of Christine Frome, things that will directly affect Gordon's campaign adversely. We see no reason to get him on the defensive before then."

"There's enough to disbar him now."

"Is there? Have you met Nancy Carter?"

"His lawyer? No."

"You know your history, Mariko. You know what they tried to do to stop the AFS happening. I want you to understand that Gordon Murcheson is a product of that, as is all the paranoia that goes along with him. When outside forces are trying to dismantle what you've newly put together you don't trust anyone. We're beyond that now. We have to move on from secrets and cabals."

She could see Mariko bristle.

"I know that. He should be disbarred on the basis his press secretary was involved with Global."

"You know what all your Family are up to? You're a senior senator, you're ultimately responsible for what activists do in the name of Lomonosov, along with Dante and River. What could disbar you?"

"That's not the same. I don't employ them."

"And you're quite sure of all your *employees*?"

Valla could see that it was slowly getting through to Mariko. Valla was well aware Nikau and Mariko had agreed someone would infiltrate Rafael Dupont's support, and that *someone* had been close to Mariko.

"What do we discuss then?"

"Delay. Leave Gordon thinking he's not under attack. Don't feed his paranoia, it makes him dangerous. Ask for a delay in the opening of the polls for the run offs till the end of Christine's trial. It will stop Gordon trying to wrap things up before anything comes out that'll hurt him. And it will look bad if he tries to stop a delay, people will wonder what's in the trial evidence."

"Damned if he does, damned if he doesn't," said Nikau.

"You don't even have to win the debate," said Valla, "you just need to have had it."

She saw Mariko sit back in her chair. She knew Daniel had liked to worked in the shadows, placing rumours and stories about people to make changes happen. This was a Daniel tactic, and she hoped Mariko would see that.

"Okay," said Mariko, "I trust you to have something concrete that will see Gordon Murcheson suffer the consequences of his actions."

The vehemence of that statement rang alarm bells in Valla's head. It sounded a lot like the tone Glenn Murcheson used to have. What was lurking in Mariko's

past that Gordon had fucked up? And was it the only
thing driving Mariko Neish?

Chapter Thirty Five - Coffee Day

It was late evening and Alison saw Glenn had finally got out of bed. He'd more or less stumbled into the apartment around eleven that morning and had slept since then. She saw he'd shaved and showered too, he was looking awake. She'd last seen him look like that three days ago, one fifty degrees longitude and nearly sixty degrees latitude away. The sleep had been understandable she thought.

"Is it safe to offer coffee yet?"

"I'll stick to water just now, thanks."

She'd offered him coffee when he'd first arrived and he'd said the only reason he was still standing was the amount of caffeine in his system, not all of it from coffee.

"Do you want to talk about it?" she asked.

"Do you want to know?"

"Whatever helps you."

"I don't want to set off any bad memories for you. They were doing exactly the same experiments there."

"I've heard some things from Cornelius Kutchner already."

"When do you think they're going to arrest Gordon?" he asked.

She noted the tactical change in topic.

"I think they need more statements, especially from the sub-committees, and they won't get them till the idea Gordon is a spent force gains ground. So, weeks, if not months."

"I don't want you here, to hear these things. Let's go away," he said.

He sounded like he didn't want to hear these things either. She was sympathetic. Who would want to hear that the worst you could think of a person had been superseded by the truth. Glenn had a very low opinion of his grandfather, but it didn't stretch to human experimentation.

"Where?"

"Stick a pin in the map. Antarctica is always a thin line at the bottom so it should be difficult to pick it accidentally ."

She laughed and he started to laugh too.

She was so glad to hear him laugh.

Valla had watched the evening news, they'd modified the article on the Melchior incident, clearly Nancy Carter had had words. She was happy enough. Christine's short campaign had already highlighted how little debate sub-committees had been allowed on policies: whether the news anchor said presidential order or mentioned some subcommittee acronym, the effect was the same. The word 'secret' had been changed to 'little known'. But this had only led various talking heads to begin discussing why there'd been a problem accessing the facility with a search warrant in the first place.

Now the late night politics show was doing a profile on Sophia Wren. It looks like Gordon had had some input into the show because it was really setting Sophia up for having gone rogue. Valla began to worry. If someone got to Kutchner, and there were plenty of someones who'd do it for enough money, then all they had was Santiago, a video link to his erstwhile assassin, some hacked bank transfers and Alison's team's narrative, which Nancy would tear to shreds without a witness to cross examine.

The Intelligence Agency was currently holding Kutchner, at their Weddell City offices. She knew Kairns would be doing his best, but Global and Gordon both wanted him silenced, and there was a lot of money between them. She could get him transferred to the Bozhinov but that wouldn't be until it arrived from Melchior early tomorrow morning.

And then how would that look? she thought. The navy, under the orders of the Defence Portfolio Holder, holding prisoners because it didn't trust the Intelligence Agency. No, what she'd said to Mariko was true. They had to move away from the paranoia. Accept sometimes shit happened and you didn't always get the guy.

But she wanted to get Gordon, almost as much as Glenn and Mariko did. He'd screwed it up, and he couldn't see it was time to let go.

An email notification pinged on the open laptop on the coffee table. It was a file on Mariko. Something Nikau had put together since the meeting that afternoon. She picked it up and read through. It made sense now. Mariko Neish's father had been one of the miners killed in Freddie's Innonnox Mine. The saser gun trial: the half truths and lies about what happened there still hadn't become clear. But Gordon was part of it. Nikau had told her what Freddie had said about Jean Mirales and his 'sound gun' idea.

She wanted Kutchner secure and Freddie somewhere safe, but there were no good options, she'd just have to trust that people could sense the old corruption dying and were willing to make better decisions. Ones that didn't lean so heavily on what Family they were but what it meant for the AFS's continued security and prosperity. She felt perhaps Nikau might not find that so easy.

The MS Bozhinov had docked at the City Quay in Weddell City. Captain Dolores McIlroy was on the bridge of the small vessel. It was three in the morning and they'd arrived earlier than expected on a favourable current and high tide. No one knew they'd already arrived, yet looking from the bridge window through her binoculars she could see movement on the quayside. She was in radio contact with Sarah, her XO. The repel team was ready and waiting. The black figures were now out from the shadows of crates and cranes on the quayside and she could see they were indeed preparing to board her. If it hadn't been for the messages from the Mercer's captain Dmitry Beardmore, they'd have been unprepared, but the Mercer had been keeping everyone informed of what was going on as much as they could. Those bastards in Global were at it, thinking they could walk over the AFS, well how about this, she thought, as she switched on the floodlights, illuminating all five figures on the quayside and hearing Sarah through the loudspeaker telling them to drop their weapons.

She saw one make a break for the cover behind him as the rest began to drop their weapons. The guy fell before he'd taken two strides. She had nowhere to hold them so they'd have to be secured and the Agency or whoever would have to come get them before they got too cold on the quayside.

She relayed the orders to secure on the quayside and called up the Intelligence Agency first. It'd be up to them whether this was a police matter. She got put through to a guy called Kairns who sounded like he was usually in charge. Within minutes she could hear sirens moving through the city and getting louder. Then saw the flashing lights momentarily stop at the security barrier. Three cars and a van pulled up alongside. Sarah was down there already and now she was talking to a fat guy who'd got out of the van and seemed to be directing the others to collect the assailants.

Dolores called up the Mercer to thank them then called Senator Torres to inform her of the latest outrage against the AFS navy. She got Valentina Torres straight away which surprised her, it was only four o'clock in the morning.

Valla took the call from the Bozhinov and then made her decision. She'd been inching towards it for some time, unlike the decisions she usually made, this one was one of those complicated ones, ones that weren't feeling right but were still somehow the right things to do. She headed over to Gordon's apartment.

There was no security at the apartment block. That she could see. Gordon must still feel safe at home, or he had ninja commandos hiding behind the ceiling panels, waiting to drop on would be assassins. She had a small quick laugh as she knocked on the door at the idea of the ninjas, born from the common perception of Gordon and his near mythical power.

She knocked again, it was half four in the morning and Gordon was an old man. She saw a figure appear out of the corner of her eye. She turned warily. They didn't look ninja. She realised she recognised the man, it was Wahid.

"What are you doing here?" he asked.

"I could ask you the same thing."

"I'm watching out for Gordon, like I always do."

"Is he in? I want to talk to him about resigning."

"He'll never do that."

"You don't know what I know. Persuade him it's the right thing to do. I can secure his legacy but not if he continues to pretend none of this is his doing."

She could see that Wahid believed her, he also seemed to have an air of resignation about himself. Like he'd always known working for Gordon would lead him to this place. She wondered if Nikau would feel the same at some point.

"I'll see what I can do. I can't promise anything."

"Neither can I, but it's for the good of the AFS, he has to see that. Doesn't he want it to continue independently, democratically?"

"Those are ideas you could spend a long time debating and still end up disagreeing over."

"For the people, then?"

She saw Wahid nod, she'd found their common ground and it was the people; the natives, the newly naturalised, the immigrants, even the long term visitors, all the people who considered Antarctica their home. She left without speaking to Gordon, hopeful that Wahid could prevail but determined to continue to pursue Gordon till he knew he was beat.

She'd slept for about three hours when she got a call.

"Valla, I'm recalling the Senate. I'll make a statement to the chamber, and then I'm asking that you're made interim president."

Fuck. Gordon. She woke up fast, thinking furiously about all the angles, and machinations and plays that were behind this, and how she should consequently answer.

"That's up to the senate," she said and left it at that. The less said the better with Gordon.

"Yes, it is, but I wanted to let you know first."

"There'll be an investigation, Gordon, even if I was president I couldn't stop that, or anything that came out of it."

"I appreciate that, you let me worry about an investigation. I hear Global tried to liberate their scientists earlier."

"You let me worry about them," she countered, wondering if Wahid had managed to get through to him, or if this was simply a fresh twist in Gordon's existing plans.

There was a moment's silence, as if he was thinking about saying something more, then he simply said goodbye and hung up.

Her head was in utter turmoil, usually she'd call Nikau and they'd strategise, but instead she called Alison.

"I need to come over."

"Valla? Yes, yes, of course. What's up?"

"I can tell you everything when I get there."

She heard Glenn asking who it was in the background, heard Alison put her hand over the receiver end and the phone change hands.

"What's he done?" asked Glenn.

"Let me come over."

She hung up.

"I don't believe it," said Glenn.

He'd listened as Valla had relayed the events of earlier in the morning. He didn't trust his grandfather, hated him with a passion that had recently been reignited and was now realising they'd have to stay in the AFS while the whole evil mess unravelled and there was nothing he could do to protect Alison from it. Worse, he did believe it, but just couldn't face what it meant.

"This is good," said Alison.

Glenn looked at her.

"Why?" asked Valla.

"Let me eat breakfast and I'll double check things, but at first analysis, I think he's calculated that eradicating Global from the AFS is worth paying a price for."

"Removing Global?" he queried.

"Breakfast," demanded Alison.

"Valla?" he asked, pointing to the cooker he was heading towards.

"Just coffee, thanks. Today is going to be a just coffee day I fear."

Alison had switched on the morning news programme. It was on mute and the ticker tape at the base of the screen carried the attack on the Bozhinov and the announcement that the Senate was to be recalled for an emergency announcement. Glenn glanced over while pushing bacon and mushrooms around a pan.

"He's wasted no time, then."

"Mariko will be pissed. She wanted to recall the senate, but not to give Gordon a platform to make announcements from," said Valla, checking her phone again.

Glenn scooped up the cooked bits and dropped them onto a thick slice of bread, presenting it to Alison with a knife and fork.

He saw Valla sipping her coffee lost in thought, staring at the screen. Glenn sipped his, starting to do the same. Did he really believe his grandfather knew what was going on at Melchior? Valla said Freddie had been sent by Gordon to find out. Was that a feint? He was properly lost about how he felt. Sometimes he believed it was all true and he rationalised it. Other times he didn't, remembering the half arsed apology decades later about not protecting the McMurdo coast and then, his own concerns while onboard the Mercer when they'd spoken. He hoped Alison would be able to give a clearer indication of what was really happening.

He heard the scrape of cutlery on the plate.

"I'm ready, it's going to take a while, I'll need sugary tea when I'm done."

He nodded at her, and watched with worry while the person he loved disappeared from the face that he loved and was replaced by emptiness.

They waited in silence, Glenn becoming agitated as the minutes wore on. He checked his watch, and held up five fingers to Valla. She was nodding back to him. He stood up and went to the kettle, he needed to do something, he switched it on to boil.

"Glenn," said Valla.

He dashed back to hold Alison.

"Tea."

He nodded at Valla, who went off to finish the process at the kettle.

"You were gone a long time. I don't want you to do this anymore."

He saw her smile weakly at him.

Valla had returned and was holding out a mug to Alison. Glenn helped her hold it to her mouth. Glenn could smell the sweetness as she drank it in one go.

"He didn't know. There's a 85 percent certainty of that. He knew it was bad but he didn't know what. He did send Freddie to find out, but who knows what he'd have done with the information when he got it. I can't predict those scenarios. He'll step down but not till he's removed Global from the AFS, probably his final executive order. He wants to drive a wedge between Torres and Lomonosov and Valla and Mariko. This is one of the reasons he's suggesting you Valla, but he was at the Innonnox Mine, he doesn't trust Mariko anyway. He'll plead diminished responsibility at any trial and you'll both be called as witnesses to that too. Take the interim presidency Valla, and make the changes that are needed. You'll have the vote if you accept the nomination."

There was silence. Glenn felt a kind of relief. To know he wasn't related to a monster, just a man who made mistakes and never admitted them was almost acceptable.

Chapter Thirty Six - Interim

The senate chamber was busy. It looked like most charter flights had been commandeered so senators could attend. The announcement had gone out at half past seven in the morning and the emergency debate booked for eight at night, even if you were coming from Saylon you'd just make it. Still, there were nine senators on screens above the chamber, who had their own reasons or had just got caught out by the announcement. The other forty senators were in the room. The chamber had been built with expansion in mind so there was room to spread out. Even so there were clumps of senators, and much catching up going on, so much had passed since the chamber had last met.

A vote in the senate was not secret, nor electronic, it was a simple hand up affair. Albeit the hand had to be grasping a senate card, colour coded by Family. A high definition image was taken of the vote and recorded for posterity. Visitors and advisors were therefore allowed to sit within the body of the chamber and not exiled to an upper storey. Nikau Burns was sitting next to Valla.

She could see Mariko sitting near to Dante and River, with the five junior Lomonosov senators spread behind her. They still hadn't managed to elect a replacement for Mariko's junior position nor to ratify Mariko as a senior senator. Not that anyone usually cared about these things but she did wonder if Gordon had some trained Glencor junior up his sleeve who'd make a bit of noise about it. That would be a mistake if they did, she thought.

She'd met with Nikau in the early afternoon, after calling him to mention Gordon's morning phone call. Not surprisingly he was sceptical. He also thought it was a wedge between Mariko and them. She tried to reassure him. After all Mariko needed Torres votes, not the other way around, and they weren't backing out of supporting her presidential ambition.

She'd told him there were things she wanted to do and it would simply be easier if she was interim president. Things like the anti-corruption unit for a start, and Dante Castillero could get his legal review. And no one would challenge the legitimacy of the investigation into Gordon or his trial, unlike the questions that would be asked about Mariko's motives once it became clear she had a vested interest in Gordon's downfall. She thought he'd come round, but now she wasn't so sure. He was almost surly, sitting next to her.

There was muted applause as Gordon emerged at the foot of the chamber and took to the podium. Valla took in who had not been clapping. That was where those who might oppose her were too.

"Fellow members of the Antarctic Free State senate, thank you for coming to this emergency debate at such sort notice. The business before the chamber is two fold. Firstly as you're all doubtless aware Global Corporation has been involved once again in attempts to undermine our state, and it is my final executive order, as president…" he paused as a few loud gasps erupted round the chamber, then continued as though he had simply cleared his throat, "that I bar all enterprise taking place on behalf of or as part of, Global Corporation, and all personnel employed, excepting native or naturalised, from the territory of the AFS. All such enterprises will become the property of the state until the senate decides how to dispose of them. There will be no negotiation with Global Corporation until a full and thorough investigation takes place into their role in the events of the last sixteen days. And secondly as was explicit in my first point I will be standing down as president of the AFS from the point at which the senate elects an interim president to preside over these and other investigations and the run-off and presidential elections. I would like to nominate Valentina Torres as the interim president. I wish to thank you all for the respect you have shown for the position of president, for having faith in me and I hope you will extend that to the interim and the future elected presidents. Long live the AFS."

There was the briefest of silences then a stomping of feet. Valla noticed some senators, mostly Glencor standing, then she saw Mariko stand. That was smart, she stood too. Soon the whole chamber was standing and clapping. She thought she saw Gordon give a tight smile to her, but it could have been to anyone in the room really.

The senate administrator took to the podium, as Gordon stepped down holding onto the rail by the steps. From the back she thought he looked like any old man, and maybe there were others who were seeing that too.

"The nomination for interim president requires a seconder, may I have a senator to second Valentina Torres' nomination."

She saw Arne Dale get to standing ahead of a few others, not all Torres either. He waved his yellow senate card in the air.

"I second the nomination."

The administrator took note and there was the flash of the recording camera.

"Are there any other nominations?"

The room went very quiet. Most senators were looking at Mariko Neish or Felix Maine, but Valla could see they were resolutely not catching anyone's eye. Whoever was the interim president could not stand in the run-offs, and that suited her perfectly.

"No? Then Members of the Senate show me your vote," asked the administrator.

Valla saw a forest of hands go up with cards representing the colours of all of the five Families. The recording camera flashed and she became the interim president of the AFS. Fuck she thought to herself, how had she ended up here, where she least wanted to be?

Someone started saying her name, Valla, and others were joining in more loudly. She stood up before it got out of hand, and made her way down to the podium. She thanked the administrator and had a brief scan for Gordon. A moment's panic seized her as she thought he might had done a runner. Her phone buzzed and she checked the notification. That might be harder than he'd realised.

She put her hand up and the chamber quietened down.

"Thank you. Thank you for your confidence. I pledge to oversee these investigations in a timely and impartial manner. To that end for my first executive order I am instigating an anti-corruption unit, with full powers to investigate everyone and anyone in the AFS from the president down, with the ability to co-opt police, intelligence, navy and militia in the course of their investigations, in line with due legal procedures. And in respect of those procedures my second executive order will authorise Dante Castillero to set up his review into the judicial and legal system with a view to making it fit for the AFS today."

She saw Dante nod thanks.

"Finally, my third executive order is to formally open nominations for the presidential run-off elections. Fellow senators please choose your candidates with the continued independence and prosperity of the AFS in mind. Thank you."

She stood down to applause but nothing like Gordon's ovation. She smiled, that was fine, she thought, that kind of adulation could go to your head.

She heard the administrator call for order then for the first nominations as the camera flashed overhead. She climbed back to her seat. Nikau patted her hand.

"Your father would be proud," he said.

She was happy to hear him say that, she hadn't wanted to drive Nikau away. Together they slipped out of the chamber, hardly noticed in the activity surrounding the nominations.

They were in her office finally, after most of the senate administration team had met them en route to offer her congratulations. She sat down in an armchair. Nikau was up at the window.

"I'm not sure it's congratulations I should be getting. I'm going to do all the hard work and be a blip in the history books."

"You wanted it that way."

"Ah, wait a minute, I did not. There just wasn't any other way to do it."

She saw him turn around, and she saw his wolf grin.

"But we have him at last."

"We do. Enya arrested him somewhere unobtrusive between the senate chamber and his office. I got the text message as I took the podium."

"Well then, how about a whisky? Tricia has found a bottle of champagne from somewhere if you'd prefer?"

"Can I have a minute? I'd like to make a quick phone call first, then I'll come out to join you in a glass of champagne, thanks."

She saw Nikau pause, like he'd forgotten something then nod and head for the door.

She called the Mercer. It was Dmitry who answered.

"Madam President," he said.

"Oh bugger, you've heard already?"

"Right this minute. I can't think of anyone better," he said.

"Yes, well, don't get used to it, I'm only interim. Is Martin around?"

"I'll put you through to his cabin, I don't think he's asleep yet."

There was a pause, a ring or two and then his voice.

"Hello?"

"It's me."

"Valla. Is everything alright?"

"I'm the interim president of the AFS."

A pause, the faintest of crackle on the line.

"What do I call you now?" he asked.

She could tell he was smiling, it helped her smile too.

"I'm taking a leaf out of Rita Hussain's book, call me Valla."

She heard him laugh and she began laughing too. She had missed this.

"How long is interim?"

"I don't know, less than a year more than a month. When will you be back?"

"It takes longer to get to Weddell City, there's still twelve days till we arrive."

"I have no idea what I'll be doing in twelve days time. But I will be there."

"Madam President I expect no less."

"XO."

"Till then."

"Yes."

It seemed impossible to hang up, but she had to. She could hear more voices in the ante-office.

She opened the door and there was Arne and Dante with Nikau and Tricia, all with glasses of champagne in hand, they held them up to greet her.

Arne held a glass out to her.

"Congratulations" he said.

"Thanks" she toasted them and took a sip.

Alison was cuddled into Glenn watching the large log burn in the fireplace. The outer layer of the log had broken up into small rectangles of orange outlined in a deeper red as the centre cooked. There was hardly any flame, just intense ember activity. She was drowsy. After Valla left, she'd eaten another breakfast, and then they'd retired back to bed. It seemed to her Glenn had wanted to shut the world out and she'd been happy to indulge him, as they lounged and ate, kissed and drank.

There was a knock at the door. She didn't really want him to answer it but she knew he would. It was Anatoli. She saw Glenn invite him in. But there was no sign of Enya with him.

"Anatoli, Is everything okay?"

"Yes. I think so. Enya is busy, and I just wanted to have some company."

She saw him properly look at the room and saw him pause.

"I'm sorry I didn't mean to intrude on your evening."

"Anatoli, sit down. Tell me what's worrying you."

She saw him perch on the end of the sofa.

"Enya's arrested Gordon. She's head of the new anti-corruption unit that Valla has announced. And I'm worried for her. You don't make friends in that kind of job. What if something happens to her?"

"Anatoli, I know you're still trying to process what happened to you in Vostok. You have to put risk into perspective."

She saw him nod, and Glenn press a glass of whisky into his hand. She took the other glass from Glenn's outstretched hand. This was a very primitive kind of healing but it seemed to work especially well in Antarctica.

Chapter Thirty Seven - Support

It was an unseasonably cold day. The sun couldn't fight through the blanket of cloud and remained a stubborn disc of light easily watched as it rose higher. Glenn stood at the window having opened the blackout curtains. Two days ago the trial of Christine Frome had finished, the jury deliberated for less than five hours and returned a unanimous verdict on the murder charge and perverting the course of justice, but a not proven verdict for the treason charge. The press swung between claiming the death penalty was what influenced the decision on the treason charge to heralding the decision as sensible for anyone who wished to do business with outside organisations.

Glenn threw the papers down onto coffee table in a mix of disgust and weariness. This would all start up again today as the trial of Gordon Murcheson got underway. Only this time he would be part of it, and Alison too, as state negotiator and the interrogator of Global's Cornelius Kutchner. As expected Nancy Carter had made a plea of diminished responsibility on behalf of Gordon. The press had mentioned it in passing but were still waiting to see the lie of the land before choosing sides for and against. Nobody underestimated Gordon, even now.

He put some music on and tried to relax. Alison was out. There was a briefing of the Kutchner team. There was a chance Nancy would call them one by one to the stand at some point to try and pick away at the narrative they had found. Kairns had put him on leave. Everyone else was busy. Enya had managed to get James Wylie, Chris Saraband and Eric Jordan onto her anti-corruption team but she couldn't get Glenn till the trial was over. He felt lonely, and tried to remember what he used to do when he'd found a day to himself. He realised that had been a long time ago now. There was the bar Wahid used to run, further back than that there was climbing. Maybe he needed a run out, away from the city. Soon enough he'd have no escape.

He left a note for Alison, there'd been no agreed time for her return and he had no idea how long it would take to shift this feeling.

Alison left the briefing session. The prosecution lawyers were good, but she felt they weren't going to be good enough. After they'd left she'd spoken further with the three students. They'd all agreed from the beginning that they'd see it through wherever it would lead to. Being part of the prosecution of the president had been an outside probability. Now it was a certainty, she wanted to give them as much support as she could, something the lawyers hadn't been able to provide. She reminded them that the Mercer had arrived with Santiago Kooper onboard, who had further testimony linking Gordon to the attempted murder of Frederika Tran, and the actual murder of the decoy inmate. They had nothing to fear from Gordon and with the removal of Global's suits nothing to worry about there either. Global had found itself under attack elsewhere. Anywhere that Cornelius Kutchner had worked was now running investigations and freezing Global operations and assets. Global had other things on its mind.

She was waiting in yet another glass foyer, in one of the anonymous skyscrapers of Weddell City for the taxi. There'd been no answer at home. The day was drab, after a run of sunny days and almost temperate temperatures it felt cold. She almost wanted to zip up her survival suit, but nobody else had, and she was trying to blend in for a change. The taxi driver had the heating on inside. He had an Indian accent without a trace of modification.

"How long you been here for ?" she asked.

"Five freezing years,' he answered, "You?"

"Ha. Not much longer. What do you do about the winter?"

"Lately been trying to stay, used to go back to South Kerala, what about you?"

"I'm thinking of moving to Melchior."

Now, she thought, where had that come from? She'd heard from Anatoli how warm Melchior had been, and had done a bit of research. They had houses, a temperate climate and nearly normal light levels, normal if you'd lived most of your life in Northumbria anyway. Clearly it had been in her sub-conscious.

"Oh, yes. Where's that?"

The taxi was approaching the apartment block.

"Up north, Torres Islands."

"Ah," he said, "I like the city, though."

She leant forward to pay him and got out, running for the airlock. It wasn't till she was inside the apartment that she unzipped. She punched the thermostat up, even though it registered twenty two degrees already. She felt light headed, must be from running she thought. She sat down on the sofa and passed out.

It would be a surprise. He'd read in the papers what was happening and school wasn't going to start for another two weeks. Gary thought it would be good to be around his mum for a while. She had a habit of relying on herself too much. Which he understood, but as he'd got older and noticed more things, he also worried about. Glenn would look after her, but still, something told him to go home and he'd been brought up to trust his instincts.

He put the key in the lock and felt it turn. It wasn't locked fully, but no one had answered the door when he'd rung or knocked. He felt a bit of panic rise in his chest. He breathed in and out. Could be nothing. He entered the flat. It looked normal, as his eyes passed through from the kitchen area, till he saw his mum on the couch. She wasn't moving. He ran over. Checked for a pulse. She was alive, breathing but he couldn't rouse her. He called for an ambulance putting her into the recovery position on the floor like it was a drill at school. He checked her pulse and breathing again.

He looked around trying to see if there'd been a trigger. A long time ago he remembered that was the thing she'd asked him to look out for. When she used to fall into a kind of dream state or black out. But that hadn't happened since they'd moved here.

He saw Glenn's note and read it. Tried him on the mobile. It seemed where ever he was 'at the coast', it was out of range. There was a knock on the open door and the paramedics arrived. They checked her like he had, but also shone lights into her eyes.

"We need to take her in, she's non-responsive."

"What does that mean?" asked Gary.

"Could be a lot of things. Are you next of kin?"

He nodded.

"You need to come with us, get in touch with whoever else you need to."

He nodded picking up the keys as they were putting his mum onto the stretcher. Who should he call? He went to the top.

"Gary, what's up?"

He heard her voice, just as he remembered it from McMurdo.

"Valla, mum's collapsed. They're saying she's non-responsive. I can't get a hold of Glenn, he's gone for a drive to the coast. She's going into hospital."

"I'll be there."

"Thanks."

Glenn was parked up on a headland looking out into the Ronne Sea, when he heard the siren. There was absolutely no one else around for nearly a hundred kilometres, he was sure. So they could only be looking for him. Something heavy sank to the pit of his stomach and turned. Horrible sensations rippled up through his chest. He fought the memories away. The car pulled up alongside.

"You Glenn Murcheson?"

"Yes."

"You need to get to the Weddell City Hospital. I'm here to give you an escort."

He had concentrated on driving. Hadn't let his mind wander anywhere near to the whys he might be being escorted to the hospital for. He ran into the main reception and met a police officer, who recognised him. "Come with me," he said.

People had turned and there was a bit of whispering in the foyer and reception waiting area. He began to hope it was Gordon and not Alison, but deep down he knew different.

He stepped out of the lift and saw Gary, with Valla. Shit, shit, shit.

"Glenn, I found mum in the flat."

He could hear the wavering in the boy's voice. He went over and gave him a hug. He wanted to say something reassuring but he didn't know what had happened so there was nothing he could say.

"What have they said?" he asked.

"They did a scan, they want to operate on her brain, isolate the bio-implant," said Valla.

"Fucking Canning," said Glenn, "If I ever meet that monster..."

"I had to give them consent," said Gary.

He could tell the boy was scared. Glenn understood. His mum, his only family, in a country far away from where he was born and having to make a decision about her life.

"She'll be alright, they're good surgeons here, and she's tough."

They were platitudes, he knew it, but what else was there to say?

"Look, I have to go, but anything I can do, call me," said Valla.

He saw her hug Gary and turn to him.

"You don't worry about anything else. I can get you a room here. Let me know as soon as they tell you anything."

She had grasped his arm at the elbow, and he clasped her's back.

He sat down, and Gary sat down next to him.

"I'm sorry I wasn't there. She was at a meeting to do with the trial."

"It's okay. She's always done her own thing. I just felt like I had to come back. Do you ever get that feeling?"

Glenn wasn't sure. If he had then he'd not have been out staring at the Ronne Sea.

"Sometimes," he admitted. This was no time for that kind of honesty.

They'd sat in the waiting area for five hours, at some point someone had arrived with some sandwiches and coffee. Gary had eaten his, but Glenn had only drunk the coffee. Gary was sat on his phone, having already charged it once on the wireless table in the waiting room. Glenn couldn't face his phone, he'd sent it to silent. There'd be messages, missed calls, not to mention the news. He half expected press to arrive at some point. Perhaps Valla had managed to keep them away.

Finally a door swung open and unlike the countless other times, someone walked towards them and not on down the corridor.

"Gary Strang?"

The surgeon was still in his green scrubs and had some notes on a board with him, which he'd just checked.

"Yes?"

"Your mother's in intensive care, but we expect her to make a full recovery. You should go home. You'll be able to visit tomorrow afternoon, unless we call you."

"What exactly did you do?" asked Glenn.

"You are?" asked the surgeon.

"Glenn Murcheson, I'm her partner."

The surgeon looked down at his notes.

"Ah. The bio-implant. Yes we treated it like a tumour, it's mostly removed, except where it would impact on function. The hypothalamus had been compromised but we believe that full functionality will be returned there. It's early days but I'm hopeful."

"Thank you," he said still not quite sure what any of that meant. Was she going to be the same person? Was she going to recognise them?

The surgeon nodded to them both and went off back through the double doors.

Glenn looked at Gary, there was relief but he was still worried. Glenn understood. The trick would be to try and get back to normal. Whatever that was now going to look like.

"Hungry?"

"Pizza?"

"And beer."

Chapter Thirty Eight - Noticing

Glenn visited her with Gary, every day for the first week, despite the progress feeling infinitesimal. Together they'd tried hard to help her remember who she was. At the end of the week he thought maybe there was shades of Alison returning. A smile, a turn of phrase. He hadn't felt able to discuss it with Gary. He felt too many resonances to be able to help him properly, and had relied on simply being around.

When they'd moved her to a private room on a ward, he'd encouraged the others to come. He'd been grateful that they'd stepped up, coming along and trying to chat while avoiding her questions about the trial. It felt like lying somehow and he knew for Enya especially, how hard that had been. Enya must have been pleased that there was a wedding to talk about, even if to Glenn, that all sounded very vague and far off.

And now, it was time. Two long weeks, but somehow a dreadfully short amount of time to be bringing Alison home from major brain surgery. He wasn't sure he was up to it. But he had to be.

It was the day they were letting her come home. Alison felt she'd spent two excruciatingly long weeks in hospital. The first week in intensive care, where only Gary and Glenn had been allowed to visit. She'd been told the first day she'd had to be reminded who they were but she had no memory of those early days. It felt a lot like the original biotech implant operation, mentally, something she tried not to draw too many parallels with. Eventually she'd regained her memories, and the second week she'd been moved into a room on her own in a standard ward she remembered that even now. She'd received more visitors; Valla and then Enya, Anatoli and James dropped by. Though she asked, no one would talk about the trial. She wasn't allowed TV or papers or her phone. It had been frustrating, they were treating her like a child.

When they said she could go home, she insisted on a day and time there and then. So it was Friday and four o'clock and she was dressed, waiting on Glenn and Gary to arrive.

As soon as she was in the car she demanded a full report on what had happened in the last fortnight. She knew Glenn wouldn't hold back now, maybe she'd even known how hard it had been for him to hold back earlier. Was that what made her relent from her questions in the hospital?

As Glenn recounted the to and fro of the trial, she understood why no one had wanted to discuss it. Cornelius Kutchner had taken the stand and refuted every line of the team's evidence. He had denied any knowledge of the server where the files were found. He'd denied knowing or contacting Santiago Kooper to break Canning out of prison and he'd denied contracting the guy in Singapore to kill Santiago. He'd denied receiving payments from Gordon.

The prosecution sounded like they were unable to pin anything on him and that confused Alison, since there was evidence linking him to the server farm, to Santiago, and to Gordon.

"What are they playing at?"

"There's still the evidence from Melchior to come," said Glenn.

He sounded concerned.

"Mum, the doctors said you weren't to get upset, that's why they banned us from taking in papers or a phone," said Gary, sounding even more concerned.

"Did they? Well what did they think would happen when I got out?"

She felt properly furious, in a way that she'd never felt before, an out of control rage almost. She wanted to calm down but none of her thoughts were working the way they used to. She tried breathing exercises and that seemed to still have some effect.

"Did you get the report on the operation for me?" she asked Glenn. She had to really try to moderate her tone.

"I did. They were a bit reluctant at first, but then I pointed out it was your brain and it was the tool of your livelihood. There's scan images in it which I almost understood, but the rest..."

"It feels like there's some issues in the frontal cortex, I can't quite control my anger. I feel like I ought to warn you both."

"We've noticed," said Gary.

She winced and decided she should try to chill and not worry about the trial right away.

They got into the apartment. She was cosseted on the sofa and watched Glenn light the fire. She realised she was really tired despite only moving from a bed to a car seat to a sofa, and let herself nod off.

It was Monday, DI Enya Zhao was to be called to the witness stand. She was feeling calm, despite having seen Nancy Carter apparently destroy Cornelius Kutchner's testimony. He was a hostile witness and it was never going to be easy to use him, but Enya had agreed with Valla, they should put him up first, make it look like there was less of a case than what had been compiled.

The fact Kutchner was a high ranking Global executive was damning enough in most people's eyes, and he was clearly aiding Gordon's case by not cooperating, so on the old principle of 'no smoke without fire' most of the AFS knew fine well the accusations against him were true. Gordon's reputation was already taking hits, and Enya knew, that was as important as getting a conviction for Valla. Not so for her. She wanted everyone to know Gordon Murcheson, senator and president had broken the law multiple times.

She felt she'd held her own against Nancy Carter. She'd dealt with that kind of person before. The trick was not to get flustered, to be clear and concise and to continue to repeat a point exactly the same over and over again when necessary.

"They need to let me take the stand," said Alison.

"No. They're doing fine so far. Enya's evidence was powerful. Santiago stayed on track even when Nancy tried to 'what if' him. The video link to Singapore was good too. They all identified Kutchner, and the guy in Singapore agreed he'd been told Gordon was paying. You don't need to do anything," said Valla.

Valla had come round at the request of Glenn to speak to Alison about the trial. All week apparently Alison had been glued to the TV, getting more agitated. It was a new week and tomorrow Glenn had been called to the stand as part of the defence case of diminished responsibility, the day after they would be calling Freddie for the same.

"Listen Alison, you're still rebuilding neural pathways, you can't be put on the stand. It's unethical. I can't let you. No one can make you. Please just accept that's the way it is."

She looked at Alison. She seemed a shadow of herself. Gary had had to go back to school at McMurdo, and while Glenn had stayed in with her, tomorrow someone would have to be with Alison, she thought.

"Look, I'll get Anatoli to come round and take you for a drive, you need to get out of this apartment. You're getting paler than Glenn."

She saw Alison smile, it was now so rare that she immediately broke out into a grin herself.

Anatoli had turned up, while they were still making breakfast. He'd sat and ate with them, and the conversation had been pleasant, skirting round the trial and what was happening today. She felt Anatoli was doing this almost as much for his own sake as he was for her. She'd kissed Glenn goodbye at the door, and then they'd gone out shortly after that. Anatoli had driven north. She'd told him she'd never really been out in the wilds surrounding Weddell City, there always seemed more going on in the city, or she had to travel somewhere. He'd sympathised, and told her what it was like growing up in Weddell City as the son of a senator, and a Glencor founder at that. She understood why he'd not wanted to get into politics. She understood why Glenn had chosen the Agency too.

They'd arrived at the headland and she got out. The wind was cold off the sea, strong enough to be lifting spray. It felt invigorating. Maybe Valla was right, sitting in the flat wasn't doing her any good.

"It's beautiful," she said.

"Isn't it," agreed Anatoli.

She had stood for a while allowing herself to be buffeted by the wind, feeling the power of nature. Eventually the chill had penetrated her survival suit enough that she moved back to the car. Anatoli had been taking pictures then had disappeared down to a small pebble beach. She waited in the car for him to return. When he did, she'd seen him reach into the back and produce a flask with soup for each of them.

"So have you set a date?"

She felt that the mood deserved a light subject matter.

"No. Enya's very busy just now, and I think she'll be that way for a while."

She could tell he was feeling a bit lost in all the goings on. She was reminded of the time they had all sat round the table in McMurdo and he'd sounded just the same. She wanted to help him. She thought about how she would have done that in the past, some ideas came back to her. She felt her mind quicken somehow, as though sparks were setting off sparks, and she began to feel alive in the way she remembered. She told him how to make space for themselves. She knew Enya could be very driven, it was important she said, to change the direction of that drive occasionally.

"Will you be doing charter work out of Weddell City now?"

Another topic of conversation that ought to help him work things out for himself.

"I'm trying. I'm thinking of doing a regular run up to Melchior. It's quite shameless really, there's been a lot of interest in the place as a result of the trial. You know, people do a bit of research and now they're finding out it's temperate, and the fishing's good, the scenery's nice, the food's cheap. That sort of thing."

"I think that's a good idea. you need to link up with accommodation as well. Tell you what," she said, entirely on the spur of the moment, "I want to look at houses up there. Why don't you take me up. What are you doing tomorrow?"

Anatoli had looked at her, like he was making sure she was serious.

"Nothing,' he said, "It's a deal."

"I'll pay for fuel. We can go early, be back late, yes?"

"Consider yourself under contract," he said.

When they'd got back to the apartment Glenn had been waiting, they'd ordered a food delivery and eaten together. Alison had told him about Anatoli's plans, and he'd encouraged Anatoli too. It wasn't late when they said goodbye to him at the door.

"He's totally lost," said Glenn.

"I know, I've tried to help. He's going to take me up early to Melchior tomorrow, I want to look at houses up there."

She saw Glenn looked worried.

"Don't worry, we can come and go. Winter up there, summer down here, that sort of thing."

"When did you decide this?"

"I said it today, but I think I've had the idea for a while, ever since Anatoli first talked about Melchior."

"A house. A whole building all to ourselves?"

"Yes, maybe run it as a bed and breakfast."

"A what?"

"A kind of home hotel, where you rent out a bedroom and give people breakfast. They do their own thing, and eat their dinner wherever they like."

Alison had managed to get to to sleep and not ask about the trial. Glenn was eternally grateful to Anatoli for that, because what had happened that day had not gone well for the prosecution. Certainly for the charges related to recent events. It looked like Nancy Carter would make the diminished responsibility stick. For the earlier events, the attempt on Freddie's life and murder of the inmate, Enya had it sewn up pretty tight, even without revealing that Jim Leavey was in fact James Wylie. But he'd not lied when he took the stand and admitted he was concerned about Gordon during the conversation on the Mercer. He had purposefully refrained from looking in the direction of Gordon when he was on the stand.

Towards the end, he'd lost his temper a bit, and had asked Nancy to stop referring to Gordon as his grandfather, saying that he hadn't considered him such since he was ten and that he felt that she was trying to create a relationship that didn't and had never existed. He'd managed to say it, but it had been ordered struck from the record. Still he noticed she stopped. He hoped Freddie did better tomorrow.

As he lay awake next to Alison sleeping peacefully, he thought he'd like to go up to Melchior with them tomorrow, and having decided that he finally managed to drift off.

The Iceberg Presidency
Chapter Thirty Nine - New Year

It was nearly New Year and the peak of high summer in Antarctica. The house wasn't quite finished, but it would have to do. Alison had bought it after seeing it when they'd gone up with Anatoli just to have a look. The agent said the seller had worked for Global and had left in a hurry before they'd got deported. They were selling with all furniture included. It was an old design with a modern extension. It seemed fated. She'd been trying to source tundra suitable plants for the garden, maybe find some hardy dwarf trees. She'd hardly seen Glenn but she'd been busy enough not to notice till the holidays swept in.

She adjusted the flowers in the vase and thought back through the last four weeks. The trial of Gordon had finished and had been a disappointment to all concerned. Gordon still got nailed for the attempt and murder, but he'd also had his plea of diminished responsibility upheld. As a consequence he was under house arrest for the rest of his life, with significant curtailments on who could visit. It was an ignominious end, but still somehow dissatisfying.

They now had Cornelius Kutchner on trial and seemed to be making a better job of it. She felt that some of the punches they'd pulled in Gordon's trial had been on purpose and now they were going to let rip at an easier target. It wasn't good but it was better, at least they'd managed to put Gordon on trial. There was a time in the AFS when that idea would have been laughed at, even while everyone laughing knew Gordon had broken laws.

She'd invited them all to the house, Valla and Martin were staying with them, but the rest had got rooms in the hotel in town. 'In town', now she even sounded like a local, she thought. She'd get to meet the 'team', as Glenn called them. She knew James, but Chris and Eric were going to be new to her. Enya and Anatoli of course. And Gary was coming. She was pleased she'd see him again so soon, usually in the summer he'd be away with friends. She had a surprise for him.

The first to arrive were Valla and Martin. She could see the hire car coming up the mountain turns. Valla wasn't going to be interim president for much longer but she'd asked Alison to help keep Martin a secret till she stepped down. The run-offs had just finished and had resulted in Mariko Neish and Felix Maine coming out on top. The presidential campaigns would start as soon as everybody got back to work from the holidays. She was pleased it was two recently turned senior senators.

Valla burst in the door. Alison felt the General was back.

"Hello," said Valla.

Alison could see she was casting an eye over the place. She wondered if Valla was assessing its defensive capabilities. Alison rather hoped those days had passed. She saw Martin hang back in the doorway with their luggage.

"Martin come in, dump them here," Alison said, pointing to the side of the front door.

"Tea, coffee, whisky?"

Valla was looking at the staircase. Alison understood why. It was an impressive bit of wood. It was a shocking amount of wood actually, but she'd moved past that thought a long time ago. It had been the reason she'd wanted the place so badly.

"You've gone native," teased Valla.

"Totally. Come on Glenn will be back soon with the 'team'. Let's get some gossip done before the drinking starts."

"I've brought my cards and poker chips, if they're drinking, I'm laughing," said Valla.

Alison headed for the kitchen at the back of the house. It was part of the extension, sleek and modern, the opposite of the ancient staircase. She'd tried to find out where the staircase had come from. The Global guy must have imported it from somewhere, but it looked like it had been 'without paperwork' as they tended to refer to smuggled goods in Melchior.

She had just poured coffee and whiskies when she heard the door again, and voices in the hallway. The 'team' entered the kitchen: all tall, Glenn and Eric, both pale, blond and ginger, James dark, and Chris sallow like Anatoli. They sat down at the table while Valla and James did some introductions. Glenn had come to her straight from the door and kissed her. She held him still round his waist.

"How are you? When is Gary getting in?" he asked.

"I'm good, better now you're home. He won't get in till ten on the last flight in, but he's getting a taxi, so we can begin drinking without him."

"He knows Valla's here. There will be poker. I'm not getting drunk in those circumstances."

"Have you told the 'team'?"

"Ha, no. James and I decided it was worth letting them find out for themselves."

The table had coffee cups and glasses in various states of fullness when Alison heard the door bell. When she opened the door there was Enya and Anatoli.

"Ah Alison," said Enya, nodding at the glass in her hand, "you've started without us."

"Come in, catch up."

Alison saw Anatoli check out the bags at the side of the door.

"I was wondering how they'd manage it," he said, "I saw the Torres Mining jet at the hanger. She always did like a bit of risk."

"The press will be too drunk or hungover to notice, if you can't sneak off for New Year when can you?" Alison said.

The table was now ringed with glasses and finished plates, in the centre was a decent pot of poker chips. There was silence. Glenn had folded, she had too.

James was sitting out, having run out of chips two hands ago. The turn of the fifth card face up on the table had wrecked any chance she'd had, and she felt everyone at the table must be bluffing. Enya playing a hand with Anatoli folded, then Chris and Eric did too. All eyes were on Martin who had yet to decide his play.

Alison was watching Valla, who was unperturbed, merely looking at the pot as if counting up the amount. Martin raised.

It was just Valla and Martin left. Alison felt those at the table had more interest in the mind games between the pair than the result of the hands. Those who knew Valla well had been intrigued to find out who this man she'd fallen for was.

She watched them turn their cards over together, one card at a time. There were a few intakes of breath over teeth then a lot of laughing. Martin had just managed to best the General. She saw Valla smiling, while James was slapping Martin on the back. Martin was leaning forward to sweep his winnings in with a big grin. She saw him hand a chip to James.

She'd just brought a fresh bottle to the table when all around there was a chorus of alerts from mobiles. She didn't know why, all her alerts had a generic tone, but she could see worried faces from those who already knew what the alert was for.

"Solar Flare,' said Valla to her, "they're shutting down the networks."

"Will Gary be okay, his flight gets in at ten."

She cast an eye to the clock on the wall and saw there was still twenty minutes till it landed.

"Yes, this is an early warning. Usually thirty minutes to an hour. They tweak the sun spot model on a thirty minute basis. It's why there's a tonne of server farms and computing power over on James Ross."

"I hope it isn't bad," she said, "isn't it supposed to be picking up?"

"Yes, you should buy a solar-safe for your portable devices if you've not got one," said Valla.

She saw Valla cast a look at Glenn that suggested he'd been remiss in his duties. She saw Glenn salute back. Clearly more than enough whisky had been consumed. Though the alerts had had a sobering effect. Alison decided more food was required and got up to find some.

Thirty minutes later she heard the door. She rushed through to find Gary in the hall, looking at the staircase.

"Gary, how are you? Was the flight okay? Did you get the alert?"

"Mum," he said sounding exasperated. Then he was nodding at the staircase, "Where did you get that from?"

"Came with the house. Isn't it grand?"

"You've got to hope the UN never manage to over run this place."

"Son," she said, reaching up to tousle his hair, "Come on you missed Valla lose a hand."

"She did? Who to?"

"Ah, indeed," she said, and caught his arm before he could go through.

"What?" he asked.

"First I have something for you. I don't know how you might feel about it, but I think you should take it."

She saw his smile fade, there were memories neither of them chose to go to but knew were waiting out there anyway. She passed him the credit note. It was for five thousand dollars. It was a lot of money, Antarctic currency was the strongest in the world at the moment. It had originally been five hundred thousand sterling, housed in a left luggage locker in a Greater Kent train station, and only recently found as a result of Doctor Canning's unfortunate attempts to bribe a member of the Alvarez crew. It was the money Canning had paid to David, Gary's father, for his part in the kidnap of Gary. She considered it Gary's, but wasn't sure if that's how he'd feel about it.

"What's this for?"

"Consider it restitution, for your kidnapping. Or maybe inheritance."

She saw him nearly take the note then stop.

"He was paid?"

"He had problems, it isn't an excuse but he was weak not evil."

She pushed the note towards him again.

"Make something worthwhile out of it. Money is just a tool."

She saw him take the note, momentarily worried he'd simply tear it up.

"Okay. But only because I've an idea for it already. I've been talking to Anatoli."

"Oh?" she said, as they began walking through to the kitchen.

"Yes, we're going to build airships."

"Are you?"

"Yes," he said.

And she was overcome with immense pride for the man he was turning into.